Where Light Comes and Goes

WHERE LIGHT COMES AND GOES

A Novel

Sandra Cavallo Miller

UNIVERSITY OF NEVADA PRESS *Reno & Las Vegas*

University of Nevada Press, Reno, Nevada 89557 USA
www.unpress.nevada.edu

LIBRARY OF CONGRESS CATALOGING-IN-PUBLICATION DATA
Names: Miller, Sandra Cavallo, author.
Title: Where light comes and goes : a novel / Sandra Cavallo Miller.
Description: Reno ; Las Vegas : University of Nevada Press, [2020] |
    Summary: "Where Light Comes and Goes" is the second novel in a trilogy
    about a young female physician. This second book takes Dr. Abby Wilmore
    to Yellowstone National Park to operate a medical clinic for the summer
    tourist season. This novel of contemporary popular fiction offers an
    insider's view of a family medical practice involving the career of a
    woman doctor"— Provided by publisher.
Identifiers: LCCN 2020017818 (print) | LCCN 2020017819 (ebook) |
    ISBN 9781948908948 (hardcover) | ISBN 9781948908955 (ebook)
Subjects: LCSH: Women physicians—Fiction. | Grand Canyon National Park
    (Ariz.) —Fiction. | Yellowstone National Park—Fiction. | LCGFT: Novels.
Classification: LCC PS3613.I55293 W48 2020 (print) | LCC PS3613.I55293
    (ebook) | DDC 813/.6—dc23
LC record available at https://lccn.loc.gov/2020017818
LC ebook record available at https://lccn.loc.gov/2020017819

The paper used in this book is a recycled stock made from 30 percent
post-consumer waste materials, certified by FSC, and meets the requirements
of American National Standard for Information Sciences—Permanence of Paper
for Printed Library Materials, ANSI/NISO Z39.48-1992 (R2002). Binding materials
were selected for strength and durability.

First Printing
Manufactured in the United States of America

24 23 22 21 20   5 4 3 2 1

To Ted and Katie:
For their endless enthusiastic support,
and for calling me out less than they should.

In every walk of nature,
one receives far more than he seeks.

—MUIR

Where Light Comes and Goes

1

Spring came to the canyon. The last snow aged, turning gray and disappearing little by little, and soon pale green spears pushed up through the rocky soil. The black nights lost the sharp edge of frost and people began putting away winter coats and boots. Miles deeper, far below the tinted layers of stone, miles even below the great dark river that twisted through red chasms, little rifts and broken shelves of the planet's crust shifted and collided, sending out vibrations, rocky ripples. Vibrations too faint for humans to feel, but the seismographs caught them and the needles waggled, tracing a jagged image of moving stone. Geologists sat up and took note.

The physicians at the Grand Canyon Clinic on the South Rim had no time to contemplate such subterranean developments. For the last month they found themselves in the middle of a measles epidemic, responding to frantic parents and treating sick children. The outbreak began seventy miles away in Flagstaff, where a cult of families who abstained from vaccinations suddenly started getting very sick. Shortly before the epidemic was realized, many of the children took a field trip to the canyon for their science lesson, visiting gift shops and stores and restaurants.

"We've got another one," said Abby as she exited the isolation room in the back of the clinic, pulling off her face mask. "She's really sick."

Dr. Abigail Wilmore rubbed her nose with her forearm. Face masks always made her itch, and even though she had just washed her hands, then applied alcohol gel for good measure, it was an ingrained habit to keep her fingers away from her face. She should be immune to measles because of her childhood vaccines, but a small chance of infection always lingered.

"So. Not out of the woods yet," Dolores sighed, printing another measles handout. One of the best nurses Abby ever worked with, efficient and competent, Dolores Diaz frowned and pushed back her dark hair, laced with silver this year. "I remember you talking with Angela's mom just last fall, about getting caught up on her shots."

"Yeah. I guess I didn't talk about it quite enough."

Abby wondered if there was another way to say it, another way to be more convincing. She wondered if all physicians harbored such self-doubts. They get so many shots, Angela's mother wailed, it just doesn't seem right. Let's wait till she's older. Abby assured her that babies often tolerated vaccines better, but the mom's decision had been made. Now two years old, little Angela baked with a fever of one hundred four, with red runny eyes and a drippy nose, coughing and crying. Inconsolable and miserable. A sandpapery rash scattered across her face, and Abby warned it was about to get much worse.

Abby pulled the mask back over her nose and took the handout into the room, reviewing the precautions personally. Acetaminophen for fever, and watch for dehydration. She explained the possible complications, pneumonia and encephalitis—brain inflammation—and when to worry. Encephalitis occurred in only one case per thousand, but was always a threat. Angela's mother clasped her daughter closely and Dolores ushered them out the back door, avoiding patients in the lobby. Measles viruses could hover in the air and remain contagious for several hours, a very tenacious organism.

Here came Priscilla from the front desk, stepping quickly down the hall in her tiny skirt and black tights, her spike-heeled boots clicking on the floor, her snug scoop-necked top reaching a new low position. Abby's eyes widened and she made a conscious effort to look away from the deep cleavage approaching. This was a brave look even for Priscilla, known for provocative attire, dramatic eye shadow, and her attraction to Dr. John Pepper. Another few millimeters, and nothing would be left to the imagination. A medical mask dangled around her neck, and she held a handful of papers and envelopes. Her eyelids glimmered bright blue and her glance flicked past Abby as if she wasn't there.

"I need to speak with Dr. Pepper," Priscilla announced to Dolores, craning her neck to look into the doctors' office where he talked on the phone, his voice low and serious. "He needs to sign these disability papers."

"You can give them to me," Dolores offered, reaching. "I'll be sure that he sees them."

Priscilla snatched the papers away, then smiled apologetically and her voice sweetened. "Thanks so much, Dolores. But I promised the patient I would take care of it myself. She had a personal message for the doctor, too. Something she asked me to tell him."

"He's talking with the medical company manager," Abby put in, keeping her head down and tapping on her laptop. "The FirstMed guy. And Pepper doesn't sound very happy. It could take a while."

"Well," Priscilla huffed.

Abby felt Priscilla look her way, sensed herself being measured and dismally failing that evaluation like she felt a dozen times every day. This had gone on now for months, ever since Abby and Pepper started dating last summer and now more or less lived together. As if Priscilla could not fathom why Pepper chose Abby. As if it was only a matter of time until he came to his senses and started looking around with his eyes wide open.

"Well," Priscilla said again. "I'll come back in a few minutes." She stalked up front to her desk, loudly asking her counterpart Ginger if Dr. Wilmore didn't have another patient to see.

Dolores sighed. "She is good at her job."

Abby nodded, leaving it at that. Feeling tired, she wanted to go sit in the office to work on her notes, but from Pepper's tone in his conversation, this was not the moment to distract him. Abby worried about how much more measles they might see and if they should distribute new signs around the village, urging vaccinations. Everyone in their patient database had been contacted, but that was only a portion of their clients. They saw so many temporary visitors from all over the country. From all over the world. More than five million people a year came to marvel at the Grand Canyon, and some days it felt like every single one of them managed to get sick or injured while they were there.

Abby heard Pepper hang up, dropping the phone into the cradle a little harder than necessary. She grimaced, wondering, and gathered up her laptop to move to the office, but Priscilla's radar was operating at an impressive stealth level—she suddenly appeared and whisked into the little room with her papers. Abby saw her bend over him, her little stretchy skirt hitching up, her hand on his shoulder, and her pale blond hair falling against him as she pointed to the documents and tilted her chest toward his face. Pepper straightened his back, pulling away, but Priscilla moved right with him, talking earnestly in a quiet, private voice.

Eventually Priscilla exhausted herself and returned to the front desk. Abby moved to the office and sat down beside Pepper, who quietly fumed.

"What's going on?" she asked.

"Nothing," he said shortly. He vigorously rearranged a stack of messy papers. "Everything is just peachy."

"Come on, John. Talk to me."

He exhaled and finally looked at her, his blue eyes chilly. "You want to take a walk? Not much privacy here."

Abby glanced at her unfinished work. "Of course."

"Don't worry. I'll come back with you and we can both wrap up then." Pepper stood and put his hand on the back of her neck, just under her hair where she gathered it into a low twist, and he squeezed gently. A reserved man who rarely displayed affection at work, he allowed himself that one gesture, that soft hold on her neck, and she loved it.

They pulled on jackets, asking the staff to lock up when finished, and cut through the woods to the rim trail. Abby slipped her hand in his and he gripped it hard, a sure sign of his stress.

"Ow," Abby said mildly, wiggling her fingers.

He looked down at her and smiled, relaxing his grasp. "Sorry."

They reached the rim and stood silently, taking it in. The sunburnt canyons fell away at their feet and the stone mesas paraded off in all directions, striped with bands of rust and buff and dusky green. Hundreds of millions of years, the planet's history laid open below, the raw exposed specter of past ages.

Abby closed her eyes and inhaled deeply through her nose, savoring the scent of limestone dust and pine. She knew about the uptick in seismic readings and tried to sense that inner crust, shifting so far beneath her feet. She opened one eye, sniffed again, and glanced sideways at Pepper.

"So what do you think?" she asked. "Does it smell like earthquakes to you? One big tremor and this very ledge we're standing on could crumble and drop into the canyon. When was that last rockslide at Mather Point, triggered by a quake? I think in the 1950s. Just a second ago, geologically speaking."

John smiled, his hair tossing back and forth in the breeze, and one hand distractedly rubbed his short beard. "I wish it would. Then I'd have better things to worry about."

"Better than what? Let me guess…Priscilla?"

"Ha," he snorted. "Thanks for reminding me." His gaze appealed briefly to the dark blue sky as it deepened, edging into night. "I suppose I need to say something to her about her tops. Or blouses, or shirts, or whatever you call them. Unless you want to? You know, woman to woman?" His eyebrows rose hopefully.

"Nice try. But since you're technically in charge of the clinic, I'm afraid that's up to you. Besides, you know it's mostly for your benefit. If I said something to her, she'd probably take heart."

Abby sat on a bench and pulled him down, snuggling against him, waiting for him to get to the real reason why they were there.

"How awkward can this get?" he asked. "Me having to tell a woman who's trying to seduce me that she has to dress less sexy. We need an office manager for these things. As busy as we are, it's ridiculous how they don't give us one. What has happened to FirstMed, anyway? They used to be so supportive. Now, instead of helping us, all they can do is come up with harebrained new ideas to send us all over the country."

He picked up a small rock and hurled it over the edge. Abby gathered her brows—there was no trail beneath them at this spot, but it was still a forbidden thing to do, throwing rocks. You could seriously injure someone below.

Then what he said sank in.

"Wait. What?" She turned to stare at him.

Pepper looked troubled. He palmed her cheek. "They want to try out a new national park clinic this summer, just for three months. Where there's lots of visitors, where they can maybe make lots of money. There's a small clinic, staffed with a physician assistant, I think. But they're busier and want to see how it goes with a doctor."

Abby let that digest. "Just you, is that what you're saying? Not me."

"Yeah." He pulled her tight. "You would stay here."

Abby bristled. "There's too much work here for just one person, and that goes triple in the summer."

"That's what I told them," Pepper agreed. "And they said they would fix that by approving the rotation for a third-year family medicine resident to help out here. I've been requesting that the last few years. Someone who could function almost independently."

"Sure, if they're a really good resident," Abby argued heatedly. "But if they're not, if they're struggling or not very polished, it takes a lot more time to supervise them."

"Yeah, well, you're preaching to the choir." He picked up another rock and Abby put her hand on his, prying it from his fingers and dropping it to the ground. He dipped his head and went on. "Besides that, there's my sodium study. We're ready to start the next phase, and I've got a professor and a medical student coming up here in June to launch it. I have to be here."

"Surely they understand that?"

"No. Just the opposite. He said he couldn't authorize me working on a study during company time. The little bastard. I assured him that I only work on it during my own hours, and I have never jeopardized the company's precious damn time."

Abby winced. How often did they come in early and stay late, taking care of patients and paperwork, following up phone calls and labs? Nearly every day; it was simply part of the job. While they theoretically worked an eight-hour day, most days it was more like ten, sometimes eleven. Occasionally more. She took a deep breath.

"So. What are you—we—going to do?"

"I don't know." He shook his head. "If I insist I won't go, it actually might put my job at risk. Or so that little weasel implied."

Abby sat back in alarm. No wonder he was upset. "Surely not."

"I doubt it. He's just full of hot air, flexing a few muscles he doesn't have." Pepper scowled, then peered at her. "I don't suppose you could work on the study?"

"Are you kidding? You want to trust me with your statistics?" Abby laughed. "How much do you care about your study? If you recall, I originally wanted to make my career in astronomy, but it was too mathy."

Then it occurred to her. She slid the idea back and forth in her brain.

"What if I went instead of you?" she suggested, cautiously feeling her way. "That way you could stay here and work on the study and work with the resident. And I can run off and have fun in a new place that probably doesn't even need a doctor, and I'll just lie around all day watching the clouds go by."

He looked at her hard, his eyes brittle. "I don't like it. I would worry about you too much."

"But maybe it wouldn't be so bad. It's only three months. Maybe we could visit each other. What's there to worry about? Where is it anyway?"

His expression went dark as he studied her, the sky nearly black now, with a few stars sparking above his head.

"Nowhere dangerous." He took her hands, bent to her, and lightly kissed the old scar on her forehead. "It's at Old Faithful, in Yellowstone. On top of the biggest active volcano in the world."

2

One of the issues Abby struggled with was whether to tell measles parents about SSPE. Every case made her uncomfortable.

SSPE stood for subacute sclerosing panencephalitis, a rare but devastating complication. SSPE could lurk silently for years after the initial infection before revealing its dreadful presence. Unknown why, sometimes the measles virus lingered in a child's brain, furtively damaging nerve cells until symptoms appeared—confusion and seizures, symptoms of neurologic wreckage—and turning fatal in a matter of months. While SSPE only occurred once in every ten thousand cases of measles, recent research suggested it might be more. Abby found no guidelines from the CDC or WHO about informing parents; it was not addressed on their handouts.

This tormented Abby. If her son or daughter had measles, she wondered, would she want to be terrified throughout their childhood by the rare chance of a deadly complication? One that wouldn't strike for years and had no cure? Eventually she rewrote the handout and, at the bottom of the sheet, she added the unlikely risk of SSPE. In case anyone read all the way down.

It still didn't feel right. The genetic disorder phenylketonuria had a similar incidence or less, and every child born in the country got tested for it. Often they were tested twice, just to be sure. Of course, knowing that your child had phenylketonuria meant you could change their diet and spare them...unlike SSPE, which was hopeless.

Abby wondered what was wrong with her, why she agonized over such issues that didn't seem to trouble other physicians as much. She worried why her brain mired itself in such dilemmas. She worried about being too neurotic, then she worried about worrying about being neurotic.

Abby closed the CDC website and forced the thoughts away. Instead, she opened the National Park Service website and clicked on Yellowstone just as Pepper came into the office, squeezing his lanky frame behind her, moving over to the other chair.

"Still thinking you might want to go?" he asked, gazing over her shoulder at a frothy geyser. Several days had passed since their first discussion. "I'm thinking I should tell them to forget it, and let the chips fall. They can find someone else."

Abby shrugged, debating when to admit how appealing she found the proposition, which wasn't exactly flattering to Pepper. Something covert chewed at her mind, something about proving herself. Besides that, she had never been to Yellowstone.

"Did you know Yellowstone has nearly two-thirds of all the geysers in the world?" Abby asked.

"Actually, yes. Because it's sitting over a gigantic ocean of magma that's hundreds of miles deep and horribly unstable. Being there is basically like walking around on top of hell." He looked gloomy and reached over, closing the screen on the geyser. His uneasy blue eyes found hers. "You want to go, don't you?"

Abby opened her mouth, but Dolores saved her by calling from the nursing station.

"Dr. Wilmore. Can you come see this patient right now?"

"Later," said Abby to Pepper, moving out and down the hall, glad to escape his cool regard. How did you tell someone that you love him, maybe enough to spend the rest of your life with him, but at the same time you might really like to go work a few months without him? They needed a serious conversation.

Dolores stood outside an exam room holding a small plastic basin.

"He just vomited," she said, nodding at the puddle of yellow gastric mucus. Bright red streaks swirled through the fluid.

"That's not good," Abby agreed. She opened the door to meet a pleasant but vexed forty-year-old man with a dark blond ponytail and weathered skin, drumming his fingers against the exam table.

Thin and muscular, he wore dusty black-and-orange high-tech hiking shoes. An ultralight backpack stood in the corner, with bright blue carbon-fiber walking sticks poking above the flap. Top-notch equipment.

"I'm sorry to be in such a hurry," he apologized, "but I need to get back on the trail as soon as possible. I'm already way behind."

Abby nodded but held up a cautious hand. "Give me a minute. I don't even have your history yet. But you just threw up blood, and you're having stomach pain, so this doesn't look like something quick. Pretty much the opposite."

"I only threw up because I missed lunch," he said shortly. "I feel fine now."

He put up with her questions, impatiently. He'd been ignoring a dull burn in his stomach for a week as he tramped the difficult trails, writing a journal he hoped to publish about speed-hiking through the canyon. He had an agent interested, and he added without humility that he was "a pretty damn good writer." But he must return to his regular job in Tucson, which left him only a few days to chronicle several more tough hikes. Worse, his right knee ached badly, an old injury, so he worked through the pain by alternating frequent doses of naproxen and ibuprofen.

"Which one are you taking now?" Abby asked, thinking she was near the root of it.

"Both," he replied shortly. "Prescription strength. On most days, I take the maximum dose of each. But I always take them with food, and I make sure there's at least two hours between each dose."

She quit typing. "Let me get this straight. You're taking full doses of two different anti-inflammatory meds in one day?"

He glared at her as if she was dimwitted. "Yes, like I just said. It gets me through."

"You can't do that," she said, appalled. "You probably have an ulcer because of that. A bleeding ulcer."

"Oh, come on. They always say you can alternate those meds."

"No, you cannot. You can alternate an anti-inflammatory with acetaminophen. Tylenol. Not with another anti-inflammatory. That tears up the lining of your stomach."

He scoffed, disbelieving.

She had him lie down. He grimaced when she palpated his abdomen, very tender over his upper stomach, exactly where an ulcer would be. At least his belly was soft, without tense, guarded muscles. Which meant that the ulcer had not perforated through his stomach, a surgical emergency. At least, it hadn't yet.

"I'm really worried," Abby told him. "This is almost certainly an ulcer caused by the medications. That ulcer could burrow through your stomach, which is a very bad development. It's called a perforation. You should see a gastroenterologist right away and get a scope, see what's going on."

"Well, it will have to wait a few days till I finish these hikes. Can't you give me something for it in the meantime?"

Abby looked him in the eye. "I don't think I'm making myself clear. This can kill you. If this ulcer perforates while you're out there hiking, far away from any help, you could bleed to death internally. Some ulcers bleed very rapidly. I can call someone in Flagstaff right now and probably have you scoped by this evening."

He nodded and made a diffident face, standing up. "I get it, Doctor. But the fact is, I'm going to finish this hiking. I'll keep my fingers crossed. Do you have any treatment for me, or not?"

"You could bleed to death," she repeated, incredulous. "You might already be anemic. We need to draw labs, see if your blood count has dropped, check your kidney function. Those drugs can damage your kidneys, too, and you've been overdosing. Not to mention hiking in the desert, which is also hard on kidneys. You can't just take off into the wilderness without checking a few things first."

"I don't think you can stop me," he replied with force, sliding on his backpack. "And I know there are ulcer medications you can prescribe. Will you or not?"

"I can only stop you if I think you're suicidal. Or if you don't understand the risk you're taking." Abby began to doubt herself again. She wondered if Pepper would have done better, explained it better, convinced him.

"Got it. I'm not stupid, and I'm not suicidal. I understand the risk. Ulcer, bleeding, death. Now please give me the prescription, okay?"

Abby reluctantly wrote for omeprazole. But first she typed out instructions to stop taking the other medications immediately, what symptoms to watch for, and the risk of dying. She included strong warnings that he not go, and had him sign it. She kept the original and gave him a copy, which he pocketed with a grin and took off, practically at a run. She even called the chief ranger, asking his staff to watch out for this patient. But Abby couldn't shake her distress. When she discussed it with Pepper, he agreed she had done all she could. Recklessness was hard to control, and the patient was willing to take his chances.

Abby found it all very unsatisfying. She knew she would keep worrying and likely never know the outcome.

That night, Abby and Pepper sat together on his back deck, wrapped in blankets against the cold spring night, watching Venus drift down toward the faint red horizon. Abby drew up her list, pros and cons. The pro list was long: Yellowstone, volcanoes, geysers, boiling mud, bison, wolves, grizzlies, change of scene, change of pace, manager experience, new challenges, new people. The con list was much shorter: manager stress, new people, and missing Pepper.

He draped his long leg over her knees, as if pinning her down to keep her, and pointed to his name on the list. "But that single item is worth a whole lot more than all the others, by a factor of about a hundred. Right?"

Abby looked sideways at him. "Are you trying to sway me with math? Appeal to my scientific logic?"

Pepper grinned. "Sexy, isn't it?"

Abby laughed. "I needed that. Between SSPE and that guy today with the ulcer, I feel sort of ineffective these days. I'm serious, I think I'm losing my touch. If I ever had it."

"Hey. No negative self-talk. We've had this discussion before." He scowled but cuffed her fondly on her shoulder.

Abby took a deep breath. Stars pricked the charring sky, and Abby pointed up.

"Orion, right?" Pepper ventured.

"Yes. But more importantly, Betelgeuse and Rigel. Orion's right shoulder and left foot. Two of the brightest stars in the sky." Abby felt her way.

"Good for them. High achievers." Pepper waved at them.

"That's the thing." She turned to him. "Their days are numbered. Betelgeuse is a red supergiant, in its final stages as a star. It will explode one of these days soon, relatively speaking, and it will be so bright that we'll be able to see it in daylight. Can you imagine? Rigel is a blue supergiant and headed for the same fate."

Pepper pulled back and squinted at her. "This isn't just foreplay, is it? Here I am, getting all turned on by these massive stars about to detonate all over the sky, and you're trying to make a point, aren't you?"

Abby smiled, leaned over, and kissed him softly on the lips. "Can't it be both?"

He lowered his brows and did not kiss her back. "I know you pretty damn well by now, and I'm not dense. You're saying life is short, and you want to go to Yellowstone. Before you blow up like a—what you called it—a superstar giant."

"A supergiant star." Abby laid her head on his chest. "They might not even want me. The whole reason they asked you, I'm sure, is because they want someone with more rural experience. It's pretty surprising, when you think about it, that they even hired me to come here."

"I'll remind you that was up to me, who to hire. I'm the one who interviewed you."

"And look how that worked out." Suddenly curious, she added, "And why did you hire me, anyway? Weren't you worried about my anxiety, my panic attacks, after I warned you?"

"Maybe I like to gamble," he teased, tugging her long hair. "But do you think you'll be okay out there in Yellowstone? What if you get panicky again, without anyone around, just in case? Anyone meaning me, of course. It's a really long drive for the middle of the night."

Abby paused, realizing what just happened. Within a few heartbeats, he was talking as if the decision had been made, as if she would go. Maybe she would struggle, and he was concerned, but he was signaling in his subtle John Pepper way that he accepted that she wanted this, and he would support her.

She smiled and shifted the blankets, climbing on top of him, sitting astride his hips.

"My anxiety has been good for a while now. I know it's always creeping around the dark corners of my brain, but you have to admit I've learned to manage it pretty well." That was one thing she did feel good about. "Besides, it's only seven hundred miles. If you drove at one hundred fifty miles an hour, you could get there in four—no—four and a half hours."

"Here you go with the sexy advanced math again. I'm not made of steel." He moved his hands across her back, down to her waist, then slid up inside her shirt with his long fingers.

"Mm." Her pelvis warmed and began to melt against him, her breath quickened. "I think that's about a sixth-grade arithmetic problem. It should take at least advanced algebra to get you heated up, what with you being so brainy and all. Maybe even calculus."

"Those roads to Wyoming go through mountains and canyons. I could probably only drive one hundred twenty miles an hour."

He freed one of his hands and seized her hair, pulling her to him and kissing her energetically, suddenly intense. His heat flared through her like a torch. She felt him rise and they started shifting together, Abby now panting as he hurriedly pulled off her clothes and she fumbled with his, his vigorous mouth never letting go, her groin flaming unbearably. They quickly escalated and she flashed like steam, unexpectedly and abruptly, bringing him with her.

"Whew." Abby lay collapsed on him, rising and falling with his heavy breathing. "That was intense."

He smiled, pulled her hair back from her face. "All that provocative math talk. It makes me crazy."

She closed one eye and peered at him. "So. You think you could drive only a hundred twenty miles an hour, huh. So that would take you about—wait a minute—"

"Almost six hours," he said.

"What the heck. You were calculating that in the middle of—?"

He grinned. "Please. I can figure that equation in about a second."

She made a face at him, then sobered. "So, you're okay with this? I mean, okay with me going to Yellowstone. If they want me."

"I will miss you desperately." He lightly touched the mark on her forehead, running his finger along her eyebrow where the scar ran through, a slightly crooked step. "But you seem to really want this. And you must promise that you'll stay out of trouble."

Abby snuggled against him. "I will miss you desperately back. I don't even know exactly why I need to do this." She closed her eyes. All the second-guessing, rewriting the handouts, arguing with patients, questioning her decisions. She had never truly been on her own since taming her anxiety; Pepper was always there to back her up. "It's like I need to prove myself. Something about independence. And not from you, either. More like independence from myself, from my own insecurities, which makes no sense at all. I can't quite figure it out."

"And you're fascinated by the whole supervolcano thing," he pointed out.

"And I'm fascinated by the whole supervolcano thing," she admitted. She took his hands tightly.

"I'm not very happy about this." His expression clouded.

"I know. And that's what makes you special. Because you're telling me to go anyway."

She hugged him and felt his breath catch, and she didn't dare look at his face.

3

A few phone calls, and the Yellowstone plans were confirmed. Suddenly it was Abby's last day at the canyon; she would leave early the next day.

The clinic overflowed. Crying babies, injured tourists, diabetic follow-ups, headaches and stomachaches and backaches and heartaches. But all the patients acted friendly and grateful, with no arguments about what treatments she advised or the dangers of immunizations. Most people became convinced after the epidemic hit. The outbreak ran its course and dwindled away. The last case of measles occurred two weeks ago, so it was probably over. For now.

The office staff threw a small going-away party at lunch. Pepper gave a funny speech, pleading with Abby not to fall into a boiling mud pot, while Dolores and Ginger chewed their cake slowly and looked morose.

The new family medicine resident, Dan Drake, arrived from Phoenix. Excited and eager, short and appealing, he seemed a little shy with a quick sense of humor, and sported a shock of dark hair and round glasses like Harry Potter. Abby saw how rapidly he bonded with Pepper, saw how after a few discussions about hiker injuries that he already looked up to John. She felt glad, for a nice, clever, temporary partner would help Pepper get through the next few months. Not that he wasn't completely capable by himself. After all, he'd been there alone three years before Abby joined him. But she also knew that Pepper was prone to dark moods, and this would help.

Dolores came up beside Abby and caged her arms around her, a mock tragic look. "Don't go, Dr. Wilmore. It just won't be right without you."

Ginger from the front desk joined her, encircling Abby from the other side. "We'll just hold you here and keep you from leaving," she pouted.

Priscilla saw them standing together and came over, lurching a little on her red stilettos. Pepper must have talked to her about the low necklines, because she now wore a red turtleneck to match her shoes, only the turtleneck looked a size too small. The fabric clung so tightly that Abby could see every line of her bra, every clasp on each strap, and her breasts stood out like a shelf. Priscilla smiled, her lipstick fire-engine red. Celebrating, no doubt, thought Abby.

"Dr. Wilmore," Priscilla gushed, leaning forward to give Abby a distant air kiss from nearly a foot away. "We'll miss you so much. You're so brave to go all the way to Wyoming. It sounds so primitive! I bet you'll meet all sorts of cute cowboys out there. Maybe even Indians, right?"

"Um, I suppose," Abby replied, thinking what on earth is she talking about? "More likely rangers and concession staff, just like here. All the tourists, just like here. And there are a lot more Native Americans here in Arizona than in Wyoming, I'd guess. What with the Havasupai to the West, and the Navajo and Hopi to the East, and the Apache over in the White Mountains. Not to mention all the smaller tribes."

Priscilla looked bored, too much information. "Well, don't you worry about Dr. Pepper, not a bit. You go off and have fun. We'll take very good care of him." Her eyes shifted across the room to where an animated Pepper spoke with Dan about heatstroke. Priscilla's mouth curved into a smile and she licked her red lips, watching both men with appetite.

Abby wondered if she should take Dan aside and warn him, then decided against it. He was a grown man, recently broken up from his girlfriend according to Pepper, and would surely figure things out. Pepper could warn him if he saw fit. And who knew, maybe they were perfect for one another. Not likely, but she had seen stranger relationships. She fell into a peculiar one herself over a year ago, so she knew better than to throw stones.

That evening, she and Pepper took a last walk along the rim, sitting on their favorite bench, not saying much. The shadows stretched, cloaking the gorges in deep blue, the stone towers glowing gold in the last light. Low tremors persisted on the seismographs, and she wondered if the panorama before her might be altered when she returned. What if the entire rim broke away, plunging everyone into rocky oblivion? She had to chide herself for catastrophizing. Abby took deep breaths and imagined slowly churning galaxies and the overwhelming distances of lightyears, reminding herself that a few months was less than nothing in the scheme of things.

Then Pepper took her to bed early, wanting to make certain she had plenty of sleep for her long drive but also, as he put it, wanting to give her something to remember him. Not likely I'll forget that, she said later, limp and spent. But she slept uneasily and found herself regretting her decision, unable to recapture that burning need to prove something, feeling his warmth alongside and missing him already. She felt numb and isolated, like one of the canyon mesas, a dull chunk of stone standing alone, brainlessly unaware of itself and its past.

He arose with her at dawn, and she knew he could sense her doubt. They stood by her loaded car, the air heavy with pine and musk.

"Don't do this to yourself," he admonished. "It's a bad old habit. This will be a great experience, and I'm a little envious. I'll come visit you soon."

"I know, I know. You're right, as usual." She forced a smile and clung to him for a moment.

"If you get tired, pull off and rest. Take a nap. It's a lot of miles. Promise me."

"I promise." She pulled back and looked closely at him, his troubled blue eyes, and knew it was the right time. She smiled genuinely now, reached up and fingered his flannel collar, brushed against his short brown beard. "Now don't take this wrong or anything. But I think there's a small chance—a really tiny chance—that I might actually sort of love you. A little bit." She paused. They had hardly said the word before. He took in a breath to speak but she put her fingers on his lips. "Don't worry, not very much. And not all the time. Just every now and then. Like, for a few seconds."

He laughed and his long arms wrapped around her and he lifted her off her feet, planting a kiss on her lips.

"I might sort of actually love you a tiny little bit too, part of the time," he said thickly. He put her down and nearly pushed her through the open car door. "You'd better leave fast before I ambush you and keep you here."

Abby sniffed and scrambled into the car, jamming the seatbelt home and revving the engine too much. Swallowing hard, she backed the car out quickly; the last thing she wanted was for him to see tears. She watched him in the mirror, standing in the road with his hands crammed in his pockets, until she rounded the curve.

Stop it, she told herself. She sniffed again and blinked away the tears. By the time she entered the highway, her jaw was set and her eyes were dry, and she made herself think of the journey ahead, all the adventure to come. Embrace it, she reminded herself. Those words formed her mantra the day she arrived at the canyon, almost exactly two years ago.

At first her trip felt counterproductive, bleak miles of broken canyons and dry plains. To reach Wyoming from the South Rim, she first had to drive backwards, southeast to Cameron then up to Page, before she could swing back west to Kanab and start moving through Utah. As the crow flew, it was only seventy miles to Kanab, but by land she must drive nearly two hundred miles before really starting the trip north, because the highways just didn't go where she needed them. Getting around the Grand Canyon was never a simple task. She planned to reach Salt Lake City the first night, three hundred eighty miles and over halfway to Yellowstone.

Normally she would stop and enjoy the vibrant Navajo trading post at Cameron, maybe find a small silver necklace, walk over and contemplate the Little Colorado River with its scanty sandy flow, headed for much greater exploits. But she kept on driving.

Willow Springs.

Bitter Springs.

Page.

Normally she would pause to contemplate the wide vista of Lake Powell, think about the drowned, devastated canyons and Edward Abbey, but she only lingered long enough to pump gas and use the bathroom. She did laugh out loud inside her car as she repeated her favorite lines from Abbey: "Saving the world is only a hobby. Most of the time I do nothing."

Big Water.

Kanab.

Panguitch.

The miles rolled and vanished under her tires and she yielded to the mindless rhythm of road and sky, moving farther and farther away. She surprised herself at how long she could go without thinking, without feeling, simply absorbing the stark crusty landscape, the jumbles of orange and rust-colored stone, and the morphing piles of cumulus, soaring and melting, rising and collapsing. It was the sort of meditative relaxation she had bettered for three years, emptying her mind, focusing on things more vast than herself and her small trifling life.

Beaver.

Meadow.

Spanish Fork.

She recited the sub-forms of cumulus as she watched them all day long, floating across the endless cornflower sky: the small low cumulus humilis, the puffy cumulus mediocris, the fat rising cumulus congestus. And finally, the towering, glowering cumulonimbus, far away on the horizon, dragging a dark purple drape of rain.

The few times she stopped to stretch or get a snack, she texted Pepper about her progress, if she could get a signal. She considered driving on because it was only late afternoon as she neared Salt Lake, but she knew she was tired and had promised him prudence. Abby drove through the city and picked a clean, simple motel at the northern edge, next to a highway diner. A quick supper, a long satisfying talk with Pepper, and she dropped into a deep, dreamless sleep for nine hours.

Up early the next day, Abby slipped into her car like a hand into a comfortable glove. Now as the miles slid along and she crossed into Idaho, she felt stirrings of excitement.

Pocatello.

Idaho Falls.

Sugar City.

And finally West Yellowstone, bustling with summer tourists, every street brimming with campers and families and hikers, every car and truck and RV bristling with backpacks and tents and fishing rods and maps, tourist buses crowding the lanes and coughing exhaust into the thin air. Not much different from the Grand Canyon, Abby thought, just a new set of hazards. Where the canyon was deep, Yellowstone was wide, covering two million acres. How curious it was, to go from a vertical to a horizontal park.

The landscape shifted quickly to pine trees, the river, and tight canyons, the road suddenly scenic and beautiful. Abby waited in line at the park entrance ranger station, caught off guard when the woman asked how long she would be visiting.

"Three months," Abby explained. "I'm the doctor for the new medical clinic. The one at Old Faithful."

The ranger looked puzzled. "But there's a clinic with a doctor at Mammoth Hot Springs."

Abby nodded. "Yes. This is a new one."

The woman waved her along, armed with maps and precautions. Abby drove slowly, following the signs to Old Faithful with her pulse quickening, trying to pay attention to the road as she craned to see the juxtaposition of forest and blighted landscape, the bright blue sky over the strange steaming terrain.

She pulled into the complex, realizing that she didn't recall exactly where to check in. It was all buried in an email somewhere. The large Old Faithful Inn stood prominently, flags fluttering gaily along the top, so she found a parking spot and decided to just go in and ask. Surely someone would know.

Walking across the pavement, she accosted two ravens having a bird party alongside a parked motorcycle. Elastic bungie cords anchored a small backpack to the seat, but the ravens had teased open a zipper and were carefully pulling items out and dropping them on the asphalt, then hopping down to peck and inspect them with their thick black beaks, sometimes crooning their approval in a coarse croaky murmur. A sock, two coins, a small church key, a tube of lip balm, and an empty candy wrapper lay scattered at their feet. Abby shooed them away and stuffed the items back in the pack, but the moment she moved on they flapped back and started in again, plucking at the zipper and tilting their shiny feathered heads as if inviting her to keep trying, that they could keep this game up all day. Since whoever owned the motorcycle might not return for hours, she shook her finger sternly at them and left.

A funny noise made her pause. A hiss and splash, then nothing. She started to move on and it came again, louder and longer, and Abby turned to notice a crowd gathered around a chalky, fuming barren space across the way. The slope behind it smoked, desolate and vaporous, draped in white, yellow, and orange drippings. A narrow wooden walkway stretched through it. Then the fizz accelerated and a tall gout of steam and spray shot high up, splashing back down noisily onto the rock.

Nice, Abby thought, that must be Old Faithful itself. Impressive, although she thought it would have been more dramatic than that. The spray settled—she thought it was over—when a harsh deep hiss issued from the ground and steam and mist burst up and up, far into the sky, cascading and rising, higher and higher, looming over the landscape. Bright white in the sunlight, the spearing chevrons of water and haze climbed over each other, soaring one hundred fifty feet and reverberating like a giant waterfall as it crashed back, gushing up and falling down on itself all at once. A warm mist drifted against her, smelling sulfurous, something from another world. Abby tried to imagine the boiling water just beneath her, the now-empty gurgling underground reservoir that would soon refill and seethe and spout again, and the deeper mass of restless magma underlying the entire area. The geyser dwindled, sputtered, and disappeared, hot rivulets of water streaming across the ground.

Abby pulled herself away and walked under the heavy timbers into the Old Faithful Inn, catching her reflection in the glass door.

She saw a wide smile on her face.

4

Not everything worked out quite as Abby had pictured, but it was close enough.

Her company procured a frontier cabin for her, in a cluster of box-like huts behind the Old Faithful Lodge. The cabins looked bland outside but rustic and cozy inside, with western furnishings and wood-paneled walls. Her stipend covered meals in the lodge and she had a mini-fridge, with a hotpot for tea and soup. Though a tiny place, it suited her, although she had a hard time imagining Pepper and his long legs sharing the double bed when he came to visit.

First things first. She drew a stick-figure cartoon of Pepper, standing by her car the day she left, pointing with a grumpy face and saying, "Get out of here." Abby credited her rudimentary drawings, which usually showed Pepper acting crabby and bossy, with why he became attracted to her, and she reminded him often. He disagreed, insisting that her damn cartoons nearly ruined their relationship, although Abby knew he collected them in a folder. In turn, he sent her ink and pencil sketches of the canyon and trees and skies, and sometimes of her.

Abby arranged a meeting with her new staff. Until now, the small medical practice at Old Faithful had been housed in a pleasant log building, shared with a ranger station. But new plans to expand the rangers' space changed everything, leaving the exam rooms stripped and empty, awaiting desks and maps.

The health center now stood, uninspired, behind a large parking lot in a generically tan doublewide trailer. Once Abby looked past all the pavement, though, she found the spot actually satisfying, tucked into a stand of pines, where birds hopped through branches and ravens patrolled with low grating mumbles, checking for plunder. Arcs of sunlight and shade danced over the roof. Short steps and a wide wheelchair ramp led to the door, where a small white sign proclaimed CLINIC.

Abby pulled out her key as she approached, but heard voices inside and found the door unlocked.

"It's never going to work if you don't fix the settings first." An exasperated female voice.

A woman in her late twenties stood scowling behind a portly man seated at the front counter, their faces illuminated by a computer screen. Her maroon hair sprouted dark roots, a little spiky on top, and fell in shaggy layers past her shoulders. A tiny diamond glinted on the wing of her nose. She had light brown eyes, wearing black jeans and a frayed black tank, but what drew Abby's eye was the rattlesnake tattoo curling down her left arm and around her wrist, the open-fanged mouth emerging on the back of her hand. The thirty-something man had a benign round face, receding short pale hair, and wore a large aloha shirt crowded with loud pink-and-yellow flowers. He reminded Abby of Winnie-the-Pooh.

"Sorry, we're not open," the woman said shortly, sending Abby a sharp look and returning to the computer. "Oh my god, Marcus. What key did you just hit?"

He shrugged and looked sheepish. Then they realized Abby still stood there and both looked up again.

"I'm Abby Wilmore. The new doctor."

They stared at her. Abby smiled, aware that in her jeans and bohemian cotton shirt, with her hair loose down her back, she didn't look quite like they expected.

The woman smiled cautiously and came around the counter, shook Abby's hand.

"Gem Bittersmith. I'm the nurse." Her light brown eyes looked levelly into Abby's, then she tipped her head toward the computer. "We're trying to get the system up and running, ma'am, but there's a problem with the EMR. Marcus here is fighting with it, but so far he's not winning."

Abby shook her head sympathetically. The EMR, the electronic medical record, was the data heart of every practice now, but it was not always a healthy heart, plagued by stutters and low output. Most systems carried glitches and non-intuitive links, full of annoying templates and awkward syntax.

The man stood and extended his plump hand over the counter, a wide smile spreading across his face. "Marcus Limerick. And before you ask, the answer is no and yes." Abby looked puzzled and he smiled even wider. "No, meaning it's not a joke—it's my real name. And yes, it is a joke—because that's sort of what a limerick is. Get it? Anyway, I'm your front desk man. At your service." He put his hands together and gave a funny little Asian bow that seemed vaguely inappropriate.

Gem rolled her eyes, while Abby moved around to the computer. "This is the same program we use at the canyon. It's kind of tricky to log in, especially the first time."

Abby closed and reopened a computer window, busy with codes and passwords, while Gem tapped her foot impatiently.

"Hopefully Marcus hasn't destroyed it already," she commented.

Marcus grinned amiably. "Yep, I could do that. Sort of a specialty of mine, messing up computers."

Gem sighed heavily and Marcus laughed, not the least shamed by his admission.

"There you go." Abby straightened. "All ready for anything."

"Thanks!" Marcus said with approval, scooting up to the keyboard and busily navigating the site. "I need to set up our first appointments. You want to see a patient every seven minutes, right?" He peered up at their alarmed expressions and chuckled. "Just kidding! Boy, you should see your faces right now. Is fifteen minutes okay, or do you want twenty?"

Abby settled on twenty minutes. Seeing over three patients an hour was difficult unless there were no complex problems, no chest pains, no older patients, no chronic pain patients, no Pap tests, no one with depression—for starters. A long list. And routine appointments often got derailed by unexpected injuries and sick tourists.

Gem motioned Abby to the back office and conducted a brief tour: three small exam rooms, a generous work station with a lab, two bathrooms (one for patients, one for staff, Gem emphasized), and a treatment room. All plain and uninspired, but adequate.

"Wait," said Abby. "Where's the x-ray?"

"Yeah, about that." Gem glared around the room as if it might materialize. "I called FirstMed and they said the old x-ray unit is kaput and they're working on it."

"Working on it…" Abby repeated. "We kind of really need that."

"Yes, ma'am, we do. Apparently we're supposed to send people up to Mammoth Hot Springs if they need an x-ray. That's just fubar. It's about fifty miles, so it takes over an hour if traffic is good. Or a whole lot longer if there's a bison jam. Two hours is pretty standard."

"Bison jam." Saying that out loud felt surreal.

"Yeah. Sometimes bison stand in the road, and they don't move until they want to. I'm pretty sure they do it on purpose. And you don't just go shoo a bison away—they'll move you before you move them. Traffic can back up for miles." Gem had her hands on her hips now, staring at Abby as if trying to figure her out. Not exactly hostile, but not overly friendly, either. "Not to mention the tourists who just stop their cars in the middle of the road to take photos. Then someone gets rear-ended, then someone else. You can imagine."

"Well." Abby found herself mimicking Gem's posture, arms akimbo. "It sounds like—"

"Excuse me." Marcus appeared, looking serious. "I know we're not open, but there's a patient here who—"

"You're right," Gem said sternly. "Not open. They can come back tomorrow."

"I think you need to take a look. He's kind of bleeding all over my waiting room." Marcus pulled a small white towel from a pile and disappeared up front, Abby and Gem close behind.

An unhappy ranger stood there, watching a distraught older woman hover over a silver-haired man. He sat on a plastic chair, blood sliding steadily from his left nostril, leaking down onto his shirt and pants. Bloody tissues piled his lap, and blood smeared his hands and the woman's hands and now Marcus's hands, too, as Marcus pressed the towel to the man's face. Marcus arched his brows at Gem, as if to say "I told you so." The ranger stepped back, relieved, the woman looked alarmed, and the patient looked lost, his eyes shifting back and forth above the towel. His wife kept tipping his head back as if that might help.

"How long has this been going on?" Abby asked. "By the way, I'm Dr. Wilmore." She grabbed a rubber band from the desk and snared back her hair. Then she corrected the patient's position, tilting his head forward, pulling on the gloves that Gem handed her. "There. That way the blood won't run down your throat and choke you. Is that better, Mr.—?"

"Mr. Trapp. Bob Trapp. So that's why he keeps coughing. Sorry, honey." The woman's hands fluttered like butterflies around his head. Marcus took her arm and tugged her gently away.

"Come over here and let me get your information, okay? He's in good hands now." Marcus had a mild, reassuring voice, which Abby appreciated.

"How long, Mr. Trapp?" Abby tried again, seeing the towel slowly turn red. She reached up and pinched his nose shut, keeping her fingers tight, and told him to breathe through his mouth. Gem took his pulse, wrapped a blood pressure cuff around his arm.

He smiled and shrugged.

"A little bit, off and on, for a few days," called Mrs. Trapp from over at the counter. "Then last night it got worse. Do you think it might be his medication? You know, that blood thinner?"

"Warfarin?" Abby and Gem said it at the same time.

"No, Coumadin. Wait, that's the same thing, isn't it? Warfarin is the genetic name." She beamed.

"Generic," corrected Marcus, nodding.

"Most likely," Abby agreed. "Can you get a medication list, Marcus?"

Marcus nodded as Gem took Trapp into the treatment room. Abby found a nasal speculum and peered up his nostril, but the bleeding source was high, beyond her view. It was like looking inside a tiny dark cave, blood welling out from an invisible spring.

"Any idea what we've got for treatment?" Abby asked Gem, withdrawing the speculum and pinching his nose again. Gem rapidly opened cabinets and drawers, inspecting supplies. "Any nasal packs? Vitamin K? I assume we have an INR test in the lab. Let me know if I'm hurting you, Mr. Trapp."

"We can run the INR," Gem replied, briskly. "I was just checking that out when Marcus broke the computer. If I can just find—ha! Vitamin K. And nasal sponges, too. We are in business, ma'am." She raised them triumphantly in the air.

"Nice," Abby agreed, making a mental note to have Gem stop calling her ma'am. "And fortunately, we don't need an x-ray for this one."

Bob Trapp sat pleasantly while Gem drew his blood and ran the INR, a test for blood coagulation. More impressively, Trapp held perfectly still and smiled at her when Abby slid the nasal sponge far up inside his left nostril. She added saline to the tip and the sponge instantly hydrated, swelling and filling his nasal cavity. The bleeding slowed to a trickle, then stopped. Abby asked if he felt okay and he nodded shyly, glancing at the bloody spots on his shirt and pants, trying to cover them with his hands. Something was off with him.

Abby asked Gem to run a blood count as well.

"Already on it," Gem said. "And his INR is high. Almost seven."

Abby threw her a look of appreciation. "Thanks. Nice work."

She gave Trapp the vitamin K to reverse the blood thinner. "Have you been taking your medications like you're supposed to? And watching what you eat?" Certain foods could interfere with warfarin.

Trapp nodded, looking at the ceiling. His lips moved silently, as if counting the tiles. Abby started to question him further when Marcus wandered in, taking in all the activity: Gem bending over the lab equipment and Abby sitting with the patient, checking him frequently for new bleeding as she wrote her notes. Marcus chuckled.

"What?" demanded Gem.

"Look at us. I can't believe anyone let us take care of him. I mean, I look like—all tropical and hakuna matata. Gem looks like a punker who lives on the street. And Dr. Wilmore looks like a hippie from the sixties." He laughed out loud.

"Hey, zip it." Gem jerked her head toward the patient, glaring at Marcus.

"You don't need to worry," Marcus said, handing Abby a list of diagnoses and medications, his writing covering most of the page. "Wilma says that he barely knows up from down—his dementia's been pretty severe the last few years. But she hates just sitting at home in Indiana, following him around and putting things back in place, so now she drives him around instead, going to national parks and national monuments with him and Brutus. Brutus is waiting out in the RV. I guess they've been to nearly half of them. What are there, like almost two hundred, I think."

"Wilma?" asked Gem, staring at him.

"Brutus?" asked Abby, staring at him and feeling like an idiot for not realizing Trapp was demented. Too busy with the nosebleed, she chided herself. She knew he wasn't right, but had not pursued it, and that was a mistake.

"Wilma, his wife. Brutus, his Chihuahua," Marcus explained patiently. Marcus patted his round stomach. "Is anyone else hungry? He's older than Bob. Brutus, I mean. You know, in dog years. But Wilma says the dog knows more than Bob at this point. Anyway, they just came up from the Tetons but they didn't like it there much. A little too remote, you know. They just love Yellowstone because you can get so close to the geysers and everything."

Marcus took a breath and Gem jumped in. "Really. I'm so glad, Marcus, that you and Wilma are out there having a nice chat while we're back here saving lives. But what we really need—"

"Calm down. You're always so tense, Gem. I'm getting to the good stuff. He's on the warfarin because he had a pulmonary embolus a few years ago when he got treated for his prostate cancer. And now he's incontinent some of the time, so Wilma has to keep pads on him, which gets really expensive on their budget. And Brutus is starting to think that if Bob can pee inside, maybe he should too, so you can see the problem. She's thinking of selling the house and just living in their little RV, following the seasons. Interesting, right? Anyway, she's worried because she thinks he takes his meds sometimes when she's not looking. Bob, not Brutus. That there might be fewer warfarin pills than there should be."

Gem frowned. "She needs to get—"

Marcus held up a hand. "I told her she needs a pillbox so she can keep track."

"You've only been with her a short time," Abby said, suppressing a smile. "How did you get so much information?"

Marcus shrugged and went back to his post. Then he stuck his head into the room again. "Oh, and I forgot to tell you that Wilma made him an appointment with an ENT doc in West Yellowstone for late this afternoon. She made it a few days ago, before things got worse. So that doc can follow up on the nosebleed." He craned his neck around Gem to look at Trapp. "Looks like you got it stopped. Nice. Shall I get Wilma?" And he was gone again.

Gem stared at Abby and shook her head.

After the Trapps left, Gem rearranged the drawers more to her liking while Abby typed his medications and diagnoses into the EMR. She mentally chastised herself again about the dementia.

"What's wrong?" Gem stood scrutinizing her.

"What do you mean? Nothing's wrong." The left-hand rattlesnake had an accusing green eye, Abby realized, which seemed fixed on her.

"You look upset."

Abby rubbed her face. Here it came already, her recurrent disquiet. Maybe there really was something wrong with her, with her ability to figure things out. "I shouldn't have missed the fact that Trapp was demented. I should have honed in on that much sooner."

"Huh. Maybe you were a little busy trying to keep him from bleeding to death. And you got it stopped right away."

"Right. Anyone could have done that." Abby stared at her laptop.

"Fine." Gem paused, as if reviewing her options. "So, are you going to be like this all summer? All like, I should have done this, I should have done that? Over nothing? Because you're not 100 percent perfect?"

Abby looked up, astonished, at Gem's critical eyes and her pale crumpled lips.

"Probably," said Abby. She was going to elaborate, say something like that's what I do, but refrained. She hardly knew this woman.

"Okay then. Now I know." Gem turned and went to talk with Marcus, but returned immediately. "Marcus has disappeared, in case you care."

"What?"

"He's not there. What an oddball."

"He didn't say anything?"

Then Marcus reappeared, juggling three cups of ice cream as he closed the door behind him.

"I got us a little snack," he said, happily handing them out. "I hope everyone's okay with vanilla. I didn't want to take a chance in case someone was picky about flavors." He looked somberly at Gem.

They sat in the waiting room, eating their ice cream in companionable silence. Then Gem went to the back and returned with a handful of disposable gloves.

"Here," she said, giving them to Marcus. "Next time someone comes in all bloody, put these on first. We don't need you getting sick with hepatitis or HIV. I know it doesn't take a lot of skill to manage the front desk, but it would still probably be hard to replace you on short notice."

Marcus laughed. It seemed impossible to offend him, which seemed to make Gem try all the harder.

"I've got a whole box of gloves at my desk," he said jovially. "It just didn't occur to me to put them on. What a doofus, right?"

"Good lord, Marcus. Use your head next time." Gem rolled her eyes.

He was still laughing when a tap came at the door and a well-dressed man poked his head in.

"Anyone here?" He entered, looking around, an attractive big man in slacks and a pressed shirt. Late fifties with gray temples, he exuded confidence and command, his dark hair slicked back and a strong handshake for everyone. Rex Wrigley, one of the head concession administrators. He managed the hotels and restaurants, visiting for a few days in his rounds about the park, and he wanted to know all about the new clinic so he could inform his staff.

"We're not exactly dressed for work," Abby confessed, slightly embarrassed by the way he kept staring at her. Was it disbelief? "We're just getting organized, and then we accidentally saw a patient."

Wrigley pulled a chair up to Abby, a little too close, and flashed her a smile, his teeth very white and even. His knee bumped into hers.

"And here I thought all woman doctors were frumpy nerds," he said, looking approving.

"Pretty much the truth," Abby asserted, inching back her chair. "I may be the biggest nerd you've ever met."

He smiled whitely again. "I don't think so."

"We need to close up, sir," Gem interrupted, abrupt.

Wrigley ignored Gem and leaned toward Abby. "We should get together one of these days, you and me. Have dinner. Those of us in charge around here ought to know each other."

Abby laughed. "I'm not very much in charge."

"Of course you are. The health of thousands of people—actually, millions—depends on you."

"Unlucky for them," Abby said dismissively, then added pointedly, "Ask my boyfriend."

He paused. "The doc at the Grand Canyon, right?" He waited until Abby nodded, then put his large hand on her shoulder and leaned closer, speaking quietly, as if no one else was there. "You must be very lonely without him. The canyon is so far away."

Abby wondered how he knew about Pepper. The realm of the national parks could be a small world, she was beginning to realize. "Of course I miss him. But we'll be getting together."

Wrigley nodded thoughtfully. He had a way of lowering his head, boring his eyes into hers, and she suppressed an urge to look away. "Of course you will. It looks like I'd better go now. But we'll talk later."

He turned, waving briefly at Gem and Marcus, then stepped quickly down the stairs and was gone.

"I don't like that guy," said Gem. She cut her eyes away to make sure he was gone, then back hard at Abby, sharp as a knife. "Stay away from him."

5

A package arrived for Abby. She smiled at the return address from Pepper, opening it to find an assortment of healthy snacks: dried fruit, almonds, peanut butter crackers. Pepper knew how she often grabbed a candy bar for quick energy. Eat more protein, she could hear him say. She unfolded a paper tucked inside, a beautiful ink drawing of a tiny Abby running past a huge foaming geyser, the page filled with complicated lines of steam and water. She felt amused that she was, in fact, still wearing her running clothes as she opened the mail. Abby decided that this summer she would train for a marathon, or at least half of one, a long-simmering goal. She had her eye on the race in Phoenix next winter.

Most mornings, and some evenings too, she ran along the roads and trails, past hot steaming ground and bubbling puddles of soupy mineral broth, scalded mists seeping from cracks, the terrain hissing and gurgling as she breathed the scent of brimstone and tasted the tang on her lips. The earth felt unsound, a little unhinged, unreliable.

Abby was fascinated with her planet in a new way, and a little more afraid of it.

Immediately busy, the first clinic days went better than she expected. Local residents immersed Abby in high blood sugars and long-overdue female exams, temperamental blood pressures, insomnia and depression. Parks were meant to be serene places, but the people she saw, both locals and tourists alike, tended to be stressed. Everyone worried about schedules and timetables; they slept poorly and ate worse. Marcus sometimes overbooked her—a malfunction in the computer program—but he always compensated by blocking space later in the day. He apologized and shrugged as if it couldn't be helped, laughed when Gem criticized him, and periodically gave Abby a few hours off to make up for it.

She and Pepper talked every night.

"Thanks for the food," Abby said affectionately. She didn't tell him that another cartoon was already on its way, one where he pointed at her licking an ice cream cone and nagged "Eat more healthy!"

"I'm missing you so much."

"I miss you, too," he replied quietly. A shadow in his words.

"Are you doing okay?" Something seemed off.

"Sure. It's just…different than I thought. It's…worse."

Abby's concern climbed. "Is everything okay at work? How is Dan Drake? Are your researchers there yet?"

"Dan is great. He knows a lot, and he's a quick learner." Pepper's voice warmed and picked up. "And he gets along with people. We're incredibly busy, and he's already an expert with heat injury. The temperature down in the canyon is over one hundred five, so you know how that goes. And it's getting hotter next week. The research people arrive tomorrow."

"And has Priscilla started following Dan home yet?"

Pepper laughed and groaned, which made Abby feel better.

Yet after they hung up, she realized she never followed up on what he said, that something was worse, and she almost called him back. She felt torn, wanting to take care of him yet not be fussy. Gem already chastened her about overreacting. But Abby felt like climbing in her car and heading for the canyon, to check on him and hold him close. She suddenly missed him dreadfully, missed his thoughtful face, missed his gentle hands, missed their talks and their quick morning coffee and their long peaceful evenings on the deck. She had to go out and walk, even though it was late, and was pleased to catch Old Faithful in a fine eruption with few tourists around. The geyser didn't care.

Late afternoon the next day, Gem brought a young man into the treatment room.

"Looks like sutures," she announced to Abby, "but the wound needs some cleaning first."

Abby nodded, knowing she could trust Gem's judgment. When Gem wasn't certain, she quickly said so. Abby saw a few more patients, a man with chronic headaches who drank far too much caffeine, and a typist with carpal tunnel syndrome who didn't want her boss to know because she didn't want to rock the boat in an already tense workplace environment. Even simple problems were often not as simple as they should be.

"Turbo's ready," Gem announced.

"Turbo?" Abby noticed Gem wore long-sleeved tops at work, usually a cotton scrub jacket tugged down over the snake. The fangs and the green eye looked pale, too. Abby suspected cosmetic concealer.

"Your next patient. Turbo Packer. His real name is Thomas, but he's called Turbo because he's a little wound up. He doesn't sit still much. Everyone in the employee cafeteria knows him. He talks all the time and sometimes doesn't make much sense. And he doesn't seem to have any friends. But I think he's harmless. So I'm always nice to him."

"He's sort of hyper?" Abby tried to make a mental picture.

"Yeah, maybe he's hyperactive or something. Anyway, he's a busboy and a kitchen aide and probably does a million other things, and he's got a laceration on his hand, from a broken dish this morning. I can't imagine why he didn't come in sooner, but that's Turbo. He wanted to finish his shift, and he probably did someone else's work, too."

"It's a workplace injury, then? Did he start the paperwork?"

"He doesn't want to. Doesn't want 'them' to know about him."

"Them," Abby nodded. Little surprised her anymore.

Small and slight, Turbo Packer sat impatiently with his hand soaking in antiseptic, his leg jiggling. Abby found him serious and pleasant enough although distracted, his dark eyes shifting constantly. His ragged hair looked like he hacked it back with blunt scissors.

"Let's take a look," Abby said. A deep, inch-long laceration split open his palm at the base of his thumb, no longer bleeding.

He tipped his head to see Abby better.

"So you're the new medicine woman. That's good. I don't usually trust medicine men. Medicine women care more about the earth and her creatures. I'm glad you're here." He spoke quickly and kept bobbing his head. "That's good. That's good."

"Thanks," said Abby, leaving it at that. "Are you sure you don't want to register this as a workplace injury? That will cover all your costs, especially if there are any complications. I really do recommend it."

"No way," he replied emphatically. "Please quit asking. The less they know about me, the better. And don't worry, because there won't be any complications. I heal really fast and this will mend in no time. Very fast, very fast. I just want to see if it needs stitches."

"Definitely, the way it's gaping open." Abby nodded. "I'm surprised they let you keep working."

"They didn't know." His eyes bounced over to hers then skipped away, around the room again. "They're mostly fools. Without me, nothing would ever get done."

Abby numbed his skin and went to work. The wound came together well, and Turbo seemed pleased.

"Nice work, Medicine Woman." He held his hand up high and tilted it back and forth, eyeing it from all angles.

She cautioned him not to work until the sutures came out next week, but he insisted he would wear a rubber glove and it would be fine. Then Abby asked about a tetanus vaccine, and he stood abruptly to leave.

"Not interested. Those vaccines have bad metals and chemicals in them—they can really mess you up. My body will fight off any infection, including tetanus. Don't worry about it." He nodded vigorously.

"Can you at least tell me when you last had one?" Abby followed him to the door.

"Don't worry about it. Thanks for helping." He peered at her, head still bobbing. "I'll remember you. When the time comes."

"Turbo…" Abby started to ask more, but he was gone.

Gem watched him leave as he trotted across the parking lot. "Pretty typical. He's a little off. But he loves animals and feeds them and talks to them, and he always does extra work for everyone else. He just says weird things."

"What did he mean? Did you hear what he said…when the time comes?"

Gem shrugged. "Who knows? He probably thinks about the end of the world all the time. But he's not alone—quite a few people around here are obsessed with that. Since we're all going up in flames any day now when the volcano blows."

"Doom and gloom, doom and gloom," Marcus chanted from the front, overhearing them. "Am I the only person around here with a positive attitude?"

"There better not be any patients in the lobby right now," Gem complained. "It's bad enough for them to deal with your shirt. It looks like ghostbuster slime."

"This is my favorite shirt," Marcus protested, running his hand across his chest, smoothing his lime green polo shirt. Then he turned to a man who just entered. "Oh hello, Ranger. What can I do for you?"

An older man, hazelnut hair and moustache striped with gray, the ranger stopped by to greet them and check the place out. Abby wondered how long it would take before every curious person quit dropping in.

Friendly and warm, Ranger Don Perkins reported how much people liked the new clinic. For being so nice, Marcus gave him a pen stamped with the FirstMed logo. Gem rolled her eyes because Marcus stood up and revealed his blue plaid slacks, clashing against the lime green shirt.

"Who dresses you, Marcus?" Gem said. "And you could give him something even more useful, like maybe a Band-Aid."

Ranger Perkins laughed and admitted he could use a Band-Aid, either for himself or a tourist, at least three times a day. Marcus happily went to the back and produced a handful of Band-Aids. Perkins asked Abby about working in Arizona, and she related all the dangers at the canyon, the prolific warning signs about heat, hydration, and deadly drops off the cliffs.

Perkins smiled, his crow's feet deepening. "Have you seen all our notices about staying on the boardwalks? Just a few months ago, a guy wandered away with his camera and fell into a thermal pool. He died, pretty much instantly. His body basically dissolved before we got to it—some of those pools are very acidic. And staying away from bison? We've got bison on the road all the time, then we've got tourists acting silly around bison, no matter what we tell them." His troubled eyebrows came together. "And now there's another dead one."

Gem stiffened. "You mean another creepy murdered dead bison, don't you? I've heard about that."

"Yes, I'm afraid so." Perkins looked unhappy. "This is the third one. Someone's killing them, and we're not even sure how. Not near the road, so sometimes we don't find them until later. I mean, maybe there's more—how would we know? They range all over the park, millions of acres. And they also die natural deaths. I mean, natural for a wild animal."

"But these don't seem natural?" Abby asked.

"No, we don't think so. They're not old or sick. And we're finding a piece of each one missing, usually an organ. It's confusing to figure it out, because scavengers like wolves come along and tear the carcass apart. First it was a tongue missing, then a piece of lung. Now this last one is missing its stomach, and we got to it before the wolves."

"Missing?"

"Cut out. Gone. We can see knife marks. The tongue would be easy to take—I mean, once the bison was dead—but the lung and stomach took some work. These are huge, strong animals, so it can't have been simple. Those bison were sliced open, guts spilled out, like a cheap horror movie." Perkins stopped. "I probably shouldn't talk about it. If you don't mind, it's better if you don't spread this around."

"Ew," Marcus recoiled. "Are you looking for someone in a hockey mask?"

"What is wrong with you?" asked Gem, swatting him on the shoulder.

Marcus chuckled. "So much, so much."

Perkins left. Abby found herself uneasy in a complicated way. Maybe it was the bison killings. Maybe it was the way Pepper sounded the night before. Maybe she was just lonely, at loose ends, in a way she had not been since joining up with Pepper last year. She hurried to finish so she could go running, which often settled her. She should find time to meditate tonight, too, a calming ritual she had lately let slide.

"Oh-oh," said Gem, looking out the window across the parking lot. Rex Wrigley approached, a lively spring in his step, dressed more casually this time in sweats, with earbuds around his neck. Sunlight sprinkled his shoulders and a damp sweatband circled his forehead; clearly, he had just finished working out. Abby thought he looked better, more relaxed, his hair flopping boyishly on his forehead. He bounced up the steps and entered, shaking hands warmly all around, saying nice things to everyone. Marcus beamed and Gem looked cautious. Maybe they had misjudged him.

"Sorry to bother you all again," he apologized, "but you were closing up the other day and I never got a good look. I just want to know what the clinic can do, what services you have, so I can advise my staff."

Abby took him around, showing him the treatment room where she could repair lacerations, remove skin lesions, lance and pack an abscess. They had fiberglass tape for casts and splints, urinary catheters, the EKG machine for chest pain and palpitations, supplies for Pap tests and even uterine biopsies. Wrigley still stood too close, occasionally bumped against her, and Abby couldn't tell if it was intentional or if his boundaries were simply different. She bemoaned their lack of x-rays, which caught his attention.

"That seems pretty important," he commented. "People are always slipping and falling down."

"Well, they have to go up to Mammoth," Abby sighed. "I have this conversation with patients several times every day. Or more."

"That's ridiculous." He turned officious, looking around. "And do you have a panic button, for emergencies? For trouble? Where is that located?"

Abby laughed. "That's a little too sophisticated for this place. We have one at the canyon, though." She sobered. That panic button probably saved John Pepper's life when he was nearly shot last year by an escaped convict, a deranged man who blamed Pepper for his incarceration. Pepper had testified against him during his trial for domestic violence.

"But don't you have drugs here? Money?"

"Not much. Hardly worth bothering about."

"The bad guys don't know that though, do they?"

Wrigley turned to face Abby. Gem worked behind him, cleaning lab equipment, her dark red hair fluttering in the breeze of a small fan she used to air out the area. She looked at Abby and wrinkled her nose as if smelling something rotten, eyeing the back of Wrigley's head. Abby glanced away so she didn't have to react.

"Listen," Wrigley said, flashing his teeth, his hand on her shoulder. "Tomorrow's my last day here for a few weeks, and I'd love to sit and talk with you. About how things are going, what you need. I've got a dinner reservation at the Old Faithful Inn tomorrow night—Sunday. That's very hard to arrange this time of year. You'll join me, won't you?"

Abby paused, perplexed. Rex Wrigley had no control over her resources; he worked for a different company. She started to point that out, but Gem jumped in first.

"Don't forget, Dr. Wilmore," she said quickly, driving her eyes into Abby like nails. "You promised to go with me to Bozeman tomorrow, to look at the dinosaurs. We probably won't get back till pretty late."

Wrigley twisted and squinted at her, as if just realizing she was there, even though Gem had been in the lab the entire time.

"Remember?" Gem's dark eyebrows rose into her maroon hair, looking only at Abby, her expression now mild and innocent. A spark jumped from the tiny diamond in her nose.

Abby nodded slowly, deciding to go along. "Yes. I'd forgotten." She turned back to Wrigley. "Maybe the next time?"

He agreed graciously. But before he left, he mentioned that he had seen her out running. "That's a pretty good pace you take. I'm impressed."

"It's slower than you think," she protested, "because I'm not very fast."

He shook his head, amused. Abby felt strangely exposed. She usually wore running shorts and a tank top, sometimes just her sports bra on a hot day, but she never thought anyone would be watching her. When he was gone, she turned on Gem.

"What the heck?" Abby folded her arms. "Bozeman?"

Gem shrugged. "I don't like him."

"I don't either," said Abby, unwilling to admit how odd she felt about his comment. "But now I think you're the one who's over-reacting."

"Yeah. Only you didn't see the way he looked at you when you were leading him around. He was practically drooling down your back." Gem eyed Abby critically. "You do know that you're pretty, right?"

Abby waffled her hand. "Maybe on a good day."

"No. It doesn't work that way. Why are you always so self-deprecating, anyway?"

Abby narrowed her eyes. "I'll tell you what—we are not going to lie about this. What if he saw us here, found out it wasn't true? So I guess we're going to Bozeman tomorrow. You'd better not have any plans. How long does it take to get there, anyway?"

Gem grinned. "A few hours plus. And you're driving. My car's a piece of crap."

That night, after darkness claimed the geyser basin, Abby wandered the paths, mingling with tourists who were out late, waiting for Old Faithful, due to erupt any minute. She sat on a wide concrete ledge near the visitor center, the surface still warm from the day, and leaned back to study the stars. Orion had moved south for his summer hunting grounds, no longer visible, no bright stars gleaming at his shoulder and foot. It made her long for Pepper and their star conversation. When she spoke with him an hour ago, she asked about his statement, that things were worse than he expected. Only now, he denied ever saying that. When Abby pressed, he made nebulous comments about relationships. But then he revived and sounded fine, enjoying Dan Drake, busy at work, having fun with the study. Disquieted, she let it go.

She watched the stars thickly jamming the sky, glittering like crazy confetti. Old Faithful fumed but stayed quiet. She heard people remark on that, how unusual that was for such a highly predictable geyser.

Abby quit waiting and turned in. Maybe she was just tired; it had been stressful to get the clinic up and running. Now with a week under her belt, she felt good about it most of the time, felt she was accomplishing things.

Nearly asleep, drifting into visions of supergiant stars, Abby heard footsteps outside her cabin. People always came and went nearby, but this was closer and slower, a hesitant tread just outside her door. A scuff of sole. She waited and waited until she thought it was gone, but then it came again, now right outside the wall by her bed. Then nothing. Was she imagining this? Or was someone outside there by her window, literally inches from where she lay? Abby found herself holding her breath, trying to listen hard, her heart thumping.

Nothing. She didn't dare pull aside the curtain and peek out.

Get a grip, she scolded herself. If anything, it was a racoon or possum, and hopefully not a skunk. Maybe a tourist, who stepped out of a nearby cabin to smoke or study the night. Abby lay staring at the ceiling, muscles tense, listening for a long time. She tried to meditate, a lost effort.

That night she had her first nightmare. She was back at the Grand Canyon, back in that terrifying night when Pepper faced the convict and his gun. Only this time Abby was too far away, unable to distract the man, unable to reach him, and the gun discharged with a roar. Pepper clutched and looked down in sad surprise as his chest burst open in a scarlet spray of blood. Abby shrieked and woke up, gasping, sweat running down her face.

She grabbed her phone and nearly called him, just to make certain he was safe. But then that felt ludicrous—she would wake him up, babbling nonsense about nightmares. He would be upset and worried about her, and she didn't want to do that to him. It wasn't a panic attack, it was just a stupid dream.

Abby did not fall asleep for a long time.

6

Originally, Abby planned to rise early and go running before they left for Bozeman, but because she slept poorly and because she imagined Wrigley's eyes on her, she put it off. Wrigley said he would be gone for a few weeks, so tomorrow she wouldn't be looking over her shoulder. She and Gem were on their way to Bozeman by eight o'clock.

"Everything is so green," Abby exclaimed as they left Yellowstone and drove north, following a chattering creek, surrounded by steep grassy ranges. "It's so green it hurts my eyes."

"That's because you're from the desert. This is actually what most people call normal." Gem wore her black jeans and a gray T-shirt, and the rattlesnake unfurled down her arm with abandon.

Neither spoke much for a while, the landscape unfolding as they flew along the road, the sky empty of clouds and vivid with summer sunlight. The distance soothed Abby, obliterating all that nonsense about night stalkers and bad dreams. Clearly, moving up here and getting started took more of a toll than she realized.

Abby asked Gem about her background.

"Army nurse for four years," she explained briefly. "That paid off my school loans."

"I thought maybe you were military," Abby said.

"Really? Why?"

Abby smiled. "Not many people say 'fubar.' And maybe the tattoo. And you say *sir* and *ma'am* sometimes. Which, by the way, you have to stop. At least the ma'am part."

Gem nodded. "Good observations."

"So how was that?" Abby asked.

Gem considered for so long that Abby thought she had forgotten. Gem gazed down the highway, then off at the empty hills, and finally spoke. "Some good, some not so good."

Abby waited. "Because…?"

"You don't want to know." Her words harsh. Then she softened a little. "No one does. Trust me."

Gem lounged sideways against the door, as much as her seatbelt allowed, watching Abby.

"You're staring at me," Abby said at last.

"I'm still trying to figure you out." Gem held up her fingers in an open square, as if framing Abby's profile.

Abby laughed. "Let me know how that goes. I'd like to know that myself."

"See? You act like you're clueless, but you're not. You're good at what you do, and patients really like you."

"You didn't tell me this trip would include psychoanalysis," Abby complained.

"Hey, you're the one who insisted we go. I was pretty content with just lying to that bastard."

"Listen, I'm no fan of his. He's definitely got a creepy vibe." Abby glanced at her, then back at the road. "But why do you hate him so much?"

In the edge of her vision, she saw Gem's jaw work back and forth. Under the shaggy layers of wine-tinted hair, Gem had small features with a few light freckles, giving her a cute, nearly pixie-like look. Until she spoke and her potent personality took over.

"He reminds me of someone who's an effing ass," she said curtly.

Abby backed off. When they talked again, they focused on safer topics—tourists and medicine and weather and bison.

"I hope you like triceratops." Gem warmed to the subject as they neared town. "This part of North America is like, triceratops central. If you're not careful, you'll stub your toe on one, just eroding out of the ground."

"I don't know much about them."

"It's Wyoming's state dinosaur. What's Arizona's?"

"Um, I have no idea." Abby grimaced. "We have a state fossil, but now it seems a little boring."

"Oh, come on. What is it? Wyoming's state fossil is just a fish."

"It's actually wood. You know, petrified wood. Like the Petrified Forest."

Gem laughed. "Your state fossil is a piece of wood?"

"Hey, it's beautiful. Show some respect. It's been there for a few hundred million years." Abby recalled those trees, rocky relics of a vast woodland, now stranded on a dry plain. Close to the same age as Kaibab limestone, Abby thought, suddenly missing Pepper. "Anyway, I used to study astronomy. So I probably know more about the extinction event—you know, the asteroid—than the animals themselves."

"Really." Gem stared at her. Again.

Abby smiled, pulling into the parking lot at the Museum of the Rockies. "Here we are, talking about things that happened over sixty million years ago like it was last month. Don't you love it?"

Gem gave her that cautious look. "What?"

"Time. Space. How immaterial we are," Abby said, solemn now, not sure if she should have gone there.

"And you're saying that's a good thing?"

"Sure. At least, for me."

"Keep going." Gem's eyes narrowed.

Although feeling cautious, something inside Abby wanted Gem to understand. "Let's face it, our lives are really minimal, especially when you put them in the context of lightyears and planets and dinosaurs. It takes the pressure off when you're just a blip, because what we do doesn't matter much. But it also means we've got this little tiny window, to find as much meaning as we can."

Gem stared at her.

"Anyway, it helps me." Abby shrugged. "It helps me with my anxiety."

"Anxiety?" Gem squinted deeper, alert in another way.

"Long story," Abby said briefly, getting out of the car. How did they end up talking about this, anyway?

Abby loved the museum. Gem insisted on paying their entrance fees since Abby drove. They stayed for hours, slowly wandering the dim exhibit halls and reading the placards, studying the fossils, saying little.

Triceratops skeletons stood everywhere, almost as large as elephants with their massive triple-horned heads and wide bony frills that flared up behind their faces. Likely gentle grazers, they only needed their spear-like horns for defense. They studied huge specimens, the grownups with imposing four-foot horns and tiny infants with simple skulls who had not yet sprouted their horns or frills. Abby found them strangely endearing and melancholy, these babies with their blank faces and partially formed skulls that had died from unknown injury or disease.

"It was millions of years ago," she muttered sternly to herself, wondering what was wrong with her, standing there mourning infant dinosaurs.

Gem looked at her, inquiring, but Abby shook her head and they moved on to T. rex. Gem remarked that's what she wanted to be in her next life, a massive tyrannosaurus. When Abby reminded her they were extinct, Gem turned haughty.

"My fantasies can travel through time," she claimed, aloof. "If I want to be a vicious crushing reptilian monster that avenges wrongs, you can't be critical."

"Little bit of anger in you?" Abby commented mildly.

"You could say that." Gem examined the bones and avoided Abby's eyes.

They ate supper at a local restaurant. Gem reminded Abby that she could have dined with Rex Wrigley, and Abby kicked her under the table. Then Abby climbed behind the wheel and they started back. Twilight tinged the sky gingery orange, the horizon striped with purple cloud streamers. Abby half expected to see a triceratops peer around a hill.

Gem turned to Abby.

"I want to thank you," she said slowly.

"Hey, it was your idea. I adore that museum—who would have thought? Out here in the wilds of Montana? I hope you had as much fun as I did."

"I did." Gem smiled. "But that's not what I meant. I want to thank you for never asking about my tattoo. You may be the only person who's spent this much time with me and left it alone."

"Really?"

"You can't imagine. I could fill books. 'Why did you get that? How old were you? Isn't that unprofessional? Don't you know it'll look bad when you get older? Aren't you sorry now? Can't you get that erased?' Maybe a few comments that it's cool, but that's rare."

"Sometimes people don't even know when they're being rude. I figured you had your reasons."

Gem huffed. "I wanted something bigger, like a T. rex. But the tattoo guy said it wouldn't look right because my arms are skinny and he talked me into this instead." Gem paused, a little mischief in her face. "I call her Bitey."

A laugh burst from Abby. "Bitey?"

"Are you laughing at my snake?" Gem stroked the fanged head with her finger.

"No, I'm laughing at you."

With Gem's prompting, Abby described how good Pepper was and how much she missed him every day. Gem remarked that she was between bad boyfriends. So Abby suggested a contest to see which one of them was the most insecure, and Gem gave the widest grin Abby had ever seen on her face.

"I'll win," Abby assured her, "because I'm insecure about pretty much everything."

"No, I'll win in the end. I just keep my insecurities hidden better than you. And I can't believe you just got me to say that."

"I'm so insecure that I'm insecure about how insecure I am."

"How about Pepper? Are you insecure about him?"

"Completely. The worst. But I still bet you believe in love, in your secret heart."

"Not hardly. Love is a fairytale." Gem's nostrils flared and her lips curled.

The sky had gone dark, only a ruddy glow in the West that made Abby think of volcanoes. She thought what a lovely day this turned out to be, and then she thought about John Pepper and how different her summer could have been without her doubts, if she hadn't felt a need to prove something to herself, if she—

Gem poked her sharply in the arm.

"Pull over," she demanded loudly, pointing. "Right up there. Where the shoulder widens."

"What?" Abby startled, braking and signaling, steering onto the crumbled pavement. "What's wrong? Do you need to pee? You scared me."

Gem unbuckled her seatbelt. "You were falling asleep. Move on around—I'm going to drive."

"I'm sure I wasn't. I was just thinking about—"

"Shut up. You totally were. I'm not going to let us both be killed just to be polite. What would Marcus do without us? Move."

Abby reluctantly switched seats, but she knew Gem was right. She probably had only four hours of sleep. She leaned back and drifted off almost immediately.

Abby found herself in a dream of triceratops, a peaceful meadow filled with the large browsing beasts, humans walking among them. The sun shone warmly, the air yellow, dancing with blue dragonflies. Then came a sound, a harsh bellow, and Abby saw the huge brutal head of a tyrannosaurus rise up. Everyone started running, and up ahead she saw a tall slender man that looked like Pepper who suddenly fell and went down right in front of a thundering dinosaur. Abby shouted at him and Gem was poking her again, hard.

"Wake up, wake up," she said insistently.

Abby blinked and looked around.

"Are you okay?" Gem asked. "You were making funny sounds."

Abby took a deep breath and nodded. "Strange dream."

"I hate it when that happens," Gem said kindly.

7

Monday came, the clinic in full swing. After returning from Bozeman the night before, Abby crawled exhausted into bed and the nightmares stayed away. Maybe now with Wrigley gone, those dreams would stop altogether. Not that Wrigley had anything to do with Pepper, but it all tangled in her mind and she just hoped it would leave her alone.

"This man's rash is terrible," said Gem. "It looks like poison ivy, but he hasn't been out in the woods."

"Are there blisters?" asked Abby. "Really painful?"

"Yes…how did you know?"

"Just guessing. I could be wrong."

A cheerful fifty-year-old mechanic who worked in vehicle maintenance, Dave Turner was an automotive wizard. He put in long hours, known for his generosity, quick to help anyone when their car misbehaved. He bore a bushy black beard and curly black hair, and was so healthy that he hadn't seen a doctor in years. Dave's low-rumbling voice made Abby think of bears.

"It kept me up all night," he said, raising his arm and twisting his neck to peer at the rash, which arched across his chest, under his arm, and around his back. The skin shone scarlet, crowded with blisters, weeping and crusted. "I thought it would just get better by itself, you know. But it's actually worse."

"It's pretty classic," Abby said after studying it carefully. "It looks like shingles."

"Shingles?" He sounded indignant. "Isn't that something old people get?"

"It's more common then. But it can strike at any age."

"So how did I catch it? Who can I blame?" Even uncomfortable and tired, his eyes twinkled.

"Blame chickenpox," she explained. "That's the virus that causes it. No one understands how, but sometimes the virus hides away in one of your nerves, and then it breaks out decades later."

It made Abby think of the measles virus and how SSPE could appear in the brain years later. Except SSPE was fatal, while shingles was usually just miserable.

Damn sneaky viruses.

"Great, a virus," Dave grumbled. "So antibiotics won't work, right?"

"Correct. I wish everyone understood that. The good news is, there's a medication that works pretty well against this virus. It's the same drug we use for chickenpox or herpes—they're all part of the same family. All those blistering infections."

"Oh wonderful. So I've got herpes now." He made a face.

"Not exactly," Abby smiled. "Without the medication, it can take a month to clear up. And sometimes the nerves stay painful—really painful—for months after the rash goes away. If you take the medication, that's much less likely."

"Jeez, give it to me. Fast."

Abby wrote the prescription for acyclovir and asked him to return in a few days, sooner if he got worse. After he left, Gem glanced up from her computer, unhappy.

"I can't believe I didn't know that was shingles." Gem scanned through images, dozens of rashes. "But in all these years, I've just never seen it. And it's pretty common."

"That's the thing about learning medicine—" Abby began, interrupted by Marcus's appearance.

"Hey, I thought that guy had shingles," he exclaimed. Colorful as usual, Marcus wore a flaming red shirt and mustard yellow pants. "I saw your diagnosis. He told me about his rash while he was waiting, and I thought it sounded just like when my grandma had it. So I was right, right?"

Gem groaned loudly and buried her face in her arms. "Even Marcus knew what it was."

Consoling, Abby patted Gem's back while Marcus crossed his arms and looked pleased.

"As I was saying," Abby continued, "the thing about learning medicine is how it's so random. You might diagnose a really rare thing that almost no one has seen, and then somehow you never see a common thing. That everyone knows but you. It happens all the time."

Her head still down, Gem groaned again.

"It's okay, Gem," Marcus soothed. "You can always ask me when you don't know what's going on."

"Excuse me?" Gem's head raised and her light brown eyes locked on his face like heat-seeking missiles.

"Oops, gotta go. I think that's my phone," he said quickly, making a terrified face and hurrying back up front.

Gem glared toward Abby, fuming.

"Oh, come on. He's adorable," Abby said, trying not to smile.

Marcus poked his head back through the doorway. "And guess what? They found another dead bison. This one had part of his liver cut out. Gross."

They all shuddered.

Abby planned two important phone calls that night: Pepper and Lucy. First, though, she vowed to attend a ranger talk. She wanted to learn more about Yellowstone, to better understand what her patients faced and what decisions they made. Especially the bad decisions.

Just that morning, she treated a stout middle-aged woman with burns on her foot who whimsically stuck her sandal-clad toes into a stream of hot water flowing from a bubbling pool. Although the burns were not deep or extensive, the tight blisters between her toes would need close attention for days. She also had poorly controlled diabetes and her sugar registered three hundred.

"I kind of take a break from my diet when I travel," the woman confessed. She hadn't been checking her sugars, and snacked on chips to stay alert while driving.

"Unfortunately, high sugars will make this harder to heal, and more prone to infection," Abby said. "Do you have your glucose meter with you?"

The woman looked at the ceiling as if she might find it there. Abby sighed, and recommended buying another one since she was ten days from home. And to snack on carrots and celery.

"Same crunch. Almost no calories," Abby pointed out.

"But I really like the salt."

Abby stared at her and felt like she was growing old.

She hurried to the talk at the visitor center, joining a large peak-season crowd. The interpretive ranger wore a sharply creased uniform, a proper young man with lively eyes. He explained the magma chambers stacked below them in giant fiery bubbles, plunging toward the planet's core. Although a modest man, he barely disguised his excitement, as if they had gathered for a big lava-themed party.

Abby noticed, though, that he did not mention the increased seismic activity. Or how the ground had risen many inches over the last few years, or how Yellowstone Lake was slowly tipping as a dome bulged under it on the northern floor. New beaches appeared in the north, and shorelines flooded in the south as lake water slipped down the tilted terrain. Abby tried to imagine the forces beneath, shoving up that huge lake that had a surface well over one hundred square miles.

As he finished, Abby waited while the ranger answered questions until just one child remained, a boy about eight years old, lingering with his parents.

"Go on," his dad urged, slightly pushing him.

The boy wore a Smokey Bear cap and looked at the floor.

"What's up?" asked the ranger, crouching down.

"I just wanted to know how hot lava is," he mumbled.

"What a great question. I can't believe no one asked me that." Abby read the man's badge: William Bridges. "Do you know how hot water is when it boils?"

The boy nodded, peering from under his hat. "Two hundred twelve degrees."

"Exactly. You must be really smart, because a lot of people don't know that." Bridges lowered his voice, as if sharing a secret. "But lava can be ten times hotter! It can be two thousand degrees."

"Wow." The boy's face lit up.

"Right? Do you think you might be a scientist someday?" The child nodded vigorously and Bridges smiled. "I think you're smart enough." The boy rushed back to his parents, who waved appreciatively.

Abby introduced herself. Bridges explained he was a graduate student completing his doctorate in geology, working as a summer ranger to help with expenses. He kept taking time off to earn money—his scholarships were not enough—which made him older than his classmates. Abby asked about the information he left out, the small escalating quakes and the rising dome under the lake.

"Well, you're right. But we're encouraged not to alarm people. Yet." He removed his Smokey hat and scratched his head, short cinnamon-colored hair, then carefully replaced the hat. Abby found his cautious decorum and childish wonder endearing. "Even Old Faithful's been a little off, and that hasn't happened in a long time."

Abby was fascinated. "I guess that doesn't get mentioned at the YVO site."

"Most people don't even know about the Yellowstone Volcano Observatory. Good for you."

"I figure as long as I'm here, I should learn something."

"Nice. I hope you keep coming to the talks." He seemed awkward then, glancing away.

"I absolutely will," she assured him, turning to leave. "Thanks so much."

"Wait," he said suddenly. "You probably shouldn't make a big deal about Old Faithful. Being off schedule." He straightened and acted official. "It's likely just a normal variation."

"For sure," Abby smiled.

Then she called Pepper. He seemed better since her museum trip, and pleased she attended the ranger talk.

"It sounds like you're getting into the swing of things," he observed.

"I think I am," Abby agreed. She began to realize how he worried about her isolation. "And it's only been ten days."

"It feels like forever. Come home."

"I'll be back before you know it."

"So, you're eating healthy?"

"Most of the time," she replied. "The food has been pretty good. Better than if I was fixing it myself, anyway."

"And you're still running?"

"That's going really well. I might be more fit than I've ever been. Is this some version of twenty questions? Do I get a prize if I get the answers right?"

"Maybe. And how about sleep?"

Neither of them slept well, even when things were good—common for many physicians. All those years of night call, adapted to abrupt awakenings, the need to be instantly alert.

Abby paused. "Probably as good as you."

"You had to think about it. And sleeping like me isn't exactly something to brag about."

"It's fine, John."

She imagined his lips tightening; he knew when she wasn't completely forthright. But she did not intend to reveal her dreams and cause him worry. She didn't tell him about the dead bison, either, or the increased seismic activity. Now that she thought about it, she was avoiding a fair amount.

"Any anxiety?"

"Nothing like that." No wonder she hesitated. "John, I said I'm fine. Quit badgering me."

He backed off then, so she made sure to sound positive and well adjusted. Which wasn't difficult since she mostly felt that. She drew him a new cartoon that showed them talking on the phone, where a frowning Pepper said "Be happier, dammit!" It would go out in the morning mail.

Then Abby called Lucy. Depending on the day, Lucy might be Abby's friend or guide or surrogate mother. A seventy-year-old gynecologist in Phoenix, built short and thick like a barrel of nails, Lucy helped Abby change her life, back when Abby finally confronted her anxiety and quit drinking wine every evening to fall asleep. Abby could tell Lucy anything. Abby's own family had not coached her much, her father long dead and her mother marginally estranged, in an inexplicable marriage to an unfriendly man.

"About time!" Lucy said warmly. "I was about to call you. Tell me everything."

Abby described her eccentric, competent team. She admitted that the clinic ran well, to her own surprise. That she handled both the patient and administrative duties without much trouble, despite their limited resources.

"I guess the canyon prepared me better than I thought. It feels good."

"Coming from you, that's a pretty strong statement. You're usually reluctant to say anything positive. About yourself, I mean." Lucy waited. "But?"

"What do you mean, but?"

"Come on, Abby. There's something else. I can hear it."

Abby sighed. Why did she surround herself with people like Pepper and Lucy—and now maybe Gem—who could see through her? She hated being so transparent. It felt like a weakness, and she wondered how to become more opaque. She longed to be tougher.

"There is some strange crap going on." Abby told her about the slaughtered bison, about Wrigley and his dimly lascivious attention, about Yellowstone itself with its escalating quakes. A sense of unbalance. "But I'm running a lot, training for a marathon. Maybe. It helps…it's a good moving meditation, and I haven't had any anxiety attacks. There's just—"

Abby stopped, wishing she hadn't said more.

Lucy waited. Lucy could wait a long time.

"I've had some nightmares. Not every night."

Lucy didn't wait as long this time. "About?"

"About Pepper." Abby suddenly felt like crying; she pinched herself painfully to block it. "About him dying. Not just dying, but being killed, being shot. Once I dreamed he was trampled by dinosaurs."

"Dinosaurs." Lucy's voice quiet with concern.

"Okay, that's not as crazy as it sounds. I had just been at a museum, looking at lots of dinosaur bones. Really big dinosaur bones."

"What do you think is going on?"

"I don't know exactly. I've never had this happen."

"But you seem okay during the day?"

"Yes. Absolutely." Abby felt Lucy move mentally around the information, poke at it. She didn't like the sensation of being an emotionally dissected specimen, like a splayed-out lab frog. "I'm sure it's fine. Don't make too much of this—it already feels better now that I've told you. It will probably go away."

"Okay." Lucy drew the word out. "But I wonder. Maybe this is sort of a delayed reaction to last year."

"Kind of late for that," Abby said, dismissive.

"It's been known to happen."

They agreed to stay closer in touch, but Abby's worry had already diminished. Talking to Lucy usually did wonders.

8

The conversation with Lucy did help. The nightmares disappeared, much to Abby's relief.

Ranger Hannah Santana came in clutching her eye. Santana was a no-nonsense Hispanic woman with a long dark braid who looked utterly miffed at being there. Superficial scrapes scuffed her forehead, slightly bleeding. Abby pried her hand away, but the lid clenched tight in spasm, protecting her injured eye. The interpretive ranger who Abby met at the evening talk, William Bridges, came upon Santana just before the accident and escorted her into the clinic.

On patrol that morning, Santana cruised between geyser basins, monitoring traffic. When cars began backing up, she correctly assumed a bison jam and crept along the shoulder until she reached the spot where a huge old bull stood tiredly on the pavement. He straddled the dotted line, a brooding gaze. Vehicles lined the road in both directions, stretching out of sight, and people tired of waiting started climbing out to see. Santana warmed to her story, enjoying her audience.

"I'm watching that old bull, making sure everyone keeps their distance. Which is supposed to be at least twenty-five yards for bison," she added for Abby's benefit. With a low warm voice, she pulled her listeners in. "Then I hear this guy talking behind me, down off the road, calling out instructions like he's taking a photo. I turn around and here this man is putting his camera on a tripod, aiming it at his wife and baby who are posed on a tree stump about thirty feet from a bison cow and her calf. Thirty feet!" She gestured and made a horrified face.

"I can see that cow's nervous. Her head is up and she's breathing hard—she's just glaring. And the clueless wife is giggling and making the poor little baby wave its little baby hand at the stupid husband, who's waving his stupid hand back at them. So I start walking over there, as quiet and as quick as I can, but I don't want to spook that mama bison. It's already plenty spooked."

"Just a sec," Abby interrupted. She tilted Santana's head back and pulled down her lower lid, creating a tiny gap and dropping in the medication. "That'll numb up in a minute. Go on, please."

Santana blinked a few times and dabbed at her eye with a tissue Abby handed her.

"So. I'm quietly telling the dad to quit and I'm motioning at the mom to stop with the baby-waving. But it's too late, because that cow shakes her big furry head and she paws the ground and I'm thinking holy crap! And so I rush off the other way and I shout and wave my hands and she whips around and her tail shoots up and she charges me. So I turn and sprint for the trees nearby, and I look back to see how close she is and Bam! I run right into a branch with my face."

Her audience stood spellbound, Abby and Gem and William Bridges, hanging on her words. Santana smiled, sheepish.

"It's embarrassing, but that tree probably saved me. I went down so fast—I just disappeared in the tall grass. One minute there, the next minute gone."

Bridges, hovering in the background, took over. "I saw it. The cow pulled up, looking back and forth. It wasn't funny then, but it is now. It was like a cartoon, like she couldn't believe it. Her calf came up behind her, so they just trotted off, and by the time Hannah got up, they were gone. And the commotion woke up the old bull in the road and he walked off, too, so the jam was over."

By now the eye was numb enough for Santana to open her lids. Abby instilled fluorescein and turned on the black light to reveal a large scrape across the surface of the eye, bright green from the dye. Abby turned the upper lid inside out, looking for bits of bark that might be clinging underneath, but everything was clear.

"You've got a corneal abrasion," Abby explained. "In other words, the surface cells of your eyeball got scratched away. Sort of like a skinned knee. So every time you blink or move your eye, that spot really hurts. The good news is that it looks superficial, and these abrasions heal quickly. The cornea grows back fast, within a day or two."

"That's a relief," said Santana. "And it feels so much better, now that it's numb. So I can go back to work?"

"Absolutely not." Abby had learned to be very specific with rangers about medical time off. "You need to stay home, rest quietly, and mostly keep your eyes closed. Boring, I know. But you don't want your eye roaming back and forth, rubbing against your eyelid. Keep it quiet and it will heal faster."

"I can work with one eye," she insisted.

"If one eye is moving, they both move," Abby said. "They work in tandem. Stay home."

Abby completed the paperwork and asked her to return the next day to confirm it was healing.

"Hannah with two H's, right?" Abby asked, scribbling.

"Yeah. My mom is white, and she liked Hannah. My dad is Latino, so Santana. And don't laugh, because I have three younger sisters, Anna, Savannah, and Rhianna. I guess we're lucky there weren't any more of us or she might have been named Banana." She shook her head. "Don't do that to your kids."

Abby smiled. "My parent days are a long way off. Here's your instructions. Please follow them."

Santana folded the paper and stuffed it in her pocket.

Santana was out the door, but before Bridges moved on he dug in his pocket for an angular fist-sized rock and handed it to Abby. The stone was fine-grained, a beautiful coppery pink, strewn with small flecks.

"Rhyolite," he explained. "From the last time the lava flowed here. I thought you'd be interested."

"Nice," said Abby, thrilled with the rock and giving him a little sideways hug of appreciation. "So it's about six hundred fifty thousand years old?"

He shifted away, disconcerted at her hug. "Yes. But of course, it's all older than that."

Abby nodded. "Because it's all part of the earth, which is all part of the universe. Back to the Big Bang."

William Bridges grinned, his discomfort forgotten. "Yes. Anyway, the rhyolite makes a really thick, viscous lava, so it flows slowly."

Abby turned the stone in her hands, rubbing the grain, imagining the lava. Over half a million years ago, she thought, indulging in a brief moment of calm at the enormous timespan. Infinities always soothed her.

"Hey," said Gem, poking his arm. "Where's my rock?"

He turned to her, perplexed.

"I didn't know you liked this stuff." He seemed baffled, standing between the two women, looking back and forth.

"I like everything," Gem told him. "And especially if you find a piece of dinosaur out there. The bigger and badder, the better."

"There haven't really been many big dinosaurs found inside Yellowstone—" he began.

"Hey," interrupted Gem, taking Abby's rhyolite, tossing it up and catching it. "I thought you couldn't remove stuff like this. That you can't take it out of the park."

Bridges looked narrowly at Gem. Abby saw that he didn't know what to make of her, saw him glance at the tiny diamond in her nose and the menacing tattoo on her hand. Abby imagined he might be thinking, as Abby herself had, that the snake was watching him.

"I was about to get to that." He turned back to Abby, now stiff and authoritative. "You can't take it with you when you leave. National park rules."

"No problem. But I can't wait to show it to Pepper." Abby took her rhyolite back from Gem, appreciating the weight, the tight texture of the stone. "Thanks so much, William. I love it."

After he left, Abby looked sternly at Gem. "I'm not sure he understands when he's being teased."

"He understands," Gem replied. "He just doesn't know how to deal with it. Poor guy. He's probably never had a girlfriend because he spends all his time with rocks and books. But he's kind of sweet and cute and way too serious. And you can tell that he wishes he could ask you out."

"No he doesn't," Abby protested. "I talk about Pepper all the time. I've made a point of it."

Gem clutched her hand dramatically to her chest. "The heart wants what it wants."

"Calling him a poor guy is right, if he ever spends much time around you," commented Abby, and they both got back to work.

Turbo Packer came in soon after, concerned about his ribs. After putting him in a room and taking his vital signs, Gem handed Abby a small plastic bag, creased and slightly greasy, filled with reddish-brown powder.

"This is from Turbo," Gem said quietly, grimacing. "He wanted me to give it to you—I think he was too shy to do it himself."

"What on earth?" Abby held it up by the corner.

"He says it's cinnamon and nutmeg. He thinks you should use it. He says that it's good for the brain and it helps reduce stress."

Abby gave her a look.

"It's his way of trying to be nice," Gem said.

The patient scheduled after Turbo had cancelled, so Abby spent extra time. His hair hung ragged down the back of his neck, and he still had his nervous nod.

"I think my ribs are growing wrong." He pulled his shirt up and fingered his lower ribs. "Something's not right."

Abby had him lie down to examine him better. She found a minor asymmetry to his lowest floating ribs, but nothing out of the ordinary. Nothing tender.

"I don't know, Turbo. It feels normal to me. Almost no one is exactly the same on both sides of their body. Someone might have an arm or a leg that's slightly longer, or one foot that's a little smaller. Some people wear different sized shoes on each foot. Your ribs are slightly uneven, but they've probably always been like that."

"I don't think so." He shook his head and slid his fingers over his ribs. "This is new. I don't know what it means."

Abby doubted she would dispel his apprehension. "Let's just watch it for now, keep an eye on it. As long as it doesn't get worse, it shouldn't be a problem. Why don't you come back in a few weeks or a month and let me check it again."

"You don't think I need an x-ray?"

"No. There's nothing painful, so an x-ray probably wouldn't help. It wouldn't change anything. Besides, we don't even have an x-ray machine here right now. You would have to drive all the way up to Mammoth."

His head bobbed. "Yeah, I don't have a car. I guess that's a good plan, Medicine Woman." He squinted at her. "I get really tired some days. Like, I can hardly walk. I can't even work those days. Then other days I've got so much energy I don't need to sleep."

Abby studied him with new concern. His face pinched, serious. "How long can you go without sleeping?"

More bobbing. "Maybe three days."

"That's a really long time." Abby wondered if it was true. There was no way to know. "Is something bothering you? Are you upset about something that's keeping you awake?"

"No way. I'm excited. I've got lots to do, and it's going to be great." His lips curved into a strange smile, showing slightly crooked gray teeth. Abby doubted he'd seen a dentist in years. "I'll surprise everyone. You wait and see."

"Okay. But these tired days—do they follow the sleepless days?"

"Nope, not at all."

"Are you taking anything? Any medications? Alcohol? Or using any drugs, marijuana, anything like that? Street drugs?"

Turbo frowned. "No way. I would never contaminate my body with junk like that."

"Maybe the next time it happens, if you came in right away, I could try to figure it out. Or I could run some blood tests now and make sure everything's working right. You know, check for anemia, your thyroid, things like that."

He nodded vigorously. "Let's do that. Just to be sure."

"We could also run a drug screen," she suggested, wondering. "Make sure you're not getting any drugs in your food or water."

He peered through his hair, lank in his eyes. "You're smart, Medicine Woman. And you're fast, too—I've seen you running. They'll never be able to catch you, that's for sure."

"They? They who?" What on earth, she thought. Was everyone watching her run?

"No. I can't tell you their names." He pulled back.

"All right." Abby spoke carefully, her worry escalating. "Turbo, are they actual people? Or are these voices that you hear?"

He tilted his head, wary. "Can't say anything. Not now. Can we hurry up with that blood test?"

After he left, both Gem and Marcus voiced their concerns.

"He seems more troubled," said Marcus. "I'm not sure why. We just had a long talk about his forest animals, how he can lie out in the woods for hours and soon birds are hopping up on his legs and rabbits are nibbling by his arm and butterflies land on his head. It sounds like a scene out of Bambi. Only Turbo is a weird-looking Bambi."

"I guess we should be glad that he finds peace there," Abby said, feeling uneasy. "I'm worried that he's developing some kind of psychosis. His story seems a little manic, a little paranoid."

"Like not sleeping for days?" asked Gem. "And I agree with Marcus. Lately he seems more…troubled. Some of the guys in the cafeteria give him a hard time, calling him names. Like whacko, nutso, the stupid things guys say. I've told them to leave him alone."

"Good for you," said Abby.

She went running at dusk, the blushing sky thronged with cumulus, bulky and bumpy. The clouds climbed through the troposphere, their rounded tops glowing in the final rays of sun. If it was darker, Abby imagined she would see flicks of lightning, the bright veins at the heart of storms. The ground by her feet steamed and slurped as she moved past hissy vents and shimmering hot pools, making her feel very small and irrelevant on her planet. A little unnerved, a little reassured, that those deep terrestrial schemes—much bigger and totally unconcerned with her small life—were busy at work.

9

"You're not going to believe this!" shouted Marcus early the next morning, happily thumping down the telephone.

"This better be good," complained Gem, coming to the front office with Abby close behind. "We're trying to get ready back here. But it's kind of difficult when you're yelling around."

The schedule stayed full now. Abby saw more locals, coming in for everything from fatigue to STDs. Especially STDs. Chlamydia ran rampant in the young, mobile workforce, and lately she also treated several cases of genital herpes. Abby was looking for someone going to West Yellowstone and back, someone who could pick up a supply of condoms so they could hand them out when needed, like they did at the canyon.

"Oh, it's good news." Marcus paused for effect, waiting until both women stood there, anticipating. He wore a hot pink polo shirt and right now it matched his flushed face.

"Guess what!" he chortled.

"Marcus, I swear. One of these days I'm just going to murder you, and no one will blame me," Gem cried, her nose flaring.

"Okay, killjoy. Don't guess. You're such a wet blanket, Gem." Marcus paused again, then proclaimed, "We're getting a portable x-ray machine!"

Abby stared with disbelief. "Are you sure?"

"The company just called to make sure we'd be here when it gets delivered around noon. A rep will come by this afternoon to go over the operations manual."

"Well, hallelujah," remarked Gem, clapping him on the shoulder, her annoyance forgotten.

"How did this happen?" asked Abby, incredulous. "I just talked to them last week, and they said it wasn't likely this summer. They basically told me to quit whining."

Marcus shrugged, still beaming. "From what the woman said just now, someone with the concessions here insisted they needed it, for when employees get injured. Like, one executive called the other. So FirstMed made it happen." A puzzled look came over him. "Who do you think could have done that?"

Their faces fell.

"Wrigley," said Gem, rubbing the back of her neck.

"Well…" Abby said. "It's still a good thing. Maybe he's just trying to be nice."

"Right." Gem's face closed.

Abby waved Gem off. She was weary of explaining to patients why she couldn't tell if they had a fracture, or whether their prolonged cough was serious. Tired of handing out maps to Mammoth Hot Springs. They often did not go. Maybe some went to West Yellowstone instead, or they just traveled on, delaying their medical care and chancing bad outcomes.

The equipment arrived as promised, sending Gem into a flurry, so Abby helped by taking over some of her duties, getting vital signs and drawing blood.

"Just our luck," groaned Abby at the end of the day, disappointed, "that we didn't need it today."

Then the next morning they used it twice, for a fractured finger and to check out a man's badly bruised and swollen foot after being crushed by a horse. Excited, Marcus looked up the billing codes.

"This should definitely make money." He cheerfully ran his finger down long columns of numbers, avidly filling out forms. "I can't believe someone had to twist FirstMed's arm for this."

"It's not even your money," Gem complained. "You act like you invented radiation."

"Lighten up, Gem. Some of us enjoy a challenge. So sorry to be positive in front of you. I forgot that happiness stresses you out."

They reluctantly anticipated an appearance from Wrigley. Abby finished the last morning patient, an older woman with swollen joints who worked in the hotel laundry. Abby suspected rheumatoid arthritis, because her hand x-rays showed irregular bone erosion in the joints. Looking up initial treatments on the computer, she heard Wrigley's deep voice greet Marcus. Marcus sounded effusive, thanking him for the x-ray machine. Both she and Gem were too busy to pay much attention, but their mood shifted in a dark way. He's just a man in hotel management, Abby reminded herself, and he has no say here. She should probably quit buying into Gem's aversion. Fortunately, Marcus kept him entertained; they heard snatches of an animated conversation.

Then Marcus appeared, shaking his head.

"You can't keep hiding," he whispered. "Mr. Wrigley's here to see the x-ray and he brought us all lunch."

Abby and Gem rallied and showed him the celebrated machine. Wrigley dressed casually in jeans and a striped shirt, his thick hair swept back. He seemed gracious and interested, kept a normal distance from Abby, and even asked Gem about her work, listening closely. Abby watched, trying to see if Gem warmed to him, but couldn't tell.

Then Wrigley gathered up takeout boxes for himself and Abby and suggested that the two of them go outside to eat, implying matters to discuss. The previous week, Marcus somehow procured a small picnic table for their breaks, now resting in the shade behind the clinic. The days were beautiful lately, sunny and warm, the air drifting with the soft scent of pine and the faint stink of earthen chemicals. Abby let Wrigley usher her out and avoided looking at Gem.

"I just have to thank you again, Mr. Wrigley," Abby said, formal but sincere. She appreciated that he sat down across from her and that he didn't bump her knees. "That x-ray has already improved our work."

"Rex. You have to call me Rex." He chewed a bite of his sandwich, serious. He looked attractive in a polished way, a sharp jaw and quick eyes. "Listen. I think we've gotten off on the wrong foot. I really want this clinic to succeed. It's good for the workers here, so it's good for our company. I don't mean to come across as pushy or anything."

"No, you're fine." Abby felt embarrassed and wondered what her impression of him would have been without Gem. Still not great, she guessed, but at least he seemed aware.

He looked skeptical but let it drop and asked instead about her medical training, her work at the canyon, how long she and Pepper had been together. Abby in turn inquired about him, and he spoke of his stress, managing so many people, driving long distances, and the constant emergencies of hotel work. He exercised to reduce tension, he said, and he soon was carried away, touting his strength and fitness, talking about his sprints and distances, his weightlifting. Abby smiled absently, bored, her thoughts drifting to her patients.

He carried on, saying how he also loved golf. This was a problem, since the nearest golf course was at Big Sky, many miles away.

"I don't suppose you play?" he asked hopefully. When Abby shook her head, he went on. "I guess your receptionist does, doesn't he? Marcus Limerick. It sounds like he's actually quite good."

"Really?" For all his gossipy attention to everyone else and his ability to plumb the tiny details of peoples' lives, Abby thought, Marcus revealed little about himself.

"Maybe I'll have to see, get up a game with him." A gleam of competition arose in Wrigley's eye.

Abby glanced at her watch, gathered her napkin, made ready to go. She had done her duty. "Thanks so much for lunch."

"Will you reconsider my dinner invitation?" he asked earnestly. "It won't be for two weeks—I'll be gone again till then. But I really miss having professional people to talk with. I miss having an intelligent conversation. I can't socialize with people I supervise." He looked a little dejected.

She couldn't see a graceful way out, especially considering what he had done for them. But Gem's worries nagged at her, and Abby valued the grains of truth.

"That would be okay, I guess." Abby gazed levelly at him. "But I need to be really clear. This is just a dinner. I sort of get the feeling you might think it's a date. But it's not. I am completely committed to my boyfriend. And if he happens to come up to Yellowstone that weekend, the dinner would be off, of course."

He smiled widely. "Absolutely. See, I knew I'd made the wrong impression. But that's the last thing you need to worry about. Just friends."

Abby smiled back, briefly. "I've got to get to work."

"Wait a second. Don't move." Before Abby could react, he reached across the table. With his thumb, he slowly wiped something from the corner of her lip. "There. That's better."

Abby stood and self-consciously rubbed the spot.

"Thanks," she said awkwardly. He could have just told her.

"Of course." His eyes caught hers. "And I hope you keep running—you're looking great. It's a wonderful way to unwind. Because we all need to unwind, don't we?"

"Of course." Abby turned away and stuffed the leftovers into the trash bin, letting the heavy bear-proof lid slam shut. He departed from there, walking briskly around the trailer and across the parking lot.

When Abby went inside, she found Gem bent over her computer.

"And what did Mr. Powerful want with you out there, all to himself?" she asked, not looking up, her face tight.

"Not much. Dinner in a few weeks." Abby knew this would be a problem.

"I hope you said no."

"I couldn't, Gem. What excuse could I make up?"

"Really? You couldn't invent another trip out of the park?"

Abby sighed. "It's just a dinner. I'm not very good at lying and making things up, I'm afraid. I think he's lonely."

"Yeah, I bet he is. For good reasons." Gem glared. Abby couldn't tell if the anger was directed at Wrigley, or at herself.

Abby changed the subject and pointed at the screen. "What are you looking up?"

Gem glanced toward the door to the front desk and lowered her voice. "You're not going to believe this. Look at all this stuff about Marcus. He used to be a golf champion. Played in college, won everything. I mean, he was really good. He was on the pro tour. And then he suddenly wasn't."

"Really?" Abby looked closer. She wouldn't have recognized him at first, because Marcus the golfer was about forty pounds lighter. But he had the same cheery grin, the same sunny face. The same colorful and mismatched clothes.

"I guess that explains how he dresses," Gem remarked.

Abby nodded. "What do you think? Confrontation?"

"Dang right," Gem said. "Marcus! Get back here!"

He poked his head through the door. "What?"

"So," Gem said slowly. "Dr. Wilmore and I just happened, completely by accident, to discover that you are a championship golfer. Like, nationally recognized for a while. How has this never come up?"

Marcus's face went blank. "Who told you that?"

"You did. I heard you talking with creepy-face out there about golf and I could tell he was impressed with what you said, so I started looking up a few things. And guess what? Marcus Limerick is all over the internet with his golf amazingness. Why don't we know about this?"

Marcus shrugged, recovered and smiling again. "Why would you?"

"Oh, I don't know. Because we have conversations all the time and you never talk about yourself or where you've been or what you're doing next? You just say you're trying to figure out what to do with your life, blah blah blah."

"All true." His face charmingly innocent.

"But why did you quit golfing?" Abby asked. "It looks like you were going places."

His face fell. "No, I wasn't. It's a tough life, and I guess I'm not very tough. Long story short, I couldn't handle the pressure." Then he turned a switch and smiled brightly. "Can we please not talk about this?"

Both Abby and Gem felt bad for pressuring him. They murmured apologies and gave him a hug, and he retreated to his desk looking wounded.

"Now I feel sad," said Abby.

What a strange day, one thing piling on top of another. She was ready to lose herself in the afternoon work, think about other things. Other peoples' problems. She hadn't run that morning and longed to get out, hear the steady slap of her feet, weave between the steaming vents and gurgling, sputtering pots of boiling water, sense the moody magma below, the lifting land. As if the entire park was sloping, sliding. She immersed herself in splinting sprains and assessing asthma and analyzing chest pains and explaining depression and treating chlamydia and diagnosing sinusitis and reassuring worriers and counseling smokers and removing suspicious skin lesions and detecting a new case of diabetes and cautioning against alcohol overuse and advising contraception.

At the end, Gem picked up Abby's cell phone and tossed it to her.

"What?" asked Abby, not seeing any messages or calls.

"Look at that new icon, the one with the big ear. That's a voice-recording app that I just downloaded for you."

Abby touched it and a screen appeared that looked like an old-fashioned tape recorder, with record and play buttons, reverse and fast-forward. "What's this?"

"I want you to use it. Please. Every time you're alone with Wrigley. Just turn it on and keep it close by, like in your pocket."

"Okay…"

"I'm serious." Her jaw jutted.

"Gem. What is going on? Do you know something about him that I should know?"

Gem's upper lip curled and she flashed her eyes toward the door as if she might escape, but instead she propped her elbows on her knees and stared at the floor. Her hair fell forward, and Abby noticed another tattoo on the back of her neck, deep into the hairline—small Asian characters. Then Gem straightened and her gaze bored into Abby.

"Don't ever ask me about this again, okay? I mean it." Her words clipped, fierce. "When I was in the army, there was this officer. He acted so much like Wrigley that I want to puke every time I see him. He even looked a little bit like Wrigley. Wrigley's taller and he's older, but the resemblance is remarkable."

Abby waited, fearing.

"He raped me," Gem hissed. "I was too young, I was stupid. I was so clueless, and I didn't know what to do. He said it was my word against his. That he would just say it was consensual, and it was my duty to shut up and take it. So I did."

"Oh, Gem," Abby breathed in dismay, her hand over her mouth.

"I took care of it—I made sure I got transferred right away." Gem raised her chin. "I went and I learned self-defense and I knew I would never let that happen again. Then I got my tattoo—my badge of resentment. It hurt a lot, getting that tattoo, and I loved every second of the pain. Do you understand?"

Abby nodded, understanding well enough. She felt miserable and horrified and put up her arm to hug her but Gem bristled, backing away.

"No, it's not a hugging thing. I don't want kisses and sympathy. I want to stay angry and pissed forever." Her face stony. "I just want you to believe me when I say that bastard Wrigley is bad news. I know how these guys act. I bet he touched you, didn't he? I bet right before he left, didn't he?"

Abby's eyes widened, staring at Gem. She remembered his thumb against her skin, skimming the edge of her mouth, her lips. "How do you know that? Were you watching?"

"Of course not. I'm not going to spy on you." Gem slowly softened. "Please tell me you'll use that app, just to protect yourself."

"I will. Absolutely." Abby nodded.

"All right, then." Gem turned her back and resumed working.

A little later Abby asked her about the tattoo, hidden in her hairline.

"It means fuck you," Gem said, not even looking up. "In Chinese."

That evening, Abby ran a long way, her mind reeling with the day. First Wrigley with his private lunch and his unwelcome feel on her face—the more she thought about it, she wondered if there was even anything there. Instead of simply touching her, it now felt like he had fondled her. The few seconds grew into imaginary minutes, and she had to make herself stop imagining. And then Marcus's painful golf background, so stressful that he asked them to leave him alone. And now Gem's dreadful assault and irreparable rage.

Abby felt no one was safe, that no one escaped disappointment or suffering or sorrow or pain, that a well-adjusted, satisfied life was a myth. That in fact her own struggles with anxiety, and at one time with alcohol, were not so significant. And she admitted to herself how badly she missed Pepper. She suddenly comprehended her depth of caring for him like a blow that nearly made her stop and double over. She increased her speed, feet slamming down, lungs rasping for air, to outrun the flash flood of emotions.

Panting, exhausted, she slowed to a walk, up the hill toward the lodges, and there came Rangers Perkins and Bridges moving toward her down the path. They seemed engrossed in conversation, so Abby just waved and planned to pass by, but they stopped to say hello.

"Everything okay?" Abby asked, still huffing. A beautiful solstice evening filled the crystalline sky, late lavender light, small rosy clouds floating near the horizon. She closed her eyes briefly, awed at the delicate display, and felt a tiny bit better.

Perkins sighed and Bridges looked away.

"You don't have to tell me if you shouldn't," Abby assured them, thinking maybe she didn't want to hear. There had already been too much for one day.

"No, you might as well know, now that you're part of this place," said Perkins. He gazed at the gentle sunset. "There's another dead bison."

Abby waited. Perkins watched the horizon and Bridges looked uncomfortable.

"So," she prompted, "was something missing?"

"Yes." Perkins glanced at her briefly, since apparently Bridges wasn't about to say anything. "This time it was the testicles."

"Good grief. I had to ask." Abby wished she had not stopped. Bridges looked discomfited, and Abby guessed he had never said the word testicles aloud when a woman was within a mile of him. Or ever.

She couldn't fall asleep that night, so she went out to survey the stars, spangling reassuringly, each distant world brightly dispassionate about humans and their convoluted troubles. Calmer, she returned to her cabin and dropped deeply into slumber until she dreamt she saw Pepper. He was hiking up the Bright Angel Trail on a moonlit night when a dark silhouette appeared on the rim and raised a rifle. The muzzle flashed like a sudden sun. Pepper crumpled on the trail and she awoke with a violent jolt.

Abby lay awake after that. She pulled her laptop into bed and tried to distract her unsettled brain, visiting the Yellowstone Volcano

Observatory website to check on her small corner of the planet. It remained quite industrious, the miniature earthquake swarms still increasing. This had officially become the most earthquake activity ever recorded there, and the ground had risen more as well.

What were the chances, she asked herself, that she would happen to be here when the supervolcano finally erupted after more than half a million years? Abby closed the computer and began her relaxation exercise, counting her breaths backwards from one hundred. Usually she was asleep before she got to sixty.

When her counting reached twenty, she gave up and moved on to a medical journal. She might as well put her messy, restless mind to work.

10

Poor sleep and nightmares aside, Abby felt good about her work. The clinic ran well, everyone pulling together seamlessly.

"We may need to rearrange some patients," Gem announced when Abby emerged from an exam room. "Ranger Bridges just brought in an older woman from Madison campground and she doesn't look so good—she might take a while."

"What's the problem?" Abby asked, typing faster, entering instructions for a patient with a painful jaw. Temporomandibular joint disorder, better known as TMJ. "Do I have time to finish this?"

"I think so. She's short of breath, so I'll check her oxygen and hook her up to the tank. And get a chest x-ray. I had Bridges bring her right back, so Marcus didn't have a chance to get her entire life history."

Abby turned and saw William Bridges sitting on the other side of the workstation, reading something on his phone, waiting for the outcome. He waved at her and she nodded, then said to Gem, "I'll be there in a minute. Do your best Marcus impression and see what you can find out."

"Right?" Gem disappeared into the room.

When Abby saw seventy-six-year-old Edna Dillon, Gem had her propped up on the exam table with oxygen prongs in place.

"Feeling better?" Abby asked.

"A little." Though tired wrinkles meshed her thin face, her eyes sparked. Far underweight, almost emaciated, Edna raised a bony hand to adjust the oxygen, speaking slowly between breaths. "I should have brought my own oxygen, but it all happened so fast."

Edna worked as a campground host. While making her rounds that morning, checking that no one overstayed their reservation, weakness suddenly seized her and she had to sit down. Then she couldn't find the strength to rise. She described an increasing cough and low-grade fever for several days. Her sister Mildred now waited at the campground in their RV, holding down the fort, anxious to hear how Edna was doing. Abby had just launched into the medical history when Gem reappeared.

"Can you come look at this? Right now?"

Abby promised Edna she'd be right back.

"Sorry to interrupt." Gem motioned Abby away from the door. "But I thought you should see this."

Abby startled at the film. Normal lungs full of air should appear nearly black on an x-ray, with a light maze of white markings for the delicate bronchial tissues. But Edna's lungs were mostly white on both sides of her chest, filled with opaque clouds and cottony masses, like storms underway. A few normal dark areas scattered here and there, but not much.

Abby shook her head. "You're right. She should go to the hospital. I don't know how she's even breathing at all."

Abby returned to Edna. "There's no easy way to say this, but your chest x-ray looks pretty bad. You might have severe pneumonia."

"Oh, goodness." Edna waved Abby off. "Most of that's been there a while. It's the lung cancer. I guess we hadn't gotten to that yet."

She hacked abruptly, a convulsive cough that shook her whole body, and she spat into a tissue. She showed it to Abby, a mustard-brown glob of mucus speckled with blood.

Edna wrinkled her nose and wadded it up.

Abby touched her arm. "Let's start over with that cancer thing."

Last winter, Edna was diagnosed with inoperable lung cancer. Although she'd quit smoking five years earlier, the cancer had already begun to silently grow. Determined to battle, she first underwent radiation, then endured a round of chemotherapy. Sick and weak from both therapies, which made minimal impact on the cancer, Edna had enough.

"I'm going to die either way," she said. "There's no point in being sick from both the treatment and the cancer." Her furrowed lips trembled slightly. "I've worked here at Yellowstone every summer for the last fifteen years. Seven of those years were with my husband, until he died. I love it here, and he loved it here, and this is where I want to breathe my last breath. I'm pretty sure that won't be too much longer."

"No one can really predict," Abby said, although she didn't doubt it. "Should I see if there are any hospice services?"

Edna shook her head. "I tried, to make things easier for Mildred. So she doesn't get stuck doing everything for me. But there's not much help, not way out here. It's not fair to her, but she insists it's okay."

"Is she healthy?" End-of-life care could be exhausting, a twenty-four-hour task, physically and emotionally draining.

"She's strong as an ox. And I told her to just smother me with a pillow when I'm too much bother. That made her good and mad."

Abby placed her stethoscope against Edna's ribby chest. Her lungs held ominously quiet in many places, no air moving through at all. As if those areas were closed down, done. Other sections bubbled and crackled and wheezed, a collection of broken noises. Abby pulled back and Edna looked at her skeptically.

"It sounds bad, doesn't it?"

"Pretty bad," Abby agreed. "Because I don't have your previous x-rays for comparison, I'll just have to guess whether it's worse or not. Unless we contact your regular doctors and get a copy?" Edna shook her head. "So this is either your cancer getting worse, or you might have a pneumonia on top of it. Or maybe both."

Edna looked solemn. "Should I do anything?"

"That's up to you." Sadness welled up in her, and Abby had to push it down. "You could go into the hospital, get some lung treatments and antibiotics, get some nutrition through your veins. You're probably malnourished—"

"No hospitals." She crossed her scrawny arms, her skin spotted with purple and brown blots. "I'm done with that."

"Okay. Then I could run some lab tests—"

Edna shook her head no.

"Okay. Then I could just give you some antibiotics, see how you do. That might help. Or not."

Edna nodded. "I like that. I was kind of hoping to see the Perseid meteor shower one last time, though it's still about six weeks away."

Abby grinned. "I'd love to watch that with you. It's my favorite."

Edna's face brightened and she gripped Abby's arm. "Let's do it."

Gem tapped on the door and stepped in, telling them about the transport to the hospital. Edna looked at Abby with alarm.

"I'm so sorry, but you need to cancel it," Abby apologized to Gem. "She's staying here in Yellowstone."

Gem stared at them, at Edna's clutch on Abby, their earnest faces. "All right then." She whirled away to make her calls.

Abby came out and called Edna's sister, explaining the plan while William Bridges sat close by, listening. After she hung up, Abby turned to him.

"Can you take her back?" she asked.

He stood and frowned, uncomfortable. "I don't know. It's kind of unorthodox. I'm not sure I'm authorized to make that decision. To just leave her to die, I mean. I'm supposed to make sure she gets whatever help she needs. There's reports I fill out, explaining her disposition."

Abby realized this was difficult for William, inclined to follow the rules even if the rules didn't fit. Letting Edna die at her campground without medical care felt ambiguous to him, a violation of stability he was meant to maintain.

Gem stood nearby and then Marcus appeared with a question, both listening.

"It's okay," Abby said to William. "I understand your position. Just pretend I never asked. I'll take her myself over lunch."

"But I'll still know," William protested. "And I still need to finish my report. Maybe I should check with my supervisor."

"Could you just let it go?" Abby didn't want this complicated by some stuffy authority. "Just say the doctor released her. That's true enough."

William removed his Smokey hat and rubbed his cinnamon hair. "I guess…"

Gem clapped him on the back. "Good for you. But you should let me take her," she said to Abby. "What if you get caught in a bison jam? You could be hung up for a couple of hours, and patients will be waiting."

"That's true—" William started to say.

"Nope, not you, Gem," Marcus interrupted. "You're more important here than me. I'll take Edna. I barely got to meet her, and she seems like a lovely person. I'd be happy to go."

William shoved his hat on and held up his hands. "Stop. Everyone just stop. You're all crazy. It obviously makes the most sense for me to take her. So I'll just do it, okay? Is she ready?"

Abby hurried to get Edna arranged before he changed his mind. "Thank you, William, I really appreciate this."

"Good man." Gem patted his back again, this time more gently. "Not everything fits inside the box."

William flushed slightly and pulled away from her. They got Edna's antibiotics and helped load her into his vehicle.

"Call us if you need anything," Abby told her. "We've never made a house call yet, but there's always a first time."

Edna leaned back against the seat as William drove away. Abby, Gem, and Marcus stood together by the clinic trailer for a long quiet moment. Then Gem looked at her watch.

"Not much time left for lunch," she announced, noticing Abby yawn. "Maybe you should go take a quick power nap. You look really tired."

"I'm fine." Abby rubbed her eyes. "I've got my Diet Coke. A little caffeine goes a long way."

"Why don't you get more sleep?"

Abby shrugged. "Old habits."

Gem looked doubtful. "Well, you'd better rest up for the next twenty minutes. Your first patient of the afternoon is Turbo Packer."

"Poor Turbo," said Marcus, heading inside.

Knowing Gem was right, Abby did go lie down in an exam room for a few minutes, slipping unexpectedly into sleep until Gem touched her shoulder.

"Time to earn your keep," she said softly. "Turbo's ready."

Abby tried to reach Turbo for several days to discuss his lab tests, but he did not return the calls. He came to see her instead, he said, because he worried that someone might be monitoring his phone. He felt pretty well, with no more spells of exhaustion.

"All your tests are normal with one exception," Abby explained. "On the drug screen, the test for barbiturates came back as 'inconclusive.' Which means it was borderline. Maybe positive, maybe not, not really able to say for sure."

Turbo squinted, wary. His head went still. "What's that?"

"Barbiturates are sedatives. It's an ingredient in some old-fashioned prescription headache medicines like Fiorinal or Fioricet. Have you been taking anything like that?"

He wagged his head back and forth, his hair flopping. "Never. I told you, I keep my body pure."

"I didn't think so, since you never mentioned any headaches." He peered at her closely, intent and suspicious, making her uncomfortable. She forged on. "Do you take any supplements or vitamins? Any herbal products?"

He stared so long that Abby thought he hadn't understood. Then he suddenly bobbed his head and looked at the door.

"Sometimes. I have these Chinese herbs that help me when I'm nervous. But don't tell anyone. They might think it's a weakness."

"Of course not," Abby assured him. "No one can see your medical records, anyway. Not without your permission."

"Right." He gave her a pitying glance, as if she must be naïve.

"You should probably stop taking those herbs. It's hard to know what might be in them, no matter what it says on the label."

"All right." He nodded, then shifted abruptly. "Hey. I heard you have an x-ray machine now. Can you x-ray my ribs?"

There was no good reason to x-ray him, but she did it anyway for his peace of mind. Abby felt a little bad about that because it was a waste of money and quite unlike her, but he was happy and grateful that his bones looked normal. She showed him the pale shafts of his ribs, the sturdy blocks of his spinal bones, his square jaw at the top of the frame. He asked for a copy, so Abby printed it out for him.

"Thanks, Medicine Woman," he said, folding it carefully, lining up the corners precisely. "You're good to me."

"I just want you to be healthy," Abby explained. "Let me know if you have more symptoms. And what about those people, the ones you've been worried about? Those voices? Is that still a problem?"

"Don't worry. I'll take care of that. It's almost time." He nodded one last time and slipped out the door.

Abby sighed. Turbo was a work in progress, but at least he didn't seem any worse than his last visit.

Marcus appeared with a clutch of wilted wildflowers, wrapped in a paper towel.

"These are from Turbo. He said they're good for your immune system." Marcus shook his head. "Should I put them in some water?"

"I think it's too late." Abby fingered the limp stems. "Just throw them out. But don't tell him." She put it out of her mind and tackled the rest of the afternoon.

That night Pepper called, brimming with pleasure.

"I'm coming to see you tomorrow!" he cried.

"What?"

Abby couldn't believe it. They had talked about him visiting in a week or two. She hoped it might coincide with Wrigley's dinner the following weekend, so she could cancel that, but of course it didn't matter now. She practically hopped up and down with delight.

"Yep. I couldn't wait, and I arranged a ride to West Yellowstone with a pilot I met. Don't even ask how much it costs. So I'll be there tomorrow—Friday night."

Abby was beside herself with joy. She hurried to clean her cabin and stock up on snacks and drinks. Unable to fall asleep despite her fatigue, she had to walk around the grounds and admire the jubilant stars, flashing ecstatically in the black reaches above. The earth steamed and percolated, and Old Faithful let loose with a magnificent outburst.

She finally managed to sleep. And the nightmares stayed away. Apparently a visit with John Pepper could fix anything.

11

Abby kept her eye on the clock, determined to stay on time, even though practicing medicine rarely meshed with efficiency. She hoped to be done before Pepper appeared, despite his uncertain arrival time. By midafternoon, she was only fifteen minutes behind schedule, an accomplishment considering three unexpected cases: a bicycle crash with a fractured wrist, an older man with congestive heart failure, and a child whose family dog bit her lip. The child and the terrier disagreed over a hot dog, which seemed amusing to everyone until the dog showed them it was not.

Carly Pendleton was four years old and terrified. Her favorite buddy just bit her and she was surrounded by adults, familiar and foreign, pleading and demanding that she hold still, be brave, quit crying, and be a big girl. Though the rip in her skin was small, it tore through the border of her lip, a cosmetic problem. Her mouth quivered and twisted, and Abby had no gentle way to inject and numb her lip; it simply took force. They wrapped her arms with a sheet, and the parents held her body while Marcus held her head, Gem held her lip, and Abby pierced the soft skin with a tiny needle of lidocaine while the child shrieked nonstop into Abby's ear.

Fortunately, Abby managed to be fast and accurate. She quickly stepped away, releasing Carly into her parents' soothing embrace for twenty minutes to calm down and discover that her lip no longer hurt. Abby wasn't certain that her own hearing would ever be right again, and Gem expressed relief that Abby hadn't missed and injected Gem's finger instead.

Abby took her time repairing the laceration, using her best pediatric skills to relax Carly and make a game of it. She asked Carly to hold her mouth very still while Abby posed funny questions, instructing Carly to answer with a variety of blinks, winks, eye rolling, finger pointing, and foot motions. Soon everyone in the room was smiling as Carly furrowed her forehead in concentration. Abby asked whether her room at home was messy, if she ever behaved badly, if her parents ever behaved badly, and what veggies she liked. For "yes" wink your eye, for "no" wiggle your foot. For "good" cross your fingers, for "bad" blink three times.

Abby used very small-gauge suture to minimize the scar—it was like sewing with a hair. She painstakingly aligned the split edges of the lip, hoping to re-create a perfect border. Not satisfied with her first effort, Abby removed the stitch and repeated it. It was one thing to have a slightly crooked eyebrow like Abby's, but if the lip was not precise, it could affect Carly's smile for the rest of her life.

Before they left, Abby warned them of the cosmetic uncertainty, since healing tissues followed their own rules. They could consult later with a plastic surgeon if necessary. Being on the road, the family needed to find a physician in Idaho to remove the stitches in five days. Carly hugged Abby and Abby gave her a big sticker that said "Brave!"

"Thanks for that teamwork," Abby said to Gem and Marcus at what substituted for lunch, grabbing bites while they prepared for the afternoon.

"That was impressive," replied Gem. "Not just the suturing. I mean the way you kept her mind busy. And it was smart to tell them that it might not come out perfect."

Abby smiled. "An old ER doc taught me that distraction technique. And you should always be humble about plastic results." Without thinking, she rubbed her left eyebrow. The skin tingled when touched, as if the flesh remembered.

Gem watched her. "What happened there?"

Abby looked at the clock. "I'll tell you someday, when we have more time. It's sort of a long story. But basically, I got hit by a bad guy last year at work."

"Geez." Gem and Marcus both grimaced. "You make it sound like the canyon's a dangerous place," Gem countered.

"Yeah," Abby laughed, "you say that, while you're sitting on a big volcano about to erupt."

Gem squinted. "That's the second time you've put me off, saying something is too long of a story."

"Someday soon…," Abby replied evasively, busy with the computer, prepping charts. There was no time for that today, and she privately worried that talking about it could invite more nightmares. Maybe the monsters would be less real if she didn't give them air.

Now she had a few hours to go, trying not to think about Pepper. He might still be in Arizona, waiting at the airport, or he might be in the sky, staring out the window at the crumpled terrain below. Maybe landing right now, the thump and bounce as the wheels found the tarmac. Stay focused, she told herself, rapidly answering messages, finishing notes as she perched at the counter between patients. She heard footsteps as Gem came and went but she made herself concentrate on the screen.

Then she felt a hand, a soft grip taking the back of her neck, and she knew he was there, early. Her heart bounded but she slowly reached up, closing her fingers around his wrist, those familiar bones. It was such a private, intense moment that she nearly choked up, then she leaped and his arms were around her, lifting her, kissing her. Smiling broadly, he set her down and cleared his throat, tilting his head toward the other side of the room where Gem and Marcus stood grinning.

"Maybe you should get a room," Gem suggested.

Pepper made a slightly abashed face and straightened his shirt, then he looked sideways at Abby with undisguised lust. Abby felt breathless and masked it by tidying her stray hairs.

"I believe there are plans for that," he said formally.

Abby smacked him on the arm. "I'm at work. Behave yourself."

Pepper pretended to look contrite and Abby gave him the key to her cabin. She recommended where to walk and see the steamy waterworks, where to find the Old Faithful schedule. They made plans for dinner the next night with Gem and Marcus, leaving Marcus to find a reservation among the overcrowded restaurants. Marcus laughed, saying that of course he had connections, no worries.

Abby never worked so efficiently in her life. She wasn't brusque, but she didn't spend time chatting, either.

"I don't think I've ever seen you look so happy," Gem remarked.

"Oh, come on," Abby protested. "I'm nearly always happy."

"Sure. You're a downright Pollyanna. Except when you worry about being perfect, which is constantly. And all the secret stuff that's a long story that you don't want to tell me."

"Stop. You're not allowed to get serious today." Abby couldn't stop smiling, though.

Gem quit teasing and Abby worked even faster. Eventually the last patient was gone, the last message was typed, and she headed out the door.

"Tomorrow night at nine o'clock," Marcus called after her. "We'll meet you at the Old Faithful Inn, if that's okay."

"Nice," Abby said over her shoulder, rushing down the steps and across the parking lot, nearly running. He might still be out walking, still exploring. If he wasn't at the cabin she would call him, go find him, feeling a desperate need to hold him and touch him and—

He must have been watching for her, because the door opened before she touched it. A long moment passed where she stared at his face and he stared back. She drank in those pale blue eyes, his rumpled brown hair, and his fine lips, kinked in half a smile. Then he pulled her in, kicked shut the door, and sat on the bed with her sideways in his lap, carefully taking down her hair.

"About time," he murmured, pulling her hair free, fluffing it loose.

"I thought you were going for a walk." She undid the top of his shirt, touched the hollow of his throat, slid her hand under his jaw.

"I did. I walked a lot and I saw all sorts of things. And I met some people and talked to them about all kinds of things."

"Things?" Abby snuggled against his chest and wondered who. His tone sounded ominous. Or maybe she imagined it.

"Later."

His eyes traveled every inch of her face, then his long fingers traced her ear and down her throat, making her shiver. He felt it, and he tipped back her head and his mouth impatiently took hers until she moaned and coiled, clutching him. He turned her onto the bed, propped over her on one arm while unbuttoning her top.

"I think maybe I missed this a little bit," he said, freeing her from her bra, taking his time, one side then the other.

Abby groaned as each nerve lit on fire, telegraphing heat all the way down. She pulled his shirt from his shoulders and focused for a moment. "You've been working out," she breathed, skimming her fingers across his chest.

"I have to do something on those long, lonely nights."

He knelt by the low bed, unfastening her, sliding everything off. Abby drew rough breaths as he rubbed her ankle, then worked his hand up. She whimpered, her whole body taut, stretched like a bow. He slowly leaned to kiss her again while his fingertips grazed her, when she shuddered and fell apart. Abby opened her eyes and found him inches from her face, watching.

"I love making you do that."

Abby groaned and wrapped her arms around his neck. He almost always did that, giving her such intense pleasure before himself. Men are easy and quick, he once explained, but women are sexually complicated and take time. Only now, he didn't wait very long.

As they recovered, he kept shifting on the bed.

"You're restless," Abby commented drowsily.

"No, I'm not. This bed is just really small. My legs keep falling off." He turned again, raised up on an elbow. "Maybe we should get a hotel room for tonight."

"Ha. Every room here has been reserved for a year. Or longer." Abby smiled up at him, touched his beard. "I've sure missed you."

He gazed leisurely up and down her. "A man could get used to this."

"You are used to it."

"Oh, yeah. I forgot, it's been so long." He lay back and picked up a thick lock of her hair, ran it through his fingers.

"Just three weeks."

"Yes, but it's been more like three week-years. You know, like light-years, only where each week seems like a year." He kept playing with her hair.

Abby shook her head. "That analogy doesn't work at all. Not even close. One is time and the other is distance."

"Sh." He put his fingers on her lips. "Quit being so damn picky about my poetic analogies."

She kissed his fingers, still slow and dreamy. "What have you missed the most? My hot body or my brilliant mind?"

He tilted his head one way and scrunched his face, then tilted the other way and made a different face. "Hm."

"Hey," she protested. "You're taking too long."

"You mean there's a right answer?"

"Yes, because what if I'm ninety years old and my body is all withered up, and all you've got is my brain?"

"Or what if you're ninety years old and your brain's all demented, and all I've got is your body?"

Abby laughed. They didn't say it, but they were talking about spending their lives together. Saying it was too predictable, trite. She pulled the sheet up and burrowed against him and fell asleep.

"Hey. It's getting late. Let's go for a walk." He spoke quietly, touched her arm. "And I'm a little hungry."

Abby blinked in the dim light. "How long have I been sleeping?"

"About two hours. A little more."

"Are you serious?" She sat up, fuzzyheaded and frustrated that she had wasted precious time with him by sleeping. "I'm so sorry. You should have woken me sooner."

"You obviously needed it." He looked concerned.

She dressed quickly and they walked past Old Faithful, fuming quietly, exhaling warm steam.

"It's like it's thinking," Abby said. "Thinking about when it wants to erupt again." The eruptions had grown more irregular, and the posted schedule cautioned that estimates might be inaccurate.

"So now the geyser has awareness?" he asked.

Abby smiled. "Maybe."

They crossed the bridge, the river gleaming darkly, a green and gold mirror. Then they strolled a long way over the boardwalks as the sky turned slate blue and the low sun tinted a crazy-quilt assortment of clouds: fat bulging cumulus and high feathery cirrus and long ripples and streamers, all going pink and red and mauve, a circus concoction overhead. Up from the deepening ground rose scattered plumes and fogs, bright brimstone vapors that caught the light and glowed eerily before dissipating into the gloom.

"I feel like I'm on another planet," he said.

"We've got more to see tomorrow. I thought we'd run up to Norris Geyser Basin. I've been wanting to go there—it's got some of the hottest and most acid springs in the park."

"That's where the new vents have appeared, right? Where part of a boardwalk just flooded?"

Abby pulled back to look at him. "Who have you been talking with?"

"I told you I'd been busy. First Don Perkins, that older ranger. Nice guy. A few other people. Then I met a young geologist named Bridges. A little quiet, seems kind of brilliant. We talked a bit—he said he knows you."

Abby nodded. "He's brought in a few patients, and I've attended some of his talks. And you're right, he's really smart. He's working on his PhD. How did you manage to meet all these people so quickly?"

"Just naturally nosy." Nearly dark now, they turned around, heading for supper. "I got the feeling that he likes you."

"He's sweet," she said. "Kind of innocent. A little stuffy."

Pepper stopped and turned to her, peering closely in the gloom. Not too dark for her to see frost in his blue gaze. "He said this is the most seismic activity ever, since they started monitoring. Why haven't you told me that?"

She shrugged. "I didn't know you'd be interested."

"Hm." His face impassive. She went to walk on, but he held her arm, kept her there. "And Perkins told me about this bison killer. Pretty bizarre…that's a fairly disturbing thing. I guess he doesn't usually talk about it, but he figured you would tell me anyway." He paused. "Would you? He seemed surprised I didn't know."

"Sure," Abby said, not very convincing.

He studied her doubtfully. "Are you trying to protect me?"

"Don't be silly. There's no point worrying about such things. They don't really affect me." She knew he saw through her, but Pepper dropped it and they went to supper.

They made love again, and talked for hours. Abby discarded her cautions and spilled everything about the bison deaths, as much as she knew, then showed him the YVO website. She knew he worried less if he could analyze things.

By the time they drove to Norris, traffic was slow. Pepper studied the bison, fascinated, watching the massive animals graze along the road and across the meadows. When cars slowed to a crawl, he leaned out the window to examine their huge low heads, their heaped shoulders and necks, the dense shaggy wool of their faces. Abby warned him about the twenty-five-yard safety zone, told him about Hannah Santana. Pepper imagined how to kill such a creature without leaving a sign, concluding it must be poisoned darts or arrows, something small, so its mark wouldn't be noticed.

"Ew," said Abby. "I hate the idea of someone sneaking around here with poison darts. Because sooner or later, that's the sort of thing that backfires and ends up in the clinic." Then she regretted saying that, likely fueling his worries. Not that he needed help.

They spent hours at Norris Geyser Basin, marveling at Porcelain Basin with its thick white deposits, the blighted expanses and noisy fumaroles that furiously hissed and growled and spat. They stared at bright green swaths of the fungus Cyanidium, unbelievably thriving in the hot acid pools. Abby loved the crystal green water of Emerald Spring, and Pepper chose Echinus Geyser as his favorite, an acid geyser with water like vinegar that rarely erupted.

Driving back, they passed through the Madison area, where Abby saw a sign for the campground and immediately thought of Edna Dillon.

"Hey," she said, turning her car. "Do you mind if we stop off for a quick check on a patient? If I can find her?"

"Of course," he agreed.

Finding Edna's motorhome was easier than expected because the first thing Abby saw was Gem's little car alongside it, and a park service vehicle as well. Abby parked under a tree across the road, seeing Gem and William Bridges standing by the RV door, deep in conversation.

His head down, Gem peered up at him under his hat, talking intently, her hand gripping his forearm. Abby watched him swipe his other hand under his nose and Gem rubbed his arm. He nodded abruptly and walked to his vehicle, climbing in rapidly and backing away. He saw Abby and Pepper at the last minute, raising his hand in greeting but not stopping.

"Is everything okay?" Abby asked Gem.

Gem nodded slowly, watching him disappear down the road. "He's having a hard time. His grandma, who practically raised him, died of cancer last year. But it was during his final exams, and he didn't make it home in time to say goodbye."

They took a moment to digest that, then Abby said, "Has he been coming by?"

"Yes. We both have, off and on. We just happened to be here at the same time today. Even Marcus has been coming."

Abby explained how they were driving through.

"Edna's cool," Gem said. "I've got to go, but she'll be happy to see you. Did you know she used to have a horse ranch near Tucson? Arabians. Talk about stories. Mildred's out making the rounds, so just tap and go in. And don't forget—see you tonight at dinner."

Edna looked a little better than when Abby first saw her, but not much. Her breaths quick, her oxygen in place. She seemed shrunken, smaller, white hair straggling across her head. But her eyes leaped with curiosity when Abby and Pepper came in.

She chuckled after Abby made introductions, and she fixed Pepper with her sharp eye.

"Don't take this wrong, but you remind me of a horse I had. A stallion named Pepper," she said with mischief. "He was one of those grays covered with black freckles, so that's where he got his name." She paused to breathe. "My Pepper was this tall long-legged stud, a very handsome boy, but he had a difficult personality. Very cautious about humans. It took a while for him to come to you, and he never quite trusted anyone."

"That horse sounds just like me," Pepper laughed.

"I thought so." Edna looked slyly at Abby and made Abby wonder if there had even been a horse named Pepper. Eyes still on Abby, Edna added, "He was an excellent stud. He drove all the mares crazy."

Abby actually blushed and Pepper looked slightly embarrassed.

They didn't stay long; Edna seemed exhausted from her visits. Abby asked about her cough and whether she was eating, receiving vague answers that she didn't pursue. Pepper leaned over to take Edna's hand when he left.

"Take good care of that filly." Edna tipped her head at Abby. "I like her."

"So do I." He grasped her fingers. "Maybe I'll see you later this summer if I make it back again."

Edna sobered. "I probably won't be here."

He nodded. "Well. If you are."

"Good enough." She closed her eyes.

They didn't talk much on their way back. Abby put her hand on the shift console and he placed his hand over it, and they drove like that a long way.

Dinner with Gem and Marcus was delightful. Pepper admitted how much better he felt knowing they were there to help Abby, which they protested, claiming she alone maintained their sanity. That Gem and Marcus probably would have strangled each other by now without her. Which led to talk about the dead bison. Which led to talk about unbalanced people. Which led Gem to mention Wrigley and how he had a thing for Abby, which she probably would not have done if she hadn't had two drinks. Abby glanced at her sharply and stepped on her foot under the table.

"Just kidding," Gem said quickly, trying to laugh it off.

Pepper's eyes went chilly as he turned to Abby. "Who is that?"

Abby waved it off. "Just this older guy from the concession. You know the type."

"He's not so bad," Marcus added, trying to help.

Gem went silent and it took a while for them to regain their good mood, but they finally managed when Abby asked Pepper about Priscilla, explaining how Priscilla had amorous designs on Pepper and patiently waited for him to dump Abby. She didn't say it, but she made the point that someone else's interest in you was meaningless if it was one-sided, and Pepper rarely missed anything. He described how Priscilla kept wavering between himself and the resident doctor Dan Drake.

"She hardly knows which side of the bread to butter," Pepper said.

"Good heavens, you're not a piece of toast," Abby said. "What is it with these warped analogies?"

Pepper argued that it was a metaphor, not an analogy, and insisted it made sense. Then Gem and Marcus had to vote on whether it did, then Pepper also made them vote on the concept of week-years and lightyears, which took a while to explain because they were laughing. They finally left when they realized they were the last people in the dining room.

Abby delivered him to the airport the next day, determined to stay positive. They agreed it was a wonderful visit, and she would come see him soon. But he shook his head at the last minute, hugging her tightly.

"I don't like the arrangement here," he grumbled. "The clinic is too isolated, way back in those trees, behind that parking lot. And there's no emergency call system. Ranger Perkins agreed, and he told me he would make sure it gets patrolled more often."

"Thanks," Abby said, not buying into it but not wanting to disagree. "That should help."

"Do you want to swap? I can stay here, and you go back to the canyon? You'd be safer, and I would feel better."

"Quit being so jittery," Abby said, reproaching him softly. "Everything's fine. Call me tonight."

He kissed her and was gone.

12

Abby took a long run the next morning, reestablishing her routine. But she missed Pepper every step of the way, disturbed because she dreamed that his plane crashed on its way back to the canyon. There was no violent scene, no blood. Instead, she awoke inside the dream and read about it in the morning paper. Which was ridiculous, since she had no morning paper and never looked at the news online until evening, if then. Yellowstone had no television reception. As if that invalidated the dream.

Abby banished it from her brain by drawing a cartoon of a stick-figure horse labeled "Pepper the Stallion" and a tall stick-figure man labeled "Pepper the Stud." She dropped it in the mail before work.

Gem immediately pulled her aside and apologized for bringing up Wrigley.

"That wasn't fair. I can't believe I did that." Her worried eyes searched Abby for forgiveness.

"It's okay." Abby sighed. "We ought to be able to talk about it, just like we talk about Priscilla. Right? He's just…intense. About some things. You saw him."

"Is he jealous?" An anxious line cropped up between Gem's brows.

"No, not at all. He knows I'm crazy about him." Abby smiled briefly. "If I wasn't, or if he doubted me, he would walk away. It's more complicated than that. He's very protective about anything that might bother me, cause me problems." She touched her forehead scar, that dull sting. "He still blames himself for this."

Marcus came back to tell them that the first patient had so far failed to arrive.

"That means we have time," Gem said carefully. "Do you want to tell us that story? You don't have to, of course."

Abby folded her arms and closed her eyes until she realized that that body language shut herself away. So she moved her hands, picked up a pen, fussed with it.

"Okay. So you can quit wondering why I'm so nutty." Her mouth twitched. "Though I was nutty before this happened, too. I think I hinted there's an anxiety problem."

"Should I leave?" Marcus asked, starting to turn. "I kind of intruded."

"No, stay." They were her friends now.

Abby explained how, shortly after she started at the canyon two years ago, Pepper had testified in a Phoenix courthouse against Luther Lubbock, a brutal man who struck his wife and fractured her skull. Being the only physician at the time, Pepper treated the wife's injury, while Lubbock raved and paced and claimed that other men attacked her. Only his story changed frequently, contradicting himself, with which Pepper informed the jury and helped lead to the conviction. When Lubbock later escaped from prison, he came after Pepper, bent on revenge. Abby stood near Lubbock when he raised his pistol against Pepper—she wrenched his arm and ruined his aim. Furious, he swung at her and struck her face with the gun.

"There's a little more to it than that, and I skipped some parts, but you get the picture." Abby took stock: her pulse ran swift but not racing, and she did not feel panicky.

Gem and Marcus stared at her.

"I think I remember hearing about this," Marcus said. "But of course, I didn't know it was you. Or Pepper."

"Not the kind of fame you really want," Abby said. "And it was old news in a few days. Thank goodness."

"So then Pepper stitched you up?" Gem asked.

"Yes, he was the only one there. So he blames himself that I got injured, and he blames himself for my funny eyebrow. But the wound was a mess and the skin edges were crushed…no one could have done better. Except a plastic surgeon, and we don't keep one of those at the canyon." Abby made a rueful face. "Anyway. That's probably why he's so protective. Overprotective."

"Were you a couple then?" Gem tried to put it together.

"No, not until weeks after that. Months. I'd been dating another guy, a ranger." Abby crossed her eyes. "That was a fiasco."

Gem laughed at her expression and Abby smiled. She had come a long way.

They heard the outer door open and Marcus hurried to the front. He reappeared a moment later.

"This guy's in a whole lot of pain. You might want to see him right away."

Abby took one look at Morris Marshall and knew what was wrong from his agonized grimace, his pale face, and the stooped way he walked. Triggered by dehydration, kidney stones were common at the Grand Canyon and she recognized it instantly.

"See if you can get a urine sample," Abby said as Gem led him into a room. "And a CBC, just to be sure."

Red blood cells crowded Morris's urine.

"Have you ever had a kidney stone?" Abby asked.

A lawyer from Los Angeles, Morris was curious and analytic about everything, even as miserable as he felt.

"Why is there blood—what's it doing there?" he wanted to know. "And if there's blood, why doesn't my urine look red? And why does it hurt so damn much?"

Abby touched his shoulder in sympathy and asked Gem to give an injection of ketorolac, a potent anti-inflammatory pain medication. "Your body is trying to pass the stone down your ureter, that little tube that connects your kidney to your bladder. It's a pretty narrow tube, so it hurts when the stone scrapes through. And that scraping causes bleeding, which shows up in the urine. It takes many more blood cells than this, though, to turn your urine red."

"Whew. I thought maybe I had appendicitis." He stifled a groan and shifted on the table. "I was afraid I needed surgery."

"We have to consider your appendix, but it's not likely," she explained. "You don't have fever, and the pain is on the wrong side. Your belly would be more tender. And your white blood cells would be higher, because appendicitis is an infection. When we add up all the pieces, it looks like a stone."

He sat up easier. "I think that medicine is starting to work."

"Good." Abby reviewed the treatment plan. Most small stones would pass on their own, in a few hours or a few days. If a stone quit moving, got lodged partway, he might need a lithotripsy scope, to break it into pieces. "We don't have the right equipment here to see the stone. So if it's not better, you should go to town for an ultrasound, maybe a CT. Maybe see a urologist. Same thing if the pain gets too severe."

Morris leaned back, more color in his face. "I'm so glad you were open. Having this clinic here is wonderful." He sighed. "I've been trying to take such good care of myself. I wanted to hike a lot, so I've been taking calcium and vitamin D to get my bones strong."

"Oh-oh." Abby should have asked about that. When patients said they didn't take any medications, they often forgot to mention supplements.

"What?"

"Too much calcium increases your risk for kidney stones. And most people don't need extra vitamin D anyway. There's already plenty in your diet, and you get vitamin D when you're out in the sun."

"Crap," he said forcefully.

Abby nodded. "Just eat healthy, with fruits and veggies. And lots of fluids. No one really needs vitamins and supplements unless they have a deficiency that requires it."

"Now I feel stupid." He looked weary, and a little embarrassed. "Can I just lie here and rest for a while? I didn't hardly sleep last night, and we've already checked out of our room."

"Of course. We're not too busy right now." Abby finished her note.

"I just need a break from my kids. I love them, you know, but they'll crawl all over me. Can you tell my wife that I'm back here recovering? So I can grab a nap for half an hour?" He looked contrite. "Just say no if that's inappropriate."

Amused, Abby delivered the message, and his wife took the children to watch Old Faithful.

Morris stopped by the next day to report that his pain suddenly resolved a few hours later. A different man, upbeat and energetic.

"I'm going to send a note to your company. Tell them how much this helped, having you here."

Abby thanked him, but said it wasn't necessary.

She didn't want FirstMed getting ideas about next summer. If she could get through this season without Yellowstone erupting, without Turbo melting down, without anyone getting hurt or dying who shouldn't, it would be success enough.

13

Abby started walking at noon. It felt good to get out, even briefly, to stretch her muscles and think about her planet. To imagine that heat circulating below, under the floating crust of land. To think about that gluey mantle supplying Yellowstone's fire, nearly two thousand miles down. And deeper to the core, where liquid metals flowed in strange currents. The solid center, stunningly hot at ten thousand degrees. Abby loved the displays, showing how the tectonic plates drifted across the Yellowstone hotspot, a few inches every year for millions of years. She wondered if humans would survive to see it move into Canada, but she doubted it.

William adored it all. His eyes shone and his voice rose and sometimes he forgot he was an introvert, growing downright chatty about volcanic apocalypses.

"I'm a little worried." Gem frowned at him. "You're so excited about an eruption, which could end the world as we know it. And all of us with it."

William looked playful. "It's not about us. It never has been."

To vary her running, Abby started roaming paths through the woods.

"I wish you wouldn't," William said, unhappily watching her unlock her car late one afternoon, bound for a trailhead. "Talk to Hannah Santana—she's my wildlife expert. Grizzlies get most active at night. And a bear's more likely to attack when you're alone."

"I didn't think there were many grizzlies around Old Faithful." Abby didn't feel that worried. "Too much traffic, too many people."

"They're out there. Do you know what to do?" William held her car door open to keep her from leaving. "We can't afford to lose our only doctor."

"Okay." Though impatient to get going, Abby decided to placate him. "Tell me what precautions to take."

"I wish you would talk to Hannah. But first off, you should be noisy." William wore his serious lecture face. "Bears don't like being surprised. Talk or sing or shout as you go. And if you see a dead animal carcass, like an elk or bison, get away from it and tell us where it is, because we might want to close that trail for a while. Bears come to feed on a carcass, and sometimes they hang around. You might not see them at first." He peered at her to make sure she was paying attention. "Don't look them in the eye. And never try to run away—they can sprint way faster than you can. Back away slowly, while you're facing them. You've got bear spray, right?"

Abby looked around as if he was talking to someone else.

William sighed, digging in a pack and pulling out a can. "Here, take this. I'll get another."

"I can't take your bear spray. What if you have an emergency?" Now Abby felt bad.

He smiled. "They'll miss you more than they'll miss me."

So she thanked him and took the bear spray and kept it handy, making a mental note to replace it for him.

Abby assumed she would return to her baseline after Pepper left. But instead of stabilizing, her longing for him grew more intense. Maybe because they had such a good time when he visited, maybe because he fit in so quickly. Maybe because she realized that she didn't need to prove herself so much, that functioning solo was something she could do if she had to, or if she wanted to. Only now she didn't want to because she missed Pepper more than she imagined possible.

Maybe it was the return of the nightmares.

And now, twice, she thought she saw the convict Luther Lubbock in a parking lot or walking down the road, a heavy man in a bulky coat. She knew Lubbock was incarcerated in Arizona, but she checked the news for escapes. She meditated more. She googled her own name, checking that nothing placed her at Yellowstone, that no one could track her down.

After a trying morning on Thursday, Abby needed her walk. A tour bus pulled up earlier, disgorging seven Japanese tourists with severe diarrhea. Only one person, the guide, spoke both English and Japanese, but the guide did not exit the bus until Gem stormed out and dragged her inside to interpret. Marcus fluttered, beside himself checking them in, spelling their names correctly, and unsuccessfully deciphering the insurance plans that came with the trip. The policies were written in Japanese.

Abby quickly realized that the tour guide was germophobic. The thin, anxious woman stood in the middle of the workstation, squirting alcohol gel into her palms every few minutes until Abby handed her disposable gloves. The woman looked grateful and loosened up a little. Meantime the patients, mostly elderly, seemed too embarrassed to discuss their bowels. Abby suspected a virus, and she cajoled two younger patients to produce stool samples, but the results would not be available for several days. Because she had seen a few cases of giardia lately, Abby decided to treat them just in case.

The guide mentioned that some of her travelers had scooped up the crystal mountain water from creeks and drunk it, admiring the pristine taste.

"It's not always as clean as it looks," Abby cautioned. Wildlife carried giardia, and wildlife didn't care if they emptied themselves in a creek.

"Here's a handout about giardia and the medication, metronidazole." Abby handed the guide a paper. She scanned the page, still wearing gloves, her eyes wide at the drawing of giardia. The microscopic parasite sprouted multiple flagella, tiny whip-like tails, and even Abby thought it looked like an evil alien. "You can translate this to everyone later. The medication often causes nausea, so you should warn them about that. And they shouldn't drink alcohol, because that might trigger vomiting."

The woman stared at her hopelessly, and Abby suggested she might want to contact her company to see if she could get some help, or if maybe they could divert the trip. Appreciative, the woman nodded and took out her phone. The single bathroom on the bus was not faring well.

Not hungry after that, Abby took her noon walk, leaving Marcus and Gem arguing how to properly say "arigatou gozaimasu" and "konnichiwa," making their computers spew loud pronunciations. Abby put her hands over her ears and fled.

The day had turned stormy. Overcast dulled the sky and fitful winds kicked up leaves, making Abby hurry along as branches clashed above her. She decided not to wander far in case of rain, striding a brisk circle around the lodges and heading back for the clinic when she heard thunder growl. As she scurried past the visitor center, the glass door swung open and Luther Lubbock barged out in a rush, straight toward her. His stringy hair flew up and his dark coat swung out in the wind, one hand deep in his pocket.

Abby's heart dropped like an anvil inside her chest and she sprang sideways around a tree. She smelled the rancid sweat of his clothes, his rank unwashed body, just like the night he nearly shot Pepper. He tramped past, looking back and forth as she huddled there, and then she saw it was not Lubbock at all but an old man with a raincoat and gray hair, looking for someone.

Crumpled against the tree, her heart clanged hard against her gut and she feared for a moment she might vomit. She held her breath and squeezed her eyes tight until the nausea slackened, but still her heart accelerated, jangling like wild hammer blows and battering her lungs. She staggered from the tree, forced herself to straighten up and walked quickly, unsteadily back to the clinic.

No one waited yet in the lobby. Abby pushed through as Marcus looked up from his sandwich and started to smile until he saw the dread in her pinched face, saw her gulping for air. He began to stand but she raised a hand against him, lowered her head, and pressed on inside, past Gem without looking, and into the treatment room where she braced her arms on the sink and leaned over it, concentrating on not puking. Her breath rasped and tremors ran up and down her legs. She held her breath as long as possible, then blew it out through pursed lips as slowly as she could.

Gem came up behind her.

Abby managed to mumble "I'm okay, leave me alone" between breaths. She gripped the sink and clenched her eyes and made herself think fiercely of black holes, made her mind heavy with the weight of a thousand dark suns, where gravity sucked all the light into a dense tiny core deep inside where no one could see her or find her. She collapsed herself into that space and became an impenetrable compressed object that could not feel or panic.

It started to work. Eventually her breathing slowed, and her heart moved back up in her chest where it belonged. She opened her eyes, sensing someone, and turned her head to see Marcus standing there.

"Are you ready to sit down?" he asked quietly. His hand held the back of a plastic chair, his expression gentle.

Abby nodded and he brought the chair, took her elbow, and guided her into it.

"Do you think you might throw up? Do you need an emesis basin?" he asked.

Abby shook her head. "I'm okay now. Well, almost."

Marcus pulled over another chair, sat by her, and said nothing. Once he reached over and rubbed her arm briefly, then folded his hands in his lap. Eventually Abby leaned back and looked at the ceiling, then over at him.

"Thanks," she said, wiping her face with her fingers. "I'm sorry."

"There's nothing to be sorry about." He went to the refrigerator and returned with a bottle of water. His bright cotton-candy pink polo shirt looked out of place in the sterile treatment room.

Abby sipped the water, feeling better now. She wondered if it was time to start seeing patients, heard Gem talking with someone, but she didn't quite have the will to turn her wrist and check her watch.

"Do you want me to cancel the patients?" Marcus asked.

"No." Abby grasped his hand, gave it a small squeeze. "That's the worst I've had in a really long time. Though I've had worse, ones I couldn't stop."

Marcus nodded. "It's a horrible thing."

Abby tilted her head. "You've had panic attacks too?"

"When I was on the golf tour. That's why I had to quit. Well, that and the fact that I couldn't putt anymore." He smiled, rueful. "Which is probably why I had panic attacks. Or vice versa."

"What do you mean, you couldn't putt?"

He shrugged. "Putting is a funny thing. You have to calm yourself to be accurate. You take your time, but not too much time. You have this routine, and I would be all lined up and ready. My practice stroke was smooth as silk. Then at the last second I would hit the ball a little too hard. Or a little too soft. I'd pull it slightly to the left. Then the next time, slightly to the right. The shorter the putt was, the worse I got. It got to the point that I started feeling panicky when I walked onto the green. Then when my ball landed on the green. Then when I started to tee off." He made a face. "You can see how that was a problem."

Abby looked at him earnestly. "And practicing didn't help?"

"I practiced hours and hours. I practiced till my hands were blistered and bleeding. I practiced in my mind while I talked to people and while I ate and while I slept. I was a wreck. So I quit."

"What a shame, Marcus." Abby felt so sorry for him. "Did you try counseling?"

"No, of course not. I'm a man—we don't do that." He chuckled briefly. "If I could do it over, though, I would."

"Can you go back, try again?"

"No." He looked grim.

Abby changed the subject. "So how on earth did you end up doing this?"

His broad face turned cherubic again. "My mom worked in doctors' offices all her life. In the summers I helped her out, her own personal volunteer. I learned pretty much everything, and I was good at it. I like talking to people, helping people. I'm not saying I'll do this forever, but it's good for me, for now."

Abby put her hands on her knees, ready to be herself.

"Are you sure you're okay?" he asked.

"Pretty sure."

"Okay." He looked cautious. "But if you don't mind me asking, what happened? What triggered this?"

Abby was blunt. "I thought I saw Lubbock. You know, the bad guy who hit me, who tried to kill Pepper. I mean, I smelled him, felt him—it was like he was there. But it was just an old man."

"Sounds awful. Has this happened before?"

Something nervous stirred inside her. "Marcus, I can't talk about it now."

"For sure," he said, standing up. "Let's go to work, okay?"

"Okay," Abby echoed. "And Marcus?" He paused, smiled. "Thanks for sharing that. I know that wasn't easy."

"It's not so hard when there's a reason," he said simply.

That night, Abby talked with Lucy for a long time. Abby felt calm, exhausted, and the panic episode seemed far away, as if it had happened to someone else.

"I'm still worried about you," Lucy said. "Your dreams about Pepper, and now this."

"Maybe." She couldn't get closer to it than that; something stood in her way, a protective wall, thick and impermeable.

"If I find someone who can teleconference with you, a counselor, would you want to talk to them?"

Abby agreed to think about it. Maybe it was a good idea. But she had other things on her mind.

Her dinner with Rex Wrigley was in a few days.

14

Getting ready for dinner, Abby felt impatient and foul.

She should have followed Gem's advice and invented a story to get out of this. Why was she so soft? Once again, she longed to be tougher, more callous, thicker skinned. Her mental list went on: more suspicious, less trusting, less forgiving. But no, she always assumed people were trying to be better, assumed that her impressions were flawed, always gave them the benefit of doubt. What a sap. She should have arranged for Pepper to be here this weekend instead of last. She should have contaminated herself with the stomach virus from that tour group and been stuck in the bathroom all night. Or just told him she was sick. This evening she could concoct dozens of ways to avoid dinner with Wrigley, now that it was too late.

Big deal. It was only a dinner, just one stupid meal, and she had firmly established the friendship rule. They would meet and depart in a public place, the lobby of Old Faithful Inn. It would be like their lunch: she would encourage him to talk, he would be boring, and she could leave.

Hurry up, she told herself. She did not want him waiting for her. Abby threw on a loose drab blouse and rejected the thought of cosmetics. Then she was out the door and halfway to the inn when she realized she left her hair down instead of dragging it back in a tight ponytail like she planned, but it was too late now. Screw it, she thought.

When she entered the inn, she didn't see him at first, the lobby crawling with tourists and staff. She glanced up at the cavernous ceiling stretching seven stories above her head, because you could hardly help from doing that. Over a hundred years old, the yawning space gleamed darkly with wooden beams and bannisters. Delicate stabilizing wires glistened in the air, steadying the grand stone chimney, and shadowed balconies and nooks stood on different levels around the perimeter, mysterious and inviting. Countless curious branches and twisted struts decorated the timbers and rails, a capricious style. High near the ceiling, a small cabin-like structure seemed to float in the air, where musicians once played for dancers below. The stairs to that platform had been shut off years ago, though, considered dangerously unstable after a midcentury earthquake shook the inn and nearly destroyed it.

Abby found Wrigley waiting at the reception desk. She reluctantly noticed that he looked good in a soft leather blazer and pressed white shirt, designer jeans, and a western belt. He combed his thick hair forward, falling on both sides of his face and masking his gray temples, which made him seem younger.

"You look marvelous," he said warmly, taking her hand in a prolonged grasp, not really a handshake. "I love it when you let your hair down."

"Thanks," she said briefly, trying not to scowl. She felt like running back for a hair-tie, felt like asking a strange woman passing by for a rubber band.

The seating host beamed at Wrigley, addressed him by name, and guided them to a central table, right under an impressive painting of Old Faithful in torrential eruption. Steam from the plume billowed across a cobalt sky, bison grazing in the foreground. Abby suspected this was considered the best table in the restaurant, and she had to remind herself of Wrigley's power here.

"Can I offer you a cocktail?" he asked, solicitous.

"No thanks." Abby shook her head. She saw no reason to elaborate and tell him that she didn't drink.

He ordered himself a martini. "So. Tell me how it's going, now that you've had a chance to get organized. And now that you can get your own x-rays."

Abby started with short answers, but Wrigley asked thoughtful questions about everything from scheduling and billing to the medical cases she saw. About the problems with transports to the hospital, the pharmacy limitations, the lack of social services for people like Edna Dillon. Abby compared it to the canyon, which conveniently led to talk about Pepper. Still, he displayed a comprehensive grasp of what she faced, and he tried to help troubleshoot the challenges of caring for the widely scattered employees and endless tourists.

By the time her red pepper Gouda soup arrived, Abby felt more at ease. He made no more personal comments and said nothing else about x-rays.

"This soup is amazing," she commented.

"Right? I'm so glad you like it. We've worked really hard on this menu." He took a sip from his second martini and smiled, looking around at the contented diners. "Can you believe most of these tables have been booked for a year?"

Abby expressed suitable surprise, then followed her plan, shifting the focus to him. He enjoyed talking about himself and told amusing stories about his management training in Europe. He advised her how to behave in France, how to avoid being a cloddish American, and he somehow carried on a great deal about pasta and how to cook it perfectly. Abby stole long glances at the painting above them, appreciating the artistry that captured sunlight on the frothing water and the sky reflected in the streams that coursed away from the geyser.

Abby excused herself to use the bathroom, relieved that dinner would soon be over. It had all been fairly benign. Washing her hands, she saw the outline of her phone in her bag's outer pocket and remembered her promise to Gem. Abby sighed and pulled out the phone, activating the voice app so she could be honest if Gem asked.

When she returned to the table, Wrigley poured her a generous glass of red wine from a bottle that had appeared.

"This is a great vintage," he said, turning the label toward her. "A magnificent merlot."

Abby made an apologetic face. "I'm so sorry. I should have made myself clear. I don't drink alcohol."

He pulled his head back in disbelief. "At all?"

"I'm afraid so. But you can probably have it recorked, can't you?"

"Are you sure?" he persisted, nudging the glass toward her. "Come on. At least have a taste."

Abby stared at him, her eyebrows lowering. "No. I'm quite sure."

He exhaled heavily, then forced a smile. "Well then. You must at least let me order you dessert. You can't leave without trying the Yellowstone Caldera."

She didn't want dessert but guessed she should go along after refusing the expensive wine. Their talk drifted to exercise, one of his favorite topics, and his golf game last week, and he soon made her laugh with stories of golf balls stolen by foxes and ravens. He mentioned several times how he usually beat everyone in his foursome.

The dessert arrived, a chocolate masterpiece.

"I wasn't even going to have dessert," Abby groaned, finishing the last bite, "but chocolate is one of my weaknesses."

"I'll remember that," Wrigley said slyly.

"Don't bother." What a stupid thing for her to say. "This pretty much uses up my whole summer's allotment of chocolate."

"That Marcus Limerick," Wrigley said, tilting Abby's glass of wine to his mouth for the last drops, pouring a little more, his own wine long gone. "Quite a golfer at one time, you know."

"No, I didn't." Abby feigned ignorance, looked at her watch, let him see her look at it. "I don't know anything about golf."

Wrigley looked thoughtful, a glint in his eye. "I bet I could beat him now. He's really let himself go. Gained a lot of weight."

"He's a very nice man," Abby said carefully, annoyed. "I don't know what I'd do without him."

"Oh, I'm sure he's great. I wonder what happened to him—he had such promise." He licked his lips, tinted red from the wine. An unnatural look. "You don't suppose I could talk him into a round?"

Abby's eyes narrowed. "You'd have to ask him."

"Maybe I will. I bet I could trounce him."

"Maybe you could just have a friendly game," she suggested, her irritation climbing.

Wrigley chuckled, a little too much, a little sloppy. "You're right—you don't know much about golf, do you?"

"No," Abby said shortly. She looked up toward the painting again, planning her exit.

"You certainly like that painting," he observed.

"It's magnificent." Unsure why, she felt perturbed that he noticed.

"You do know about the increased seismic activity lately, right?" He watched her closely.

"Yes. Of course."

"Even Old Faithful's been unpredictable. Unfaithful, you could say. Most tourists are too clueless to realize what that might mean. And of course we play it down. Can't have people cancelling their vacations to our hotels, can we?" He chuckled again, then leaned forward. "What would you do, right now, if you knew Yellowstone was going to erupt tonight? If you realized this would be your last night on Earth?"

Abby sat up straight. "I'd find a pilot and I'd fly to the Grand Canyon and spend it with my boyfriend."

Wrigley didn't miss a beat. "And if you couldn't get there? If you were stuck here?"

"I'd spend the night with my friends. My staff," she added pointedly.

"Don't forget, I'm your friend too." He grinned.

"I need to go," Abby said, pushing back. "Listen, thanks. Thanks very much. This was nice. But I'm really tired, and I think all that chocolate upset my stomach."

"Of course." He stood with her. "I'll walk you to your cabin."

"No," she said abruptly. What an idiot—why didn't she see this coming? And suddenly she found it, discovered a kernel of that toughness she craved, an ability to dodge on the spot that she never knew she possessed. "You can't. I mean, I can't. I promised Gem I'd stop by her place. We've got some things we need to discuss. About work."

"Really? On Saturday night?" He looked incredulous.

"Yes, well, every day is pretty much the same here."

"Not really, since you don't work tomorrow." He studied her. "Maybe I could help. I'm pretty good at brainstorming. Solving problems."

"It's kind of personal," she explained. They stood in the lobby and he towered close to her, brushed against her, as she moved toward the exit. The gnarled branches and railings bowed and curved above them in the shadows, now feeling strange and sinister.

His hand landed heavily on her shoulder. Abby turned.

"What's her deal? That Gem?" he asked, an edge of disdain. "She looks like she's been around the block a few times."

"Excuse me?" Abby stiffened, her voice icy.

"I mean," he backpedaled quickly, effortlessly, his expression shifting into concern, "she looks like she's had some troubled times. I worry about her. Well."

He put a hand on each of her shoulders, leaning forward cheek to cheek, air kiss, then switched cheeks. Only his second kiss lodged against her face and held. Wine fumes rolled from his mouth, and Abby felt a damp, sticky smear of saliva against her skin. She pulled away and he straightened and swayed.

"I'll be back in a few weeks," he slurred slightly.

"Not likely," Abby said coldly. "I'm really busy."

"I understand. You're very…devoted to him. I admire that. But you seem so…lonely." He paused and his eyes slid down her figure.

"No, I'm not," Abby said tightly and spun away.

She hurried across the lobby and out. She didn't think he could move fast enough right now to follow her—she doubted he could walk across the parking lot—but just in case, she trotted rapidly to Gem's building. Going inside, she hustled through the first floor and exited out the back door against the dark woods. She made a circle around to her cabin, where she locked the door and put up the chain. She didn't turn on a light, but went to the sink and ran hot water, scrubbed her face where his lips had been. She felt like showering all over again, rinsing every molecule of him off her.

Instead, she climbed into bed with her phone under the blanket. She played the recording app and listened again to everything he had said, knowing he was likely blackout drunk and would remember nothing.

It really wasn't much, she realized. He made a few disparaging comments about Gem and Marcus, which he backed out of, and he said she looked lonely. And he eyed her lewdly. And then gave her a more-or-less acceptable peck on the cheek, even though it felt disgusting. Since when couldn't she deal with an irritating lush without freaking out?

She went back to wishing she was tougher, and deleted the recording.

15

The dome under Yellowstone Lake rose a little more, settled, then rose again. Such a wide placid lake, Abby thought, the surface buzzing with activity as people took scenic cruises, rented boats, caught fish. Not everyone appreciated that the lake existed because water filled a gigantic gaping caldera, the cavity from a massive eruption. Gases bubbled up from hundreds of ruptures on the bottom of the lake, discharging hot water and carbon dioxide. The magma stayed busy. And close.

Yellowstone Lake stood high on the list of places that might erupt.

Frequent subterranean tremors continued. Indolent geysers woke up and active geysers fell quiet. Fluids below ground shifted, flowed, rearranged. With summer now half over, Abby studied her calendar and counted the days, wondering if she would make it back to the canyon before the place exploded. If she talked about it, Gem shook her head dismissively while William looked a little too enthralled. Marcus just laughed. Needless to say, she did not bring it up with Pepper.

More than a few geological sites online noted that if Yellowstone erupted, there would be enough ash and lava to fill the Grand Canyon many times over.

"Take your lava and go fill something else," Abby muttered, thinking of Pepper there.

When he called her, she could tell he'd been checking the YVO.

"This doesn't look good," Pepper said. "Makes me wonder why the park is even open."

"They say it's just breathing," Abby assured him. "That when it lets off thermal energy like this, it's actually a good thing. Keeps the pressure from building up."

"Is that what William says?"

"William can't be trusted because he sort of wants it to erupt. I keep reminding him that he wouldn't live long, so what's the point of seeing it happen?" Then Abby wanted to kick herself for saying that.

"Good logic. Disturbing, but good." He paused. "I think you should come home. Now."

"Very funny."

"I'm not joking."

"John. You're overreacting. Do you really think I'm going to make them shut down the clinic, just because we're jumpy?" She said *we're* but meant *you're*. "When everything else in the park is business as usual? Besides, then Marcus and Gem would be out of work."

"I don't think that closing down boardwalks is business as usual."

"I'm pretty sure it happens all the time." She had no idea whether that was true.

The next day, Abby had Marcus block the last two afternoon appointments so she could make a house call on Edna Dillon. That pleased Gem, because she wanted a few hours of peace and quiet at the clinic to reorganize supplies. Abby also planned to visit the mud pots, one of her favorite spots, and William would be there later, patrolling and giving a talk.

Abby found Edna outside her RV under a tree, tucked into a chaise with pillows and blankets despite the warm afternoon sun. A powder blue sky backed up fluffy clouds, like great piles of whipped cream, floating and melting. Mildred sat close by, reading out loud to Edna, with skeins of bright yarn in a box alongside.

"A perfect day for a visit," sighed Edna, rubbing her cheek, the skin blotchy from her oxygen tubing. Her hand, wasted and bruised, slipped back under the blanket.

"I'm impressed that you could walk out here," said Abby.

"I didn't," Edna said. "A neighbor carried me."

Mildred pointed with her chin down the road. "Mr. Barnes, from over there. He comes by every day. He's a big man, picks her up like she's a stick of straw. He'll be back soon to toss her back inside."

"There's no point staying here if I'm stuck indoors," Edna remarked. Her head wobbled and she leaned back against the pillows, gazing at the sky from sunken eyes, her hair like thin white smoke, wisps rising above her. "If it happened right now, I'd be happy."

Abby pulled over a lawn chair and sat, went through the motions of taking her pulse, took out her stethoscope and listened to her chest. The lungs gravely silent, not enough air moving through to make a sound. Then a cough rasped up, gurgling and thick. Edna's face turned red as she choked and fought through it, finally collapsing back into her blankets.

"Does that hurt?" Abby asked. "When you cough like that?"

"A little." Eyes shut, her skin dull ivory. "But Mildred keeps me on my pain meds. So if I seem goofy, blame her." She opened one eye, rolled it toward Abby. "Of course, I've been kind of goofy all my life."

Abby smiled. She checked her legs for edema, pressed her belly for pain. "Are you drinking enough fluids? You seem a little dehydrated."

"Does it matter?" Edna shrugged, while Mildred shook her head no. Mildred picked up the knitting, her long needles clicking, a soothing rhythm.

"Well, you might feel a little bit better. Your heart might not race as much, like it is now."

Edna nodded, not really listening. "I think I'll take a nap now," she murmured, falling asleep.

Abby got up, squeezed Mildred's hand and Mildred gripped back. Not wanting to wake Edna, Abby left quietly.

William was finishing his talk when Abby arrived. He nodded her way and went on about the acidic mud, the hydrogen sulfide gases emitting the foul smell, the tiny organisms remarkably thriving in the hot murky pudding as they disintegrated rock into clay, cell by cell. Abby listened from behind the little crowd, enjoying the earthen reek that blew across the burbling holes. She imagined the masses of magma below, pushing and bulging, rising and falling. She mused about Edna's ashes and wondered if Edna had specific places she wanted them scattered. Becoming part of a mud pot might be a curious fate.

A family quarrel broke her reverie. A boy of five or six years clung to the barrier fence while his parents scolded and pulled at him, insisting loudly it was time to go. He wrapped his thin arms around the lower rail and plopped down, drumming his heels on the planks and releasing a murderous shriek. Exasperated, embarrassed, his dad said, "Fine, stay there, but we're going." His parents turned their backs and walked away, no doubt expecting that he would follow shortly. Abby gave up on her reflections.

His talk over, William headed her way, but a small clutch of tourists trailed him with questions. He paused, answering, so Abby leaned against the fence and waited. She still had Edna in her mind. Edna would not likely live much longer, hardly drinking or eating. Her kidneys would start shutting down, and she would slip away.

Abby stretched and looked around. William chatted with the last tourist. She glanced over at the mud pots and froze.

The stubborn little boy stood by himself above the caldron, far beyond the fence, on a crumbling tenuous shelf of pale gray crust, leaning over to stare below at the hot stewing sludge as it popped and burped, releasing caustic gas and acid. Little bits of grit and pebble flaked from the ledge beneath his feet and dropped into the steamy murk. He had paused just inches from the brink. She saw him shift his foot to take a step closer, to see a little better.

"Hey!" Abby shouted to him, terrified the ledge would collapse and plunge him into the deadly muck. "Don't move!"

She didn't take time to look for his parents. She hoisted herself to the top rail and swung her leg up when an arm hooked around her waist and hauled her back. William let go then, throwing her a hard glare.

"Don't you even think of it," he muttered fiercely, his face intense. "You stay right here. No matter what happens."

He climbed quickly over the fence and moved toward the boy in a graceful fluid motion, almost catlike. Somehow cautious and swift at once, he wove across the brittle surface, rapidly testing each step with the toe of his boot, then rolling his foot into place and pressing down before raising the other foot and committing his weight. And the whole time, he talked to the boy in a mild singsong voice, fixing him with his eye, saying "Hey, guy, you might want to be careful right there where you are. Just stay still for a second, okay? I'm going to come help you, okay? Don't you love that mud? It's just the craziest stuff, right?"

The boy's head came up, his face streaked with dirt and tears, staring at William as if mesmerized. Abby clenched the rail as more flakes tumbled into the boiling mud. She bit her lip to keep from yelling another warning, not wanting to break the spell. William flowed next to him, still talking quietly and, incredibly, the boy smiled. William scooped him up, tucked him on his hip with his right arm, moved away from the edge without ever stopping, and began sliding back across the hot foggy crust. Abby had just begun to breathe again when his left foot suddenly turned and sank, pitching him sideways onto his left knee and elbow as he twisted to keep the boy up. Steam puffed around them and everyone watching gasped at once.

Then William was on his feet again and finished the last few steps. He passed the child over the fence into waiting hands as the parents rushed up, just realizing the danger.

Everyone talked at once, thanking William, slapping him on the back as he climbed over. The mother cried and the father, overwhelmed, had to sit down with his subdued son in his lap. William made sure everyone seemed all right and asked their names, just in case, although Abby noticed he didn't write them down like usual, didn't pull out the small notebook he kept in his pocket. People began wandering off and Abby came up to him at last.

"Are you okay?" She saw his compressed lips, the way he kept shaking his left arm.

"A little burn," he said between clamped teeth. He flicked her a glance, his eyes dark.

Abby took his left hand and turned his arm over, saw the shiny red skin from elbow to wrist. A bumpy line of blisters rose across the burn. Then she saw that his lower pant leg was soaking wet and looked up at him.

"There, too," he nodded tightly.

"Come on," she said, drawing him away. "Let's get you to the clinic."

He walked with her, breathing hard. She knew he still felt the adrenaline of his rescue, the shock of his pitch into scalding water. He kept moving his arm with pain. Abby led him to her car, but he stopped and shook his head.

"I can't leave my vehicle here," he insisted, turning to his park service truck.

"Give me your keys," Abby said. "We'll lock it up and someone can get it later."

"No. I shouldn't do that." He awkwardly opened the driver's door and climbed in, his face pinched. "I can drive."

"Don't be ridiculous." Abby pushed him over. "I'll drive you."

William nodded, leaning back against the seat, then bolted upright. "No, wait. You can't drive a park service truck."

"Of course I can. It's an automatic, right? If it was a stick shift, I wouldn't even try." Abby reached across him and pulled over his seatbelt, buckled it by his hip as he raised his arm.

"No, wait," he shook his head, as if trying to think. "I mean, you're not allowed to drive it. You're not authorized."

"William, just sit still and be quiet. No one will care."

Abby cranked the truck into reverse. Unaccustomed to the powerful engine, she spun the tires backing up, gravel spitting and flying. Then she shifted into drive and did it again. He glowered at her in alarm.

"Calm down," Abby said. "I'm getting used to it. Pour some water on your arm from that cold water bottle. Right now. And take off your boot to cool your foot. You don't want to hold in the heat against your skin—it might make the burn worse. And pour some water over your foot and leg, too. No, no—after the boot is off."

Abby tried to keep an eye on him and drive the unwieldy truck and watch traffic and get out her phone. Not the time to tell him she'd never driven a truck. She finally managed to juggle it all and call Gem and warn her not to leave, that she was coming in with a burn patient.

"You can't drive and call at the same time," William groaned. "There's regulations."

"Yeah? Well, you're not allowed to talk right now, because it's against my regulations." Abby scowled at him. "Because you're annoying me and you're going to make me crash. And besides, this is an emergency."

Gem's eyes widened with surprise when Abby and William came in. Marcus had already left. She took one glance at William's drawn face, his boot in one hand as he limped through the door, and she took him from Abby and into the treatment room.

"Get his vitals, and he'll need to take off his pants so we can see that leg," Abby said as she washed her hands. "Let's start some cool compresses."

William clumsily tried to unbuckle his belt, gingerly and ineffectively moving his left arm.

"Lie down," Gem told him, pushing him back. "I'll do it."

First, she placed a cool wet gauze on his forearm. Then she removed his other boot, undid his khakis and pulled them off, easing them carefully over his left lower leg. But the fabric brushed against the burn and his breath hissed.

"I'm sorry, William," Gem said softly, applying another cool gauze to his leg. He turned his head away, clearly ill at ease lying there in his boxers, so she drew a sheet across him. He closed his eyes and sighed.

Abby was pleased to see that his foot had been spared. The water-resistant boot probably saved it, and he was so quick leaping up that his contact with the steam had been fleeting. A wide scarlet sheen ran down his left lower arm and lower leg, scattered with pearly blisters, but the skin was intact.

"It's mostly first-degree burn," Abby said thankfully. "Some second-degree, but not much. That's the blistered part."

"So that's good?" William asked faintly, breathing deeply.

"That's very good, considering what might have happened." She looked closely at him. "That took some nerve, doing that."

"What else could I do? And it sure doesn't feel like it's very good," he complained. "It hurts like hell and a half. Though the cool stuff really does help."

Gem laid on new gauze. "Catch me up. What exactly happened?"

Abby told the story, how William pulled her away and went after the boy. She tried to find words to describe his graceful agility, flowing like silk, moving soft as a cat…so quickly across the precarious footing. How the crust broke into a shallow puddle of steaming water and he still managed to hold the boy up, to shift and rise, regain his balance and keep going.

"If that shelf had broken off—" Abby started.

"We both would have died," William said simply. "No one could have saved us. No one could have helped us without falling in themselves. And once you're in a mud pot—or a hot spring, or anything like that—you're a goner. Fast. If the heat doesn't get you, the acid does. But usually it's both."

Gem stared at him, digesting Abby's story.

"Those moves sort of sound like ninjutsu," she said.

A smile touched his lips. "Yeah. Since I was little. My grandma signed me up when I was being bullied by some older kids."

Gem grinned, then sobered. "Me too. Other reasons."

"Cool," William said.

"What are you two talking about?" Abby asked.

"Ninja stuff." Gem winked at William.

Abby raised her eyebrows and left it alone. William called his supervisor, but Abby ended up on the phone, saying he would likely be back at work next week. Maybe desk work in a few days.

"The best thing about this kind of burn," Abby told William, "is that the pain improves quickly. Within a day or two. But the pain can be terrible at first, worse even than a much deeper burn. It's all those touchy little nerves on the surface. And right now they're screaming."

Abby dispensed pain pills for the night and Gem offered to help him home. Abby considered asking Gem to hurry since she needed a ride back to the mud pots for her car. Then she thought better of it, seeing Gem's tender touch as she wrapped his burns, and Abby called Marcus instead. Marcus was happy to play taxi.

Abby had a great deal to tell Pepper that night. Before she hung up with him, she had to promise not to fall into boiling mud.

As she fell asleep, she hoped this escapade would not provide her nightmares with new dreadful ways for Pepper to die.

Unfortunately, it did.

16

Abby knew she must fight through this. Surely it would fade; she just needed to keep herself together until it did. She meditated, she ran mile after mile, she committed to eating healthy every day. Pepper would be proud of her, and she told him so. If only the nightmares weren't so vivid. If only she wasn't exhausted from jerking awake over and over, with just an occasional peaceful night. She tried to nap, too, with mixed success.

After three days in succession of treating patients with heart attacks, Gem declared it was Myocardial Infarction Week and began posting a running tally:

_0_ Days Without Calling for Medical Transport

The little sign hung in a niche where no patient could see it, but so far that week the number stayed zero. Every day, they summoned an ambulance or helicopter for the hospital. On Thursday, it seemed they would finally make it, and Gem was about to erase the "0" and replace it with "1" when a sixty-eight-year-old man appeared at five minutes till five o'clock, short of breath, with crampy pains down his left arm. The zero stayed up. Finally, on Friday, there were no cardiac cases. But an elderly woman took a crooked step coming out of the visitor center and fell, fracturing her hip. Still zero.

For Abby's upcoming trip to the canyon, Marcus insisted on being her travel agent. He quickly found her a flight because he knew who flew and when.

"Maybe you should become some tycoon's personal assistant—you could make millions," Abby suggested.

Gem rolled her eyes. "You're right, if his tycoon didn't mind going to the wrong place on the wrong day every now and then."

Marcus just laughed, conceding that was bound to happen.

"Just make sure you end up at the Grand Canyon," Gem cautioned Abby, "and not Yosemite."

Ranger Perkins came in, bringing a teenage boy who slid on a rock in the river and now bore a black eye, a two-inch laceration above his ear, and a sprained wrist. He and his brothers had been playing in shallow water, jumping from one slippery stone to the next. Now the two brothers crowded around, fascinated by the bloody wound and suture equipment, promising to stand quiet and still. But they couldn't. They kept wanting to try out the needle holder and see what the suture felt like, and they watched the scimitar-like needle pierce the numbed skin to choruses of *Wow!* and *Cool!* and *Sick!* Abby eventually sent them out with their dad, having the mom stay until the stitches were done.

Ranger Perkins lingered after the patient left, asking how things were and did they feel safe. He promised they would monitor the clinic better. Abby felt Pepper's influence, but she didn't really mind because she liked Perkins.

Perkins also reported another dead bison.

"It's been a while," he sighed. "We hoped maybe it was over. But this one was badly hacked up, and a kidney was missing. Kidneys are hard to reach, you know? They're way up under the ribs behind the intestines and—" He stopped and laughed. "I guess I don't need to tell you where the kidneys are."

Abby grimaced and Marcus said "Yuck."

On Saturday afternoon Abby tried to nap, but nearby tourists came and went, car doors slamming and children shouting. She tossed restlessly, imagining mutilated kidneys, so she gave up on sleep and went for a long run around Firehole Lake Road. The heavens shone pale aqua between a cobblestone of little round clouds as a light breeze stirred the warm air. A sublime day. Pleased with her pace, Abby took a break and slowed to a walk beside a wide meadow, feeling much better. At the far end of the grassland, a small herd of bison grazed, a quarter mile away, and nearby people congregated, setting up cameras around a steadily steaming geyser. The steam billowed and rose higher. Abby couldn't remember the name of the geyser, though she recalled that it used to erupt a few times every day. Now it had not vented in a week.

She decided to wait—it would be nice to see the geyser spout, and it might be an impressive discharge. Moving away from the road and people, away from the crumbling, ashy ground, she sat in the grass under a tree and took out her phone in case she wanted a photo. Abby leaned back against the scratchy bark and savored the drowsy afternoon, pastel moths wafting by, a few birds squawking above her. She closed her eyes and waited.

Bump. Bump.

Someone pushed her leg, her foot. Abby took a deep breath and slowly opened her eyes, sluggishly emerging from sleep. A large brown dog stood by her feet and nudged at her ankle.

"Hey, go away," she called out, pulling up her knee.

She looked closer and stiffened.

Not a dog. A bison calf, nibbling the grass by her foot, its nose bumping against her. With the sound of her voice, both the calf and its mother raised their heads, staring at her. The cow was no more than twenty feet away. Maybe less.

Abby stayed very still. Only her eyes moved, roving without turning her head, and she saw that the entire herd had wandered up around her. People no longer waited near the geyser, so it had either erupted or they had given up. How long had she slept? Maybe fifteen minutes. Maybe an hour. Maybe longer. She heard hooves brush through the grass, heard the soft ripping sound as they tore off each tuft, heard them chewing and munching. She smelled the crushed green stems, the warm dusty hides, the dark tang of manure.

She had no idea what to do.

The sun crept down the sky, shadows stretching. Although darkness remained hours away, what if the herd decided to spend the night here, bed down around her? Several bison lay in the grass not far away, gazing across the meadow. No one knew where she was and no one expected her. While she guessed she had the endurance to wait out the night under the tree, it hardly seemed feasible. She wouldn't be missed until Pepper tried to call, possibly not until nine o'clock, and she already knew the bison didn't like it when she spoke. She wouldn't dare talk to him, and he would grow upset when he couldn't reach her. Maybe frantic, knowing him.

Very slowly, Abby moved her fingers to her phone lying in her lap. It felt like hours. She thought of Pepper's week-years and how she was now experiencing minute-hours, and she nearly laughed from sheer nerves. The calf had moved behind her and the cow stood closer, no longer grazing but staring into space above Abby, grinding her cud.

Abby wanted to contact Ranger Hannah Santana—William considered her his wildlife expert—but didn't know how to reach her. Instead, Abby texted Gem to see if she could locate Santana. She remembered William's warnings about grizzly bears becoming active at night, and then she thought of wolves. Her uneasiness climbed.

When she tapped her phone, each digit peeped and the small sound clanged like a gong in the quiet world under the tree. Three nearby bison, two with calves, startled and raised their furry heads, eyes wide. Their big wet noses twitched, smelling her, and Abby noticed the size of their horns. Curved, pointed, solid spears of bone. She sat motionless, feeling stupid, and furtively moved her finger to silence the phone. Minutes passed, Abby like stone, and the bison slowly returned to grazing. Across the field, another one shook its head and heavily laid its body down. Abby finished her text and waited.

If it weren't for the calves, she thought, she would just carefully stand up and back away. But Hannah's story, being charged by the cow protecting her calf, sat fresh in her mind. She looked up at the tree and saw the branches were low enough—she could climb up if needed. But spending the night in a tree would likely be more miserable than under a tree. Unless you factored in the bears and wolves, which made the branches look suddenly inviting. Of course, bears could climb trees.

Her phone vibrated. A text from Santana: "I'm coming. Don't move."

Abby leaned back to wait, made herself relax. She thought about running water chuckling over stones, the shining gold and green rocks, the sunlight bouncing. She thought about saguaro cactus, how slowly they grew. Barely a few inches tall after ten years but eventually reaching fifty feet, weighing thousands of pounds after a cloudburst, engorged with water. She imagined herself as a saguaro, growing cell by cell, her spiny arms, her spreading shallow roots.

A park vehicle moved slowly along the road and stopped. Hannah climbed out, and then Gem emerged from the passenger seat. They stood a moment, and Abby could see Hannah look back and forth at the herd, pointing first at herself, then pointing at something else. Her long braid swung down her back. A tourist car slowed and paused, but Hannah waved them on. Then she shoved her hat down tightly on her head and motioned for Gem to stay put, and she started walking toward the herd, but not near Abby. Gem stood by the vehicle, shading her eyes with her hand as she waved toward Abby with the other. Abby stayed still and watched flies lazily circle the cow beside her.

Hannah neared the bison and began hissing, a shushing sound, slightly raising her arms, just a little. Then she paused, waited for a reaction, and took a few more steps, repeating. A few bison watched, unimpressed, then ambled away from her. Hannah circled, keeping up her gentle noises and subtly lifted arms, and more turned their backs and strolled off. Seeing their friends walk away, the two lying in the grass near Abby seemed to look at each other and make a decision; they groaned and heaved to their feet and followed. Then another one rose. Hannah continued her gentle prodding. Soon they all drifted out across the field, and Abby stood up stiffly.

Hannah came over. "It's a good thing you got hold of me. They looked settled in. They were definitely going to spend the night."

"I'm so very sorry." Abby felt terrible that she had put Hannah at risk. "I feel like such an idiot."

Gem trotted over and took Abby by the arm, surveyed her up and down as if looking for damage. The tattoo snake glared at her. "Are you okay?"

"I'm fine," Abby insisted again, shaking out her legs, stamping her feet to get the circulation going. "I'm just embarrassed. What a stupid thing to do. And you could have been hurt, trying to help me," she added with chagrin.

"No worries. It's basically my job." Hannah smiled, then her face crinkled, puzzled. "And now how exactly did you wander out into that herd?"

Abby sighed. "It was the other way around. I sat down under the tree to wait for the geyser. The bison were way off, out there." Abby pointed. "Only I fell asleep, and when I woke up, here they were, all around me. Getting ready for bed."

Gem's eyes flashed. "Damn it, Abby. You've got to get more sleep. What's wrong with you? You're scaring me to death."

Abby shook her head. "It's not that bad."

"Like hell." Gem threw a worried glance at Hannah. "She fell asleep behind the wheel once, too. Good thing one of us was awake."

A loud sputter and splash. They turned to see the geyser burp up a large cloud of steam and a spurt of water. It fizzed and hissed in little fits and let loose, a tremendous high jet propelled into the air, crashing and rising. The few straggling bison scuttled off. A dense mist of water and haze sailed away on the breeze, catching the low sunlight and turning iridescent, a fluctuating curtain of rainbows. They stared, enchanted, as it gushed for minutes.

"Wow," said Hannah when it finally dropped and dribbled away. "I can't wait to tell William about that. I should have timed it—that went on and on. Did anyone think to get a picture?"

"Nope," said Abby, holding up her phone, completely forgotten in her hand.

Hannah drove them back and Abby insisted on treating them to supper.

"Pepper's sure going to think this was funny," commented Gem, biting into her hamburger. When Abby looked dismayed, Gem relented. "As if anyone's going to tell him."

Abby decided to ignore her and made an observation. "I had a lot of time out there, pondering about those bison." She paused, thinking it through. "If you were a very patient person, it wouldn't be all that difficult to get next to one. That calf was practically in my lap, and its mama was only a few feet away. What I'm trying to say is, you could probably get really close, if you were patient and wanted to kill one."

Gem looked skeptical, but Hannah stared at Abby.

"Huh," she said, squinting.

"Forget those crazy ideas," Gem said. "And as soon as we're done eating, you're going back to your cabin and going to bed."

"Gee, Mom, it's still light outside. Can't I stay out and play a little bit longer?" Abby complained.

Hannah laughed, but Gem shook her head.

"It's not funny," she said, perturbed.

Abby nodded, then changed the subject.

17

When Abby arrived at work Monday morning, Gem anxiously waited for her, with Turbo Packer already in an exam room. Marcus came early to open up and found Turbo huddled at the clinic door, baking with fever, shaking with chills. Marcus helped him inside and gave him a blanket. Turbo's vital signs included a throbbing pulse of one hundred ten and a temperature of one hundred two.

Turbo looked bad, enough to trigger Abby's alarm. His clothes clung damp with sweat, his wet hair hung in strings, and he groaned with discomfort every time he moved. She gave him acetaminophen, which he studied suspiciously but swallowed, and she started the long, detailed investigation of putting it all together. This did not have the feel of something ordinary.

"You've got to help me, Medicine Woman," he moaned, rolling his head back and forth on the pillow. "I think they're trying to kill me."

"They who?" Abby asked.

He pressed his hands against his temples. "My head hurts so bad. Make it stop. Make it stop. Make it stop."

Abby performed a quick neurological exam to make sure there were no signs of anything dangerous in his brain, any bleeding or an infection like meningitis, but found nothing.

"Give the medication a little while to work," she suggested. "A high fever can cause a bad headache. When did this start?"

He had gradually grown ill over the last week. Fatigue, achy joints, poor appetite, chills at night. He wondered if they had contaminated his food, his water. Abby again asked whom he meant, but he just shook his head. No exposures to anyone sick that he knew of. He didn't drink alcohol, didn't use drugs, didn't inject anything or share utensils. He didn't have sex. Abby pushed through her list. No vomiting, no nausea, no diarrhea, no stomachache, no cough, no sinus symptoms, no sore throat, no ear pain, no dental pain, no shortness of breath, no asthma or wheezing, no chest pains, no urinary pain, no blood in his urine, no testicle pain, no penis discharge, no swelling, no bruising, no numbness, no localized weakness, no problems with speech or hearing or understanding, no racing heart until today, no irregular heartbeat, no tremors, no injuries or cuts or burns or scrapes or sprains or punctures. Nothing she could narrow down and nothing she could eliminate.

Abby remembered all too well her worst case at the Grand Canyon, a severely ill man with bubonic plague, contracted from infected fleas that lived on infected rats or squirrels or prairie dogs. She failed to make the diagnosis at the first visit, and the man nearly died. Abby knew she would wonder forever if another physician might have done better. Now when a patient came in seriously ill, she always considered zoonosis, an infection contracted through an animal.

For the last few years, Turbo reported, he worked in veterinary offices across the northwest. A total of five or six practices, mostly small animals. Although some of the vets cared for livestock, he had not gone out with them on those cases. He loved the dogs and cats and little rodents, the occasional reptile. But that was almost a year ago, too long ago to be affecting him now.

"Animals admire me," he said, sitting up, feeling better. His fever had dropped and only a mild headache persisted. "I even have a rabbit friend out behind our dorm that I feed, right from my hand. I mean, it's wild, but it comes to me. It understands me. And some birds. Ravens. We connect. Spiritually."

Abby started her mental list. Rabbits could carry tularemia. Birds could carry psittacosis, and ravens could carry West Nile virus. There was no bubonic plague in the area, and Turbo had not traveled since arriving at Yellowstone. But there were certainly mosquitoes, and mosquitoes could be tiny transport machines for microbes, equipped with their own injection apparatus. Abby's differential included several types of infections spread by mosquitoes. Not Zika, because Wyoming had the wrong kind of mosquitoes. But the world teemed with little organisms hiding and traveling inside bigger organisms and finding their way into humans.

The lurking possibilities were overwhelming. She must narrow it down or the labs would cost thousands of dollars. But she had nearly run out of questions, and Abby felt her old insecurity raise its head, unsure where to turn next.

"Have you eaten any strange foods?" she asked. "Been out camping? Did you drink any unpurified water from lakes or streams?"

Turbo's face locked, his eyes nearly shut. "What do you mean… strange foods?"

"You know. Raw seafood, like sushi. Undercooked meat. Raw eggs or cookie dough. Unpasteurized milk or cheese. Anything that was left out too long—what?"

His face changed. Alert, almost cunning.

"My friend," he said slowly.

Abby waited, but he didn't continue.

"What about your friend?" she prompted.

"I had a friend visit me. Not quite a month ago." Turbo counted on his fingers, calculating, for a long time. He still looked pale, but he started bobbing his head, his familiar tic. "I knew him from Washington. He brought me a bunch of food here, fresh berries and jam. And some homemade goat cheese. It's healthy, right? He said he got it along the road. You know, how people sell their farm stuff."

"I wonder," Abby mused. "I want you to rest here while we run your basic labs." She started to leave, then turned back. "You don't happen to still have any of that cheese, do you? Or the container it was in?"

Turbo shook his head, lying down and closing his eyes.

While Gem put his blood through the machines, Abby searched her medical resources online. It didn't take long. His symptoms and his exposure to unpasteurized cheese matched well for brucellosis, a disease caused by the bacteria Brucella. She called her favorite consultant, who happened to be John Pepper, and reviewed the case with him. He agreed. By then, the labs were done, showing mild anemia, slightly low white blood cells, and borderline liver function. All possible in brucellosis.

Turbo's reaction to her diagnosis was mixed.

"So…I've got this strange bacteria inside my body? Bruce who?" He looked down at himself, ran his hands slowly across his chest and abdomen as if searching.

"Brucella. Most likely you do," Abby replied. She wrote the name on his instruction sheet. "We'll send out the test, but it might take a few days or maybe even a week to get the report. In the meantime, you should start antibiotics. You actually need to take two antibiotics at the same time. For six weeks."

He looked sourly at her from the corner of his eye. "That's a lot of chemicals. For a long time. I don't know about that."

Abby spoke slowly. It was critical that she get him on board. "I know, Turbo. And you're right, antibiotics are chemicals. But right now you have a microbe in your body that doesn't belong there, something that we need to get rid of. Brucellosis won't go away by itself, and you're very very sick. You might have to go to the hospital if you don't get better."

He twitched, wagged his head. "No, no, no. That's not happening."

"Well, I figured you wouldn't want that." Abby touched his arm, looked in his eyes. "But that could happen, if you're not treated. You trust me, don't you?"

Turbo blinked. "You've been good to me, Medicine Woman."

"And you've been nice to me. I appreciate the little gifts, I really do. So you know that I wouldn't recommend anything unless I really thought you needed it."

His head started bobbing again. "Okay. All right."

"Good. And you can't work for a little while, not until your fever's gone. Okay?"

He jerked. "What do you mean? I have to work."

"I'll write you a note, a medical excuse for your boss. And we can fill out the paperwork for FMLA—that's the legal form about your absence. That way your employer can't fire you if you can't work for a while."

He eyed her. "That FMLA. That's a government thing?"

"Yes, it's to protect you. It's a good policy."

"No way. Don't do it. I'll get by. They need me—they're not about to let me go." More bobbing. "Yep, yep, yep. They need me. And they know it."

"Well, I do advise it." Abby knew she would get nowhere.

Feeling better with his fever down, Turbo left holding his instructions and an appointment for the next day.

"So," said Gem after he was gone. "Isn't brucellosis one of those infections that you have to report to the health department?"

"Absolutely," said Abby. "But not until we're sure. We'll wait for the blood test."

"He already worries that the government is watching him."

"I know." Abby felt sorry for Turbo and his convoluted, uncomfortable world. "It's bad enough that he's a bit delusional and paranoid, and now he gets this infection on top of that."

At the same time, Abby grew excited about her upcoming weekend at the canyon. Incredibly, she had only five more weeks in Yellowstone. And while she longed fervently for her old routine, longed to be back with Pepper every day and night, she ached at the thought of missing Gem and Marcus. She could hardly imagine not working with them. Gem had only vague plans for her next job. More than once she mentioned Australia, maybe New Zealand. Marcus had no plans at all. Abby secretly pictured him working alongside Ginger at the Grand Canyon Clinic, replacing Priscilla. What a relief that would be.

Turbo felt about the same the next day, weak and sweaty, but he had only taken one dose of each antibiotic so far.

"It's really important to take those medications correctly," Abby said. "Don't skip any doses. Otherwise the bacteria become resistant to the antibiotics. The antibiotics quit working."

"Have you seen all the side effects?" Truculence reined.

"Yes. But remember, the side effects are uncommon. Of course, you should tell me right away if you think you're having any problems."

Turbo scowled.

"And something else," Abby said carefully. "You might think about going home. I mean, the clinic here will close up before long, and most services around Old Faithful will shut down for the winter. I'm assuming your job is just for the summer? You won't have any medical care here. You'll need to see your own doctor."

"Where will you be?" He stared at her.

"I work at the Grand Canyon. I'll be going back there."

Turbo nodded. "Maybe I'll get a job there."

"Well. You certainly can try. But the canyon cuts back in the winter, too." Abby doubted anyone would hire him. "Do you have a permanent home? Like, with your family?"

"My parents are dead," he remarked quietly. "To me."

Abby waited, but he said nothing more. "Well. I'm sorry to hear that. But you must have some plans, right? For what you'll do this winter?"

An uneven smile distorted his face and his upper lip rose. "Yes. I've got plans. You bet I've got plans."

Something quailed inside Abby. It sounded like a threat. "What do you mean?"

The look faded and his head bobbed. "Don't worry. You'll be fine. You'll be fine. But they won't."

"Can you tell me, Turbo? Can you explain what you're talking about? I just want to help you." She wished she knew the extent of his delusion. "You don't plan to hurt yourself, do you? Or anyone else?"

"Leave me alone," he replied sharply. "You'll be fine. Stop worrying." He slid off the exam table and left.

Turbo returned for follow-up in two days. He felt less achy and the fever was gone, and he insisted that he could work, but Abby told him he must wait until the next week for the labs, that for now he needed to rest.

Turbo departed, reluctant and surly, without a note to return to work.

18

Abby arrived at the canyon after dark, swept into the eager arms of Pepper. He hurried her to dinner at El Tovar, the beautiful old lodge on the rim.

If Pepper wished for an intimate dinner, he was foiled, but Abby didn't mind that everyone stopped by their table to say hello and tell her how much they missed her. A few divulged their medical developments, one young woman now happily pregnant and another whose back pain had finally improved with daily walking. Chef Nutter, Abby's patient for the last two years, emerged smiling from the kitchen and presented them extra treats. They even enjoyed a furtive appearance from the infamous ring-tailed cat who roamed the ceilings and hidden spaces of El Tovar, its clever masked face peeping over the rafters before scampering away with a flourish of its long striped tail.

"Let's get home," Pepper said as they stood at last, regarding her with yearning, "before someone else snares you."

"But wait. Let's walk along the rim first," Abby pleaded.

"Really? You can't wait until tomorrow? Besides, it's too dark to see much."

Abby took his hand, pulling him. "Come on. Just a little walk. If I don't, it would be like going to Hawaii and staying at the beach, only waiting till the second day to put your toes in the ocean."

"It's nothing like that," he protested, knowing he was defeated.

They strolled down the path, away from the buildings and lights, and finally stopped in shadows by the low stone wall. A quarter moon swung out West, a pale arc, and shimmering stars sprayed the sky, tiny gleaming crystals. The canyon stretched away, illuminated faintly in that improbable glow, the towers and gorges turned every shade of black and gray, rising up ashen and sinking into obsidian depths. Abby loved sensing the layers, the primeval landscapes compressed beneath her, fractured open in this startling spectacle.

"Where's Orion?" he asked, playing with her hair. "I want to see those giant superstars."

Abby shook her head. "Supergiant stars. And Orion's out wandering this time of year, gone south to hunt."

Pepper stood behind, his arms crossed over her. She knew he wanted to allow for her reflections, but soon he was rubbing her forearms, massaging her shoulders, his fingers starting to wander. Abby warmed and dissolved a little, leaning back into him, feeling him rise against her.

"We should head home," he warned, his caresses more enthusiastic.

Abby turned from the view and wrapped her arms around his waist. She gripped his slim hips, felt him shift.

"Okay, that does it," he said roughly, and he drew her into the woods. He kissed her urgently and tugged off his shirt, spreading it on the pine needles and bearing her down. An owl hooted and floated darkly away with a sigh of wings, leaving them to their privacy.

Eventually they made it back to the house where Abby showered off her extensive day, along with a fair amount of forest duff and bits of bark. They curled up on the back deck and she fell asleep, feeling safe and content.

In her dream, Pepper stood on the rim of the canyon and gazed at her, reaching toward her as a dark man in a heavy coat charged him from the side. Abby shouted a warning and rushed forward, running faster and faster, but she couldn't make it and the man collided with Pepper and thrust him over the edge. Abby sobbed and lurched up. Pepper grasped at her, telling her to wake up.

"You're okay, you're okay," he kept saying. "I'm right here."

Abby gulped and puffed and tried to slow her flailing heart. She put her hands on his face and stared at him, then closed her eyes with relief. He stroked her hair and rubbed her back until she could speak.

"I'm sorry." She felt confused and wary of herself. This had never happened when she was with him.

He held her hands, his face grave. "What the hell was that? What were you dreaming?"

Everything clashed around in her brain. She wanted to tell him, and she was afraid to tell him. She needed to reason it out and decide what was right or wrong or wise or stupid, and she felt unbalanced and foolish.

"Nothing. I mean, I can't exactly remember. Scary. Some kind of a monster." True enough. She drew a long uneven breath, getting better.

He looked skeptical. "Really?"

She nodded and put her head on his chest. He let it go and held her and, finally, they fell asleep.

The next morning they lounged with books and coffee until finally rousing themselves, taking a long hike through the woods, away from the rim and summer crowds. Cumulus crowded the sky, muscular clouds that shouldered against each other, shoving and breaking apart, dark gray bellies, skating heavily through the air and pondering rain. Then Abby and Pepper hurried home to prepare a cookout for Dolores and Ginger and even Priscilla, and they invited Dan Drake as well since he was moonlighting that weekend. Drake now had his state medical license and sometimes worked weekend shifts, giving Pepper a welcome break.

Abby loved seeing them: Ginger with her boyfriend Diego, and Dolores with her husband Mack. Dan Drake still reminded Abby of Harry Potter with his round glasses and a mop of dark hair on his forehead. Already he seemed more mature and confident, and she knew that came partly from working alongside Pepper.

Then Priscilla showed up late, after everyone had nearly finished their grilled fish and corn-on-the-cob and coleslaw, so Pepper put more fish on the grill just for her as she stood next to him and teased about men in the kitchen. Abby saw him move sideways, a little away from her, and she stepped right over, bumping against him, unsteady in her plaid fashion hiking boots with impractical two-inch chunky heels. Her tight denim leggings looked like they might split her in half. When Pepper dished the fish onto her plate and returned to Abby's side, Priscilla seamlessly switched her attention to Drake and slid in next to him at the table. Abby saw her tug down her top to expose more cleavage.

But it was a lovely evening. Abby asked Ginger about her squirrel bite reports, for Ginger managed the clinic task of logging all the squirrel nips from tourists who disregarded the warning signs and unwisely handfed the cute little begging rodents. Ginger took her job seriously, recording supplemental and unrequired information about the appearance and facial expression of each furry critter. She shared a few recent descriptions from tourists: the shy reddish squirrel that squinted and seemed nearsighted, and maybe that's why it missed the food and bit a finger instead; the sly dark squirrel with black fur, long claws, and a diabolical expression that looked satanic; and the fat, drab mousy-brown squirrel that seemed depressed and probably had low self-esteem.

They caught Abby up on local gossip and she told Yellowstone stories, while Pepper sat back and looked content, reaching over now and then to clasp Abby's knee or place his hand on hers. Abby loved it and loved seeing him relax. Once alone again, they cleaned up from dinner and made love and sat on the deck to watch lightning tickle the clouds, hearing an occasional growl of thunder.

"I can't wait to be back for good," Abby admitted, lying with her head on his abdomen.

"You mean you've had enough of steam burns and brucellosis?"

"Ack. Don't remind me of Turbo. I feel really bad about him and I can't figure out how to help him." Abby sighed. "He doesn't seem dangerous, but I still worry. He keeps making veiled comments about 'them' and what he's going to do. It's upsetting, but it's probably just talk. He's actually a meek person, and he's often kind. Like bringing me little presents, nature things, like herbs and flowers."

"It'll be good when you're away from all that." He toyed with her hair.

She nodded. "Yes. Though I'll miss Gem and Marcus. A lot."

"Maybe they can come visit?"

Abby hoped so. She watched twigs of lightning twitch in the clouds, listened as the thunder faded away. Pepper's abdomen rose and fell gently under her head, and she floated off. In her dream, she stood with him near Old Faithful, laughing and joking, waiting. It erupted, a feathery white fountain. The water changed color, as if under lights: yellow then pale orange, deepening to bronze and then darkening to crimson, and suddenly no longer spewing but heaving up fiery blobs of lava, plopping down and splattering, catching trees and cars and people on fire. Her hair burst into flame and Pepper's shirt ignited and she shouted and jerked awake, jumping up and crashing into a chair, stumbling to the deck as Pepper scrambled after her, caught her up. She struggled until his voice broke through and then collapsed against him.

He waited until she calmed, wiped the sweat from her face with his hand. His expression turned hard.

"What's going on, Abby? You have to tell me. If you say that you don't remember that nightmare, I won't believe you."

"I've been afraid to tell you," she admitted. Miserable, she looked away, then met his stony gaze. "It's so unnerving. And so stupid at the same time."

"How long has this been happening?" He brought her a glass of water, which she took gratefully.

No more second guessing herself…she knew she must be honest. "Most of the summer. Not every night."

He closed his eyes, as if it was more than he could bear.

"Tell me about it," he said quietly.

Abby felt her lips quiver but she refused to cry. He would blame himself, and crying would only make it worse. She plunged in, talking too fast. "I dream that you're killed, over and over. Sometimes by Lubbock. Sometimes not, sometimes something else. And I'm there but I can't help, I can't get to you. And then you're dead. And then I wake up."

She couldn't describe the horror, the shattering emptiness that followed. How demoralized she felt that she couldn't make it stop, or at least ignore it better. Disregard it. Laugh it off. She seemed so weak and flawed.

Abby appreciated his silence, felt him examine and analyze her words. Felt him take it apart and put it back together. She thought he would find a logical solution, make it scientific. She was wrong.

"Oh, Abby." His voice broke. "I'm so sorry."

His face—agonized and sad. Which Abby could not tolerate. She would not do this to him.

"No. This is not your fault." Vehement, she sat up and turned resolute, even angry. "It's just my stupid, messy brain. If it can't be anxious in one direction, it finds another way. Like it's determined to outsmart me and torment me, find a weak spot, push the button. I hate it."

Pepper's expression softened. "You can't hate your own brain."

"I most certainly can," she replied with force. "You have no idea."

"All right, then." He rallied. "How should we tackle this? Tell me what to do. And if you don't know, then we'll figure it out."

They talked about anxiety and flashbacks and dangers, real and imagined. Abby relayed her conversations with Lucy, and how Lucy thought she might want counseling to fight her way through. How Abby put it off, tried to fix herself with exercise and vegetables, and avoided calling Lucy back. How badly she felt to be failing, how defeated. That she now embraced the challenge openly and would seek help.

She promised Pepper she'd contact Lucy the next day, to ask Lucy's help in finding counseling. Otherwise, Pepper declared, he would go to Yellowstone himself instead. Although Abby knew now that it had nothing to do with where she was, she agreed, because it was time for another strategy.

Before he took her to the airport, she drew a new cartoon where a stick-figure Abby pointed at the canyon and insisted on walking along the rim, while a grumpy stick-figure Pepper tried to pull her home. She left it on his pillow.

19

Turbo's blood test came back positive for brucellosis. By the time Abby saw him on Monday, he had taken the antibiotics for a week and felt much better. He looked better, too. He gained a pound and the night sweats disappeared.

"You've got to let me go back to work," he pleaded. His eyes darted around the room and he kept getting up, pacing back and forth, sitting down, starting over. "I need the money. I'm not going to make it if I don't get back to work."

"All right," Abby agreed. "You shouldn't be contagious now, and it's not usually spread between humans. But you can't work with food that's meant for other people. No preparing or cooking food, serving food, anything like that."

His head bobbed and his eager words rushed. "No problem. No problem at all. I don't work with food. I do all the cleaning up. And I fix things. I keep things running. And I watch them, all the time. I watch them when they work and when they sleep. They think they're so smart, but they're not. They'll get what they deserve, don't worry. Don't you worry."

"Turbo. Who are you watching?" If only he would confide, give her a trace of insight. "Why do you hate them? Can you tell me?"

His chin rose. "Why should I?"

"I just want to help you." Abby searched for the right words, as if she walked a delicate tightrope. "I worry about you. Sometimes you seem so upset."

"Yeah." He jumped down and yanked open the door. "I'm upset all right. I need my note to go back to work. Now." He eyes skimmed around the room until his gaze bumped into her, then he softened. "Please."

Abby wrote the note and he left quickly. She watched through the window as he hurried across the parking lot, saw him pull up short once and look around before continuing.

During a small break between patients, Abby called a psychiatrist she knew in Phoenix. She described Turbo's case, his paranoia and veiled menaces. The psychiatrist guessed that Turbo suffered from a paranoid delusional disorder. But since Turbo could hold a job and had done nothing illegal, nothing dangerous, since he didn't seem to have weapons and made no specific threats, there was little anyone could do. People like him muddled along for years on the fringe of society. Sometimes their whole lives. No system existed to monitor him or help him unless he got worse.

"Even if he was willing to take behavioral drugs, they might not help him," the psychiatrist said. "And I doubt he'd be willing. These disorders are really difficult to treat, hard to impact, because the delusions are so entrenched. Even with excellent psychotherapy, he might only get a little bit better."

"He would never want drugs," agreed Abby. "As it is, he's barely taking antibiotics for a serious infection."

"Just try to keep an eye on him."

What an unsatisfying conversation. And now she had to file a report with the state health department about his brucellosis. She hadn't yet informed Turbo, but she needed to soon.

Gem interrupted her uneasy thoughts.

"We've got an emergency—it might be a stroke. And the patient's only fifty years old." She hurried back to the exam room.

Fred Galligan looked terrified, for his mother suffered a stroke when she was eighty; she died a week later. He noticed his face that morning, glancing in the mirror as he brushed his teeth: his lip sagged and toothpaste leaked from the corner of his mouth, dripped down his chin. Things worsened over the day and now the right side of his face slumped. His cheek drooped and his right forehead shone flatly without its usual wrinkles. He looked unbalanced, and his eyes gleamed with fear.

"Don't panic yet," Abby told him, not wanting to jump to conclusions until she performed a thorough evaluation. "This is probably not a stroke, but let's be sure."

As she anticipated, his history and exam were otherwise benign. No weakness of his arms or legs. He walked in with a normal gait and spoke clearly. Except for his slack right face, being unable to completely close his right eyelid no matter how hard he tried, his neurologic exam raised no further alarms.

"I think you've got Bell's palsy," Abby said. "It's an inflammation of your facial nerve. No one knows exactly why it happens, but it's temporary—it usually clears up. But that can take days or weeks, and sometimes even months."

Galligan explored his face with his fingertips. "How did you know? I mean, you figured it out so fast."

"A stroke comes on quickly, in just seconds or minutes. And a stroke usually affects the lower half of your face, not your eyelid and your forehead, and it often bothers your speech or your limbs. Or both." She smiled. "Besides, you're awfully young to have a stroke. It happens, but not much. Especially since you have no risk factors—you're not a smoker, and you don't have high blood pressure or diabetes."

He began to relax, then realized what she said. "But wait. I'm going to look like this for months? I'm in sales. I can't talk to people looking like this. I look like a clown."

"No, you don't," Abby protested. "You look like a person with Bell's palsy. I'll give you prednisone, which reduces the inflammation. You might recover faster. And you need to patch your eye so it doesn't dry out, because that can damage your cornea. Recovery still might take weeks, though. And a very small percentage of people don't fully recover, just so you know."

"Is there someone else I can talk to? Like a specialist?"

He didn't seem disrespectful, just desperate. Abby understood. He did look lopsided.

"I'm afraid I'm all you've got, for quite a few miles. You're welcome to get consultation with a neurologist, but that might be a hundred miles away. Or you could head home—you're from Seattle, right?"

"Can I drive?"

"Yes, technically. But with your eye patched, you have to be extra careful. Especially changing lanes, passing, things like that. Could someone join you, drive back with you?"

"Maybe…I'd better make some calls."

At noon, Abby sat with Gem and Marcus under the pines, strewn with slices of sunlight. Crisscrossing contrails checkered the sky, as if pilots were laying the board for an aerial game of tic-tac-toe. Gem remarked how she learned something new every day, impressed with Abby's quick diagnoses. She held an article about Bell's palsy but wasn't really reading it. She kept pausing, grinning at Marcus, who shook his head.

"Come on," Gem insisted, poking him with her left hand. "Tell her. Or my snake will get you."

"Ew," said Marcus, cringing away from her finger. He looked at Abby. "Gem wants me to tell you that Wrigley came here last weekend. While you were at the canyon. He dropped by Friday afternoon, right after you'd left. We were just closing up."

Abby's eyes widened. "Good timing for me."

"Right?" he said. "Only, when he found out you were gone—and he wasn't too happy about that—he asked me to play golf with him. His treat, because he was staying up at Big Sky. So I told him I couldn't get there because my car was in the shop, even though it wasn't. Because I don't golf anymore. I don't even have my clubs here."

Marcus found some invisible crumbs on his electric blue polo shirt, brushed them away, looked for more. Gem poked him again, impatiently.

"And—" she prodded.

Marcus shrugged. "So he sent a car and driver for me. Can you believe that? I mean, I still had to rent clubs, and of course it's harder to play without your own clubs. It's like trying to dance if you're wearing someone else's shoes that don't fit. But he really wanted to beat me."

"So you went?" Abby was incredulous; she never thought he would. "What about…you know." Abby glanced at Gem, realizing midsentence that he may not have told Gem about his golf anxiety.

"It's okay. Gem knows." He looked back and forth at them. "And you know a funny thing? Since I talked to you that day, and then later with Gem, I feel better about it." He beamed.

Gem poked him again. "Keep going."

"Ouch, Gem, stop that. You're so mean." He rubbed his arm. "Well, I kept thinking about Wrigley and how he acted around you and what Gem says about him being a nasty old man. I decided I wanted to put him in his place. If I could. I knew it might backfire. But so what? It's not like my golf self-esteem could fall much lower."

"And did it? Backfire, I mean." Abby felt reluctant to ask.

"Heck no. Basically, I sort of killed him. By ten strokes." Marcus smiled, smug.

"Way to go, Marcus!" Abby cheered and Gem high-fived him, and Marcus sat back, basking in their praise.

"Did you putt very well?" Abby wondered.

"I got a little anxious," he admitted. "I missed some putts I should have made. But I did sink most of them. And anyway, he's not that great. He thinks he is—or at least, he used to think he was, until now—but he has lots of problems. He aims wrong and he puts the ball too far forward in his stance. And he lifts his head when he chips. I think he probably cheats when he plays with his buddies."

"Why would you say that?"

"Because he tried to cheat with me twice. Amateur stuff. As if I wouldn't notice." Marcus shook his head, acting disappointed. Then he folded his chubby hands behind his head and smiled.

"I'm so proud of you, Marcus," Abby said. "And I don't mean for beating him. That's just frosting on the cake."

Sitting cheerfully in the splintered sunlight, Abby knew this was the time.

"I have to tell you both something."

She took a deep breath and told them, revealed her nightmares and fears. Gem and Marcus expressed both relief and concern, finally comprehending her fatigue. They wanted to know how to help.

"You don't need to do anything," Abby said. "I'm just done pretending and hiding. I'll start counseling soon and if I need your help somehow, I'll let you know. But if you see me freak out, now you'll understand. And if you see me fall asleep, just smack me and get me some caffeine."

It felt liberating. She wasn't fixed, but it helped.

Abby saw Edna Dillon the next day after the clinic closed. First, though, she changed out of her work clothes because a baby with an ear infection had spit up on her slacks and shoes. It wasn't much, but even a little bit of sour infant puke went a long way, and Abby felt better in her comfortable jeans anyway. Edna wouldn't care.

A soft evening breeze filled the air by the time she entered Madison campground, clouds sailing like tall ships across the warm blue ocean of sky, the west edged in amber as the sun slipped down.

Abby saw Gem's car there, a nice coincidence since neither had mentioned their plans to visit. Laughter filtered through the door, and Abby felt a brief moment of confusion, seeing both Gem and William standing over the tiny stove, their backs to her. Gem's left hand, snake and all, rested at his waist, her thumb hooked through his belt loop and her fingers trailing into the rear pocket of his khakis. His head was bare and his hair mussed because Gem wore his Smokey hat, too big and bumping down on her nose as she laughed. His right hand lay across her shoulder as they crowded before the stove, and Gem raised a wooden spoon to his lips for a taste of something chocolate.

Such an unexpected, intimate moment—Abby hesitated and nearly backed out the door, feeling like an intruder, even as she glimpsed Edna on the couch. A cupcake crowned with creamy white frosting stood on a plate beside her, a tiny bite missing.

"Thank goodness you're here," cried Gem, seeing Abby. "I need a better critic. William likes everything, so he's no help telling me if this is right. We got tired of vanilla and wanted to make chocolate. Because we baked way too many cupcakes. It's Edna's birthday! Well, yesterday, but who's counting?"

William straightened stiffly, reached behind and pulled Gem's hand off his belt. He flushed—or maybe it was the heat from the stove—lifting his hat from her head and placing it on a chair. He tried to look more proper, but the chocolate smudge on his chin prevented that. Abby pointed to her own chin, and he quickly swiped off the frosting.

"It sure smells good in here." Abby savored the fresh-baked aroma. Edna looked smaller than ever, tiny and curled, huffing faintly. Another scent underlaid the baking, something corrupt, a faint odor of waste and decay. Every now and then Edna made a small rasping noise, an extra gulp of air, then resumed her rapid breathing.

"How's it going?" Abby sat next to her and took her hand. Edna's fingers stiff and icy. Her peripheral circulation was shutting down, Abby thought.

Edna just gave a small nod. Something like a smile tugged her lips, and she glanced toward Gem and William by the stove.

"Mildred's gone to the store," Gem explained, stirring in the pan, turning off the heat. "I told her I'd stay with Edna while she was gone. I was on my way, driving away from the clinic, and here comes William just off his shift, so I asked him along. Then I found out about the birthday and we had to make cupcakes. Though we'll have to give most of them away since we made so much."

"It's awfully nice to have homemade stuff," admitted William, joining Abby. He looked kindly at Edna. "I've already eaten three of them, I'm afraid. At this rate, there won't be any left to give away."

Edna winked. "My geyser guide," she puffed.

"What?" Abby and Gem said together.

Edna closed her eyes, so they stared at William, who mumbled it was nothing. But they wouldn't let it go, so he described how a few nights ago after work he took Edna and drove her around to look at geysers and thermal features, the places where she could see them out the window.

"The park service should sign you up for tours," Abby suggested.

"I didn't use a park service vehicle," he said, taken aback. "I used my own car."

Abby assured him she was joking.

Abby stayed and ate two cupcakes herself. They talked about William's upcoming classes at the university that fall and a paper he was writing about Yellowstone, and Gem started calling him Professor

Bridges, which he pretended annoyed him. They imagined where Gem might go to work after Old Faithful closed down. Abby voted for Australia so she could visit her and meet a kangaroo, while Gem considered someplace exotic in Indonesia where she could be courted by an island prince. William pled for Montana or Wyoming so she could bake cupcakes in her spare time and send them to him. Then William pointed out that if the supervolcano erupted, none of them would have to worry about anything.

"You could at least act like that would be a tragedy," Gem scolded, smacking him on his shoulder.

"Experience of a lifetime," William said and he swatted her back, though it was soft, more like a touch. "You can't blame me for being excited about that."

Abby caught Gem's eye for a long moment; Gem made a bemused face. Edna lay on her pillows half asleep, nodding her head now and then as she listened to them talk and tease.

This time Abby did not pretend to listen to her lungs.

20

Abby's running strides felt confident now. Every time she ran, though, she found herself counting down the days, as if each step measured the steady beat of time and minced her emotions into relief and regret. Just three more weeks and she would be back with Pepper, but Gem and Marcus would be out of her life. She never expected this to happen, these deep new friendships.

Abby hurried home because she had her second counseling appointment that evening and wanted to collect herself. She stopped to pick up her mail, pleased to find a package. Abby cheerfully tore into it, anticipating a healthy treat from Pepper. But Pepper had not sent it, and it was not healthy. Instead, she held a box of expensive chocolates, accompanied by a small card from Wrigley.

So sorry I missed you last weekend. Saw these chocolates and remembered your fondness. Enjoy on me.
Special friends always, Rex

What an odd phrase, enjoy on me. That juxtaposition of words bothered her: fondness, enjoy, me. Abby was surprised he even remembered the dessert, as inebriated as he'd been. And special friends?

She stared distastefully at the box, then walked outside to the nearest trash bin and stuffed it in. She didn't even want it in her cabin.

Enough of that. She needed to focus on her counseling assignment.

The last time they met through a videoconference, but tonight the connection faltered and Abby talked on the phone instead with Dr. Karen Goh, her new psychologist. Dr. Goh practiced in Cheyenne and Abby liked her immediately, a sharp-witted Korean woman with penetrating eyes and a calming voice. Since Abby's breathing methods had failed her lately, Karen began coaching her in progressive relaxation.

"I like the exercise," Abby said. "I think I'm getting better. It's hard, though."

"Tell me exactly how it goes," Karen prompted.

Abby described lying down and beginning, contracting one set of muscles, holding them tight, then relaxing. Her feet, then calves, then thighs. Her belly, then her back, on up to her arms, shoulders, and neck. She took her time and worked each muscle group twice, focusing on the fibers, squeeze and release.

After that, Abby mentally scanned her body for tension. And she usually found it, most often the scar on her left forehead, sometimes her shoulders or back. Next came the most difficult step, where she had to mentally color those stressed regions, as if splashing them with paint. She chose green and painted each spot a gaudy neon lime. Then very slowly, she visualized dialing the color down, down to a soft mossy hue. At that point, her tension was supposed to improve.

"I don't always get there," Abby said, "but I feel closer."

"Pretty good," Karen agreed. "Keep working on it."

They talked about Abby's stressors: the earthquakes, Wrigley, Turbo. Her fear that another man in a dark coat might spark a panic attack.

"You certainly have a lot going on," Karen observed with concern. "And except for the coat thing, the rest of it seems very present. Very valid. What I'm saying is, it's normal to be anxious about those things."

Abby sighed. "You mean that a supervolcano about to erupt, and a creepy drunk trying to hit on me, are not things I can fix with imagery?"

"Let's talk about the coat," Karen suggested.

They tried, but just thinking about Lubbock's heavy coat made Abby edgy. She knew she would soon smell his sour stink and her heart would begin to skitter, so they backed off to less-provoking associations. Like the time of day when it happened and the weather that evening. Abby could recall those without strain, so they saved more for later.

The session left her exhausted, but it felt like exactly what she needed, and she made another appointment in six days. Abby slept fitfully that night, pestered by dreams where she and Pepper fled from a shadowy threat. But no one died and she barely woke up.

The next morning, Ranger Santana brought in a tired forty-year-old woman who she found doubled over, vomiting and clutching at her abdomen, behind the crowd of watchers at Old Faithful. For three days now, Betty Appleby felt jittery and slept restlessly. Waves of dizziness rolled through her. But except for a rapid pulse, Abby discovered no clues. She did notice a faint cigarette odor from her skin and hair, even though Betty claimed she quit smoking several weeks earlier.

"I'm not finding much," Abby admitted, studying Betty's normal labs.

Betty ran her fingers through her messy dishwater-blond hair. "Please don't tell me it's all in my mind."

"No," Abby smiled. "I don't think it's all in your mind."

"I've worked so hard on my smoking. Could that make me sick? Quitting smoking? I mean, I've smoked one cigarette every now and then just to see if it would help, but it hasn't. Like, I just finished one this morning, then I started throwing up." She absentmindedly patted her pocket where Abby imagined she used to keep her pack, a slight tremor in her fingers.

"Not likely. Nicotine withdrawal doesn't last this long."

"Well, I don't think it's nicotine withdrawal. I've been wearing a patch, or two patches, every day—I just removed the last one. And I've been chomping on nicotine gum like crazy."

Abby squinted at her. "You've been wearing two patches at a time? You're not really supposed to do that."

"Yeah, but I still had cravings, so I put on the second patch, too."

"And you're also using nicotine gum? While you're wearing two patches?"

"Yeah. My mouth feels like a campfire. Have you ever tasted that stuff? It's like chewing on charcoal."

Abby started putting it together. "Did you read the instructions on that gum? You don't chew it like regular gum. You take a few chews, then you park the gum along the inside of your cheek for a while. Then a few more chews, so you release the nicotine gradually."

"Huh." Betty looked blank. "Who knew?"

"You might be overdosed on nicotine," Abby explained. "You might have nicotine toxicity."

"Ha!" Betty laughed out loud. "And here I kept using more and more, so I was just making it worse?"

Abby nodded. "I think you're getting way more nicotine than when you were smoking."

"Why, I bet this happens all the time! So I'll be okay, right? What's the worst it can do?"

"Nicotine is pretty nasty, actually. It's a good thing Ranger Santana brought you in. High doses can be dangerous." Abby refrained from saying she had never seen this before. She almost shared the fact that nicotine could be used as a deadly insecticide, and that concentrated nicotine darts were rumored to bring down elephants. But she didn't want to terrify the woman.

"Wow. Oh, my goodness." Betty's eyes opened wide. "What's the treatment?"

"Nothing, I'm afraid. You just have to let the nicotine levels go down." Abby cautioned Betty to expect agitation, anxiety, rapid pulse, poor sleep. She asked Betty to remain nearby and return in a few hours for another check as her nicotine levels fell.

Hannah stayed, curious about the nicotine paradox, how a person felt bad whether the levels were rising too high or dropping too low. As they talked, Abby received a long-awaited call from the health department about Turbo. They were trying to reach him about the brucellosis, but he never answered his phone and did not respond to their letter.

"He's a little odd," Abby explained, unsure how much to reveal. Since brucellosis was a matter of public health, though, they needed some insight. "He doesn't like the idea that the government is investigating him."

Not uncommon, the man on the phone replied. And when Abby recounted Turbo's story of unpasteurized cheese from an unknown farm in an unknown state from a friend whose whereabouts were unknown, he sounded ready to give up. He asked Abby to please have Turbo call them. As if that will happen, she thought.

Hannah looked up with interest when Abby disconnected.

"Brucellosis, huh? Sorry—I couldn't help but overhear that. I didn't even realize you can get brucellosis from contaminated cheese."

"Absolutely," Abby said. "It's the most common way, from raw milk or cheese that's not pasteurized. A cow or goat can carry it and pass it along. Just because something is natural doesn't always mean it's better. I mean, think about it. Natural things include poison mushrooms and rattlesnakes and lightning. Bacteria and viruses are natural. And tobacco."

Hannah nodded. "I thought it was just from eating the meat, if it wasn't cooked well enough."

"Yes, that too."

"Too bad it's such a problem in bison. It creates a lot of tension with the ranchers around Yellowstone—they're always afraid that the bison will contaminate their cattle. Since the bison herds roam all over the place."

Abby stared at her. "Bison carry brucellosis?"

"Yes. Didn't you know that?" Hannah looked surprised. "I guess you wouldn't, since you're new here. No reason it would come up. Anyway, there's been another bison death. We couldn't figure out what was missing, but it had a big gash in it, like from a knife, so that obviously isn't normal."

Hannah left and Abby returned to her patients. She felt unsettled, her thoughts a tangle of brucellosis and bison and Turbo. Turbo worked in a kitchen, not outside, and certainly not with large wildlife. While he had his curious relationships with the little forest creatures like squirrels and birds, they didn't harbor brucellosis. Then she recalled that bison meat was on the Snow Lodge menu, and Turbo worked at Snow Lodge. It made Abby wonder if Turbo had taken raw bison steaks from the kitchen and fixed them for himself, maybe not cooking them thoroughly. Maybe he concocted that story about raw cheese to throw her off. Fleetingly, she tried to imagine him as the bison killer, but it made no sense. A small man and not very strong, and he loved animals.

At the end of the day, Abby and Gem stayed late to tidy loose ends. They finally relaxed on the picnic table with leftover pizza from lunch, enjoying the slanting sun as it cruised westward.

"This may be my supper," Gem remarked tiredly, flicking a scrap of broken crust toward a waiting squirrel. The squirrel pounced on it gleefully and fled, carrying it up a tree. "What a day."

"Not seeing Edna tonight?" Abby asked.

Gem shook her head. "Tomorrow. William and I told Mildred we'd be there after work."

Abby decided to say it. "What's going on there? I mean, with you and William."

Gem flashed her eyes at Abby, then away, up where the glistening pine needles fractured the sunlight, then slowly came back. "We just get along really well."

"Are you dating?"

"No," Gem snorted. She thought about it, then tilted her head and rubbed her ear. "Well, not exactly. Well, I guess maybe. Sort of. Not really."

Abby considered her affectionately. "It looked like you were pretty close. When you were making cupcakes."

Gem sighed. She suddenly looked soft, younger. Her wine-tinted hair had grown out, now deep sable brown with dark red tips. "I don't know what I'm doing. He's just nice, and he wants to do everything right, and he's still sad about his grandma's death. It really helps him to spend time with Edna. And he's gentle but he's not weak—he's actually strong in his convictions and he wants to make a difference in the world and he's a lot deeper than you'd think. And he's lonely, too."

Abby smiled. "That's quite a list."

Gem's face twisted. "I'm more used to men who aren't so nice. Maybe I pick them on purpose. Because maybe I've forgotten how to do that—be nice. Me and my smart mouth. But he doesn't deserve that. And he's amazing with kids."

Abby remembered how William captured the attention of the little boy at the mud pots, remembered him talking with the child after a lecture. "He is good. And it looked like you were relating to him pretty well yourself, over those cupcakes."

"Ha." Her eyes danced, impish. "I like to touch him because it throws him off. And because he likes it, too." Gem put her chin in her hands. "It's just weird. We can talk about everything. Anything."

"I'm not sure that's considered weird."

"It is for me. I mean, I even told him about what happened. In the army." Her face went very still.

"Really." Abby felt astonished, tried not to show it.

"I know, right? I never talk about it. I don't even know how it came up, but suddenly there it was." She went on slowly, as if analyzing. "And how he reacted. He just took my hand and held it really hard and he looked at me like he was sad for me but not like I was damaged goods, you know? Like he was upset, but really cared.

"Then he asked me if I was okay and I said I thought so, that I was doing better this summer, and he said that's good. He just held my hand for a long time, and we didn't even talk. I mean, for like twenty minutes. It was strange, but it was good, too. It's like he was cautious, and at the same time, not cautious at all. Like he was sending me all this energy. He made me feel like I really was okay."

Abby felt so moved. She nodded and sat there in the filtered light, the flickering shafts. Eventually Gem took a deep breath.

"So. Like I said. I don't know exactly what I'm doing any more."

"Then maybe you should just keep doing it while you figure it out."

Gem nodded, a tiny smile. "Maybe I should."

21

Edna Dillon died the next day.

Gem told Abby how Edna left them in the early evening, just as dusk took the forest and stars stippled the sky. Both she and William were there. Edna was neither awake nor aware all day, so they sat and talked quietly to her in case anything got through, until she was gone. Gem called Abby to let her know, and Mildred called the funeral home. Gem offered to spend the night so Mildred wouldn't be alone, but Mildred declined, telling Gem to go home and get some sleep. Mildred said it would be peaceful—a different and needed kind of peace—to be by herself.

Abby walked that night until she found a dark place. She sat with the ebony sky and waited for the arch of the bone-white moon to set, waited to see if there might be a few meteors. The Perseids would peak in three days, the meteor shower that she and Edna talked about watching together. Abby sat back and surveyed the sky, emptied her mind. She followed the tiny winking path of a satellite, bound in its solitary orbit, and tracked the lively blips of aircraft, bearing humans from one city to another. She knew if anyone up there looked down, they would see just blackness; she felt at the center of a quiet nothing. Finally two evanescent streaks flew by, meteors there and gone, just minutes apart.

That weekend in Edna's honor, Marcus secured a table at the Snow Lodge dining room. William waited until everyone else said a few words, then he stood formally.

"This summer has been incredibly meaningful for me, knowing Edna," he said gravely. He sniffed once but his eyes were dry. "She

153

loved you all and wished she had more time, but she was grateful she got to know us. She told me what a treat that was. We talked a lot, and she showed me to never take any day for granted, because you never know what's coming next." He swallowed and looked earnestly at each person: Mildred and Abby and Marcus and Gem. And he kept looking at Gem. "I think this is the finest summer of my life. And I also think this is the longest speech I've ever made."

He sat down abruptly, self-conscious or overcome, maybe both. Abby almost laughed, for he gave much longer lectures about the park all the time. Gem leaned to his ear, spoke softly with her hand on his back, and he smiled.

William wanted to pay for everyone's dinner, but Mildred wouldn't have it.

"Edna made a small fortune when she sold her horse ranch," she said, grabbing the bill and clutching it to her as he tried to claim it. "And she hardly spent any of it. Now I guess it's mine, because there's no one else left. So William, sit down. You're a student with barely enough to get by. Don't you dare take out your wallet."

Mildred thanked them for everything. But she was tired and left, leaving them lingering over the dregs of their meals. William told how he and Mildred had plans to scatter Edna's ashes around Yellowstone together.

"Is that legal?" Abby wondered. "I mean, not that I care. Not that anyone would know. I'm just curious."

"It's not illegal," William said, a small shrug. "Let's face it, Yellowstone is sort of covered in ash anyway. Millions of tons of ashes. A tiny handful more won't make any difference."

Abby nodded, thinking how much he had loosened up. Not completely, because that would be out of character. She fingered the menu, toying with thoughts of dessert, and her eye caught the bison burger and bison short ribs. Which made her think of brucellosis, which made her think of Turbo.

"Have there been any more murdered bison?" she asked William.

He shook his head. "Not that we've found."

Gem looked across at Abby. "Do you really think it could be Turbo?"

"What?" William looked surprised. "Turbo? Are you kidding? He's so—timid. I mean, he talks big, but he never does anything."

"Sh." Abby glanced around. Turbo usually took the early morning shifts, but still. "He works here."

"Sorry," Gem and William said together, contrite.

"Anyway, there's nothing to go on except the brucellosis. Which is most likely a coincidence."

William lowered his voice and leaned toward Abby. "How could he possibly do it, anyway? You can hardly get close to those big buggers without riling them up."

"And he loves animals," Marcus added. "That's all he talks to me about."

"I know, I know," agreed Abby, wiping the thoughts from the air with her hand. "Forget I said anything. I'm just jumpy because I didn't know that bison carry brucellosis."

"Red alert. Dr. Abby Wilmore didn't know something. Oh my god, she's not 100 percent perfect." Gem reached across and poked her.

Abby made a face and changed the subject. She had not forgotten, though, how effortlessly she found herself amidst the herd. Maybe it wasn't as difficult as people thought.

William talked about new developments at Norris Geyser Basin, jarring Abby from her musing. A stretch of boardwalk collapsed overnight when a forty-foot section of terrain disintegrated into a bubbling, boiling pit of acid water. Yellowstone gained a new thermal feature, yet to be named, but no one would see it anytime soon because they shut down that area to visitors. William spent the day there, surveying the damage and trying to assess other dangers, an impossible task.

"No wonder you look tired," Abby said. "Edna, and now this."

"I'm okay. I've got tomorrow morning off. Then they want me back at Norris. But this is just Yellowstone. You can't expect things won't happen, not when you go and put a huge park over an unstable hotspot. Probably not the smartest place for thousands of people to be milling around every day. We'll keep that part closed up for a while. They'll need to make new boardwalks. I'm just glad it didn't happen during the day, when people were there."

Abby passed on dessert. She felt weary and said her goodbyes, leaving the others chatting. Only once she settled in her cabin, she found herself annoyingly awake. She kept thinking about the Perseid meteors zinging above and the magma stirring below. By midnight she roamed back outside and sought out her dark quiet spot. The ivory scoop of moon had gone and left the sky to itself, teeming with sharp stars, blinky satellites and airplanes, unseen planetoids, and far-distant mysteries of collapsing black holes and dark matter, the countless wonders of aching infinities.

A brilliant streak whooshed across the sky, making Abby grin: remnants of a comet's tail, tiny bits of meteoroid burning through the atmosphere at forty-five thousand miles an hour, disintegrating at reckless speed. Most little meteors incinerated entirely, never reaching Earth. Abby tried to make an analogy, something about the dazzling journey and not the destination, but it seemed trite and she lacked the energy to work it through. Then two more little ones zipped through the black dome. Abby heard voices exclaim at the meteors from the walkway near Old Faithful, saw two people standing and pointing, arm in arm.

She recognized it was Gem and William, strolling slowly. Suddenly Gem's leg licked sideways up behind her and landed a playful kick on his butt. William crouched and darted behind her, then she ducked and nipped around him in turn. They worked their way along the path in a ninja sort of dance, making poses and patterns, dodging and turning, laughing at each other. Then William stopped and slid his leg around hers. He bent and lightly, tentatively, kissed her. Gem's hand curled around his neck and he wrapped her close, kissing her more keenly.

Abby realized she shouldn't watch and closed her eyes. She knew they couldn't see her—not that they were looking—so she turned her back and surveyed the sooty sky instead. Another meteor whizzed, leaving a glowing afterimage on her retina. Abby blinked until it faded, waiting a long while, then stole a glance to see if Gem and William had left. They had moved to a bench, a tangle of arms and legs. Abby smiled and settled into her spot. She watched a few dozen meteors zoom and zip and burn their fiery way through the atmosphere before she fell asleep.

When she drowsily awoke in the middle of the night, roused by Old Faithful erupting, she found herself alone and carefully walked through the pitch-black grounds to her cabin, where she dropped into a deep, dreamless sleep.

22

It was a bad day for common sense.

Like everywhere, Yellowstone had its share of ordinary problems: people who knew better, people who assumed nothing would happen to them, and people who thought the rules were guidelines at best. People being just plain careless. Abby managed two car accidents: one when a driver oversteered a curve going too fast and crossed into an oncoming car; then, someone else abruptly stopping to watch an elk trot by, calf trailing behind. The car was rear-ended, of course. Though mostly minor, the injuries still took a great deal of time to evaluate. Wrenched necks and bruised faces and stiff backs, and one fractured nasal bone in a woman who "forgot" to buckle her seatbelt.

Abby saw a man who stepped off the boardwalk for a better photo, failing to notice the steam vent next to his mesh sneaker, which produced a brightly blistered foot and ankle. And a grandpa with a carload of children who grew cranky waiting at a bison jam... he stalked up for a closer look and slipped in a pile of dung, cracking his coccyx and cussing loudly with words not meant for children.

But the worst visit came early. Turbo, the second patient of the morning.

"I don't know why he's here," Gem said, upset. "He's just a wreck, and he only wants to talk to you. He brought you some herbs, too... Marcus has them."

"What do you mean, he's a wreck?"

"He's really agitated and he won't sit still. I could barely get his blood pressure."

Abby sighed. "If I'm in with him longer than twenty minutes, come get me. Things are about to get very busy."

Gem's face tightened. "Leave the door open a crack, so I can help keep an eye on him. Really. I'm kind of worried."

Abby nodded and went in. Turbo rushed up, gripping her arm. "Medicine Woman!" His words tumbled and ran together. "Help me. Please help me. I think they're on to me. That bastard fired me this morning. He's trying to get rid of me, but of course he's too late. They're all too late. Too late. Way too late."

He let go and paced the small room, his head nodding furiously, touching things. He straightened the frame on the wall and his fingers tapped the otoscope box and he adjusted the paper cover on the table. He sat down then sprang up, pacing and repeating everything. He noticed the door slightly ajar and pulled it shut.

"Turbo. Hold still a second. You've lost your job?" Abby felt bad. She stood there, the laptop in her arms, not yet typing. She knew how important his job was to him, knew that his job may have been his only anchor. "What happened?"

"It doesn't matter. He said I missed too many days. Who cares? I don't care. This just speeds everything up. Oh boy, does it speed things up. Now they'll be sorry. So very sorry." He bent and peered under the exam table, leaned over and searched behind it. His eyes never quit moving, his dark glance flying about, wild and disturbed. He reached above the counter and opened the cabinet door, scanning through gauze and Band-Aids, peroxide and elastic wraps.

"Turbo, please stop." Abby quietly closed the cabinet, touched his shoulder. Maybe she should have insisted on the FMLA paperwork to protect his job. Maybe she should have just filed it regardless, although that surely would have breached his trust. Besides, he had to sign it and she knew he wouldn't. "How can I help you? Why are you here?"

He halted and stared, his small mouth gaping. His unkempt hair flew around his head as if electrified. He gripped suddenly at her arm again and she almost dropped the laptop, clutching at it, and he let go to help her.

"Sorry. Sorry. You understand me, Medicine Woman." His head bobbed rapidly. "Is today the day? Should I do it? Help me."

"I don't know what you mean. You have to explain," Abby implored. She felt completely inadequate.

"Okay okay okay. I get it. I have to figure it out. That's my task. I understand." He looked straight into her eyes and a peculiar smile warped his lips, showing his mottled gray teeth. "I understand. We both understand."

"Don't go." Increasingly apprehensive, Abby wished she could somehow detain him. Search for help, mental health resources. "Please stay here. Maybe lie down, take a break, and I can check on you in a little while. Did you sleep last night? I'm really worried about you."

He laughed, a short bark. "I may never see you again, Medicine Woman. Take care of yourself. And don't go out tonight, okay? Stay in at home. Stay safe."

He jerked the door open, dashing out. Abby saw Gem speak to him. He paused as if listening, then he turned and roamed around the workstation, touching things, pushing and moving things, tilting his head back and forth. He picked up a blood pressure cuff and put it down a foot away, stroked the x-ray machine and touched the dials, hopped briefly on and off the scale, fiddled with a pile of notepads. He peeked under the sink, then picked up a ballpoint pen, clicking it open and shut a dozen times in rapid succession.

Gem threw Abby a look of dismay and Abby began to think she should call for help, notify Ranger Perkins, when Turbo bobbed his head one last time and slipped out the door.

Abby decided to call Perkins anyway, just a precaution, but the patients from the car wreck came clattering in, talking loudly. Someone was crying and Marcus was busy signing them in and collecting insurance cards and a ranger needed to speak with her, so Abby made a mental note to talk with Perkins when she had a free moment.

The day offered few free moments. Everyone worked through lunch, though Marcus taped a BE RIGHT BACK sign at his desk around one o'clock and ran to get sandwiches. In the midst of it all, Gem could not find her phone. She looked everywhere, beside herself, trying to remember if she brought it that morning or whether she somehow forgot and left it in her room.

"Do you want to go check?" Abby suggested.

"No, we're too busy. I can't leave you alone. Besides, it just started raining." Gem tapped her foot and chewed a fingernail, uncharacteristically impatient. "I was just really tired this morning. I probably left it there."

"Wait, I'm the one who's supposed to be tired," Abby reminded her. "How come you're not sleeping?"

Gem folded her lips. "I was out late."

"Really?"

"Stop it. You've probably guessed I was out with William." Gem raised her chin, a little defensive.

"Nice?" Abby asked.

Gem let a tiny smile curve her lips. "Yes. He's a little…naïve. I'm showing him a few things. And he's very…eager." Then she grimaced. "But I need my phone. He said he'd call me this afternoon."

Abby glanced at the clock. "It's only a few more hours."

"I know, I know. I just—never mind."

Abby patted her arm. "He knows where you are. And he knows that you're working."

Gem scrunched her face. "I just worry about him. Out there at Norris. What if something happens?"

"He'll be fine, I'm sure. I looked at the YVO last night, and the tremors are way down for the last twenty-four hours. The supervolcano is taking a break. Come on, let's get these people out of here."

The afternoon passed quickly. Near closing, Abby realized she never called Ranger Perkins so she tried then, but the main number had shut down for the day and went to voicemail. She did not have Perkins's personal number, and she could not really claim Turbo was an emergency. Abby left Perkins a message, that she had concerns about an employee and asked him to contact her as soon as possible. She did not leave specifics because the line was not confidential.

Abby hurried to her cabin and shed her work clothes, pulling on shorts and a T-shirt. She wanted a run before dark to work off the hectic day and clear her head, so she jumped in her car and drove toward Firehole Lake Road. When she returned she would practice her relaxation, for she had a telephone appointment next evening with Dr. Goh. Though troubled dreams continued, they contained no violence, which Abby considered quite an improvement.

Her phone chimed with a text from Gem. Thank goodness she found her phone, Abby thought.

Please come back to the clinic right away. Something urgent.

Once the clinic closed, all emergencies went to the evening rangers, so this felt unusual. Abby called, but Gem did not answer. Abby turned the car around. Although frustrated, she could hardly leave Gem there alone waiting, and she doubted Gem would call without good reason. The sun hung low anyway, shadows spreading—Abby hadn't allowed for the earlier twilight of late summer. Maybe after seeing this patient she could manage a short run nearby.

The clinic trailer waited deep in gloom under the pines. No cars stood parked in front, but Gem and almost everyone walked around the Old Faithful area instead of driving. Although the entry and lobby looked dark, light shone through the small windows in back. It seemed odd that Gem hadn't turned on the front lights, but not odd enough to make her pause.

Abby pushed open the door and stepped inside.

Someone slammed against her and she went down abruptly, landing hard, knocking the air from her lungs. Disoriented in the dark, her mind reeling, Abby fought for breath and felt a brief stabbing pain in her upper arm. A harsh smell of blood and dung. In the dim light she saw Turbo, Turbo's hand helping her up, pulling her through the door and into the lighted workstation.

"Sorry sorry sorry," he said rapidly, peering at her as she bent over, puffing. "You'll be okay. Really. Really really."

He set something on the counter. Abby saw a small syringe, saw traces of bright pink fluid puddled in the empty cylinder. She touched her sore upper arm and a strange horror washed through her.

"Turbo."

Alarmed, disorganized, Abby stared back and forth from his wild face to the syringe. He was filthy and rank, streaked with dirt and blood and something sticky, his shoes crusted with manure. His jeans torn, a ragged rip across his thigh, thick with matted blood.

Her eyes ran back to the empty syringe.

"Turbo. What just happened?" It felt unreal. "Did you inject me with something?"

"Don't worry." His head bobbed and his clotted hair bounced heavily around his face. "Just a little bit. Just a little. Just to slow you down. You're too fast, too fast, the way you run. I need your help and now you can't run away from me."

Her thoughts spun. How could this be happening? Where was Gem?

Then she saw Gem's phone near the syringe and it dawned on her. Turbo texted her. He used Gem's phone, must have taken it that morning when he fumbled around the clinic. Which explained why he didn't answer.

But the syringe? She knew no medication colored like that, bright pink. His grubby backpack slumped on the counter, and alongside it laid a stained hunting knife. The long blade caught the light, gracefully curved and razor-sharp, the back edge deeply serrated and clumped with dark furry hair.

A blunt cold fear turned and froze in the deepest pit of her, a jagged lump.

"Turbo. Please. What was in that injection?" Abby heard her voice climb with distress. "You're really frightening me."

"Don't worry. Don't worry. You're fine. It was just a little bit. Just be quiet and help me. Just do what I say." His voice rose and fell unevenly, punctuated by his nods. His eyes glittered and he looked down, fingering the congealed blood on his thigh. A glimpse of raw muscle underneath. "I thought he was down, but this last one was very strong. Very strong. He didn't go easy—he got me good. But that's excellent, right? Because now his strength is part of me and that just makes me better. No one can stop me."

"Are you talking about the bison?" Abby tried to be calm. But she kept staring at the syringe, her mind racing and stumbling. What could it possibly be, to slow her down? The only injectable sedative they carried was Benadryl, which was clear, not pink. Nothing was pink. They had Valium for seizures, but that stayed in a locked cabinet, and Abby could see that those supplies were untouched, still locked away in the corner, the little door secure.

"Of course. Of course. You knew that. You've always understood me. Every organ I ate made me stronger. The bison flesh and bison spirit are part of me now—we are one. And today I've had the brain. I saved the best for last."

His mouth broke open in a zealous grin and he licked his lips. Dried blood cracked on his chin, his gray teeth gummed with gore. Her stomach curled.

"Come on," he ordered. "Help me with my leg. Hurry hurry hurry. I have things to do."

"How? How did you kill them?" Abby tried to concentrate. Maybe it was her nerves—her mind distracted, jumbled. She gathered supplies, had trouble deciding what she needed. Her eyes ran to the long knife, and she wondered if she could grab it. Snatch it up and try to stop him, hold him at bay while she phoned for help.

Or maybe she could just seize the knife and run, out the door, across the parking lot, shouting for someone. Surely he couldn't follow very fast, not with his injury. But she felt oddly weak, strangely drained, and doubted she could pull it off. She imagined grappling with him over that brutal blade and her stomach turned again.

She abandoned that idea, took a bottle of Betadine and had him sit down. Her fingers trembled and she used both hands to steady the bottle.

He tilted his head back, haughty as a king.

"It's easy when you understand them. Bison love apples. Love love love apples. They understand me, and I understand them. They are my brothers, my sisters. I sit in the field until they come to me, then I roll the apples to them. Apples that I've injected full of xylazine or detomidine. And pretty soon the bison get dopey and lie down and they sort of pass out, and then I can inject them with the killer. But I pay my respects first. Always always always. Pay my respects. Honor them. For the gifts they give me." He stared, eyes glowing.

"Xylazine? Detomidine?" Abby had never heard of them. Or could she just not remember? "I don't think I know those drugs."

"Of course you don't. They're veterinary drugs. Sedatives. For horses and cows. I told you I worked for veterinarians. It's easy to take the meds, take a little cash, make it look like a robbery. Everyone's such fools."

"How many bison have you killed?" Abby tried to imagine.

He narrowed his eyes and did not answer.

She tried to fix on her task. His wound looked terrible, his thigh split open, a gash ten inches long and deep nearly to bone. It bulged and glistened with fat and muscle, littered with bits of grass and powdered with dirt. Abby screwed up her face.

"Turbo. This is really bad. It's filthy and it needs irrigation. Deep irrigation, in an operating room. You'll need antibiotics, special dressings, special drains. You have to go to the hospital. I can't treat this."

"Don't be stupid," he sneered. "Just fix it up and I'll be gone. My body's strong now. It will heal itself. So much to do. Hurry hurry hurry." His head nodded in rhythm with his words and he chanted them again. "Hurry hurry hurry."

Abby tried to pour Betadine into the wound but her hands shook and the fluid slopped out unevenly, missing his leg. The bottle slipped from her grip and fell, splattering dark liquid across the linoleum, a pungent odor of iodine. She stared at the mess, muddled, thinking she should put down some towels. Turbo grabbed up the bottle and poured it himself, twisting his neck with pain.

"Anything else?" he snapped, impatient with her now.

"We have to lush it…I mean flush it…with saline." Her mouth didn't work quite right. She gazed dully at the deep puddle of iodine in the wound. "You can't leave it like that."

Abby moved slowly, took a fresh bottle of saline, but she could barely make her fingers grasp the lid. Her hands felt wooden, unbending. Fear mounted in her again, thickly, a dense syrupy panic.

"Turbo. What did you give me? I can't…" She forgot what she wanted to say. She needed help. What drug was pink? Pepper would know, he knew everything. She fumbled for her phone, pulled it out. She touched the screen and Turbo rose up, snatched it from her hands.

"What the hell do you think you're doing?" he yelled in her face, slamming the phone on the counter.

"Please," she blinked, reaching for it. "Pepper can help. He'll know what to do. Just let me—"

"I know what to do!" he shouted, slapping her hand away. Then his head jerked around as the front door banged open.

"Hey, Abby! What are you doing here?" Gem's voice called through the waiting room and the lights out there snapped on. "I saw your car here and the lights on in back, and I thought I'd come look for my phone again. Geez, what is that smell? What are you—"

Gem halted in the doorway, staring, dumbfounded.

"Oh, Gem," Abby called with relief. She took a step but her foot felt wrong, not quite belonging to her, and her leg didn't know where to go and she staggered and fell to the floor. Gem rushed to her and tried to help her up, but Abby only got partway and couldn't collect her legs and she fell again.

"What's wrong with you?" Gem demanded, gripping her arm.

Abby squinted. Gem was a little out of focus. "Something. Pink. A drug."

"What's wrong with her?" Gem cried, turning to Turbo.

"Nothing," he said disdainfully. "She's weak. I'm surprised how weak she is. A good Medicine Woman should be stronger. I hardly gave her anything."

"What do you mean? What did you give her?" Gem's voice worried, frantic.

Abby sat up straighter, forced herself to concentrate. He could hurt Gem.

"Shut up," he said shortly. "You have to help me now. She's worthless. I have to get out of here. Hurry hurry hurry. So much to do. Get that saline over there—she said to wash the wound out with saline. Hurry up, damn it."

Gem grabbed the saline, poured it recklessly over his leg, glancing at Abby where she sat on the floor, leaning against the wall, then looked back at his leg. "Your leg is just awful, Turbo. We can't begin to treat that. You have to go—"

"Shut up," he repeated, getting louder. His dirty face pinched and irate. "I'm not going anywhere so just shut up. Shut up shut up. Do what I say. Wrap this up, okay? Bandage it up or something. You know what to do. Do it do it do it."

Gem pulled packets of gauze and elastic from cabinets, knocking things over in haste. Abby saw Gem look sideways at her own cell phone there on the counter, which she wisely ignored. Abby rallied and somehow pushed herself up from the floor, propping up unsteadily against the wall.

"Let me help," Abby said. They had to get Turbo out of there.

"Abby, for heaven's sake, please sit down before you fall again." Gem stepped over to her, pushed her into a chair. "I've got this."

Gem ripped the packets open and stuffed the wound with gauze, and began wrapping his thigh. She talked quietly and steadily, giving him instructions about how long to leave it wrapped and how to flush it again, explaining the signs of infection, a soothing stream of words. Her voice seemed to calm him. He quit bobbing and actually closed his eyes for a few moments as Gem worked on his leg.

"There," she said, stepping back. "Does that feel better?"

He inspected his thigh and nodded. The wide white wrap looked tight and professional.

"Nice work," Abby said out of habit. Gem sent her an incredulous look.

"It seems good," Turbo approved, taking a few tentative steps. "And it feels better, too. Good job." His face darkened and he glared at them. "I have to go. Don't follow me or you'll be sorry."

"We're not going to follow you," Gem promised. "Just go. Hurry and get out of here. Before someone comes. They'll be here any minute."

His head bobbed furiously. "You're right. You're so right. Don't tell anyone." He grabbed his backpack and the wicked knife and limped quickly to the door.

"No, wait!" Gem rushed after him. She clutched his arm, disregarding the knife, and she fell to her knees, pleading. "You have to tell me. What drug you gave Abby. She's always been good to you, Turbo, you know she has. She's really sick. Please tell me."

Turbo stared down at her.

"Fine. Okay." He eyed Abby critically, disappointed. "I only used a little bit. She's so weak. It's pentobarbital. You know, cattle killer. What they use to put down sick livestock." He paused and his head tipped, and then his face softened as he continued to regard Abby. "Yes, you take care of her. She's been good to me. She'll be fine. She'll be fine. Fine fine fine."

He scuttled unevenly out the door and disappeared into the night.

23

Before Turbo was down the steps, Gem grabbed the phone and called the emergency ranger number. Then she rushed to the bulletin board on the wall where they pinned miscellaneous information, found Poison Control, and dialed it quickly. Abby watched in a daze, wanting to lie down. But her relief felt huge, that Turbo was gone, the icy lump in her gut beginning to melt.

"Pentobarbital," Gem said to Poison Control. "I don't know how much! Too much! About twenty minutes ago, maybe more. No, I don't know what she weighs…one hundred thirty? One thirty-five?"

"Hey. Not that much," Abby protested slowly.

"Jesus, Abby. It doesn't matter." Gem knelt beside Abby while waiting on the phone, her fingers pressed into Abby's wrist, taking her pulse. Gem braced the phone under her chin and wrapped the blood pressure cuff around her arm.

"I think I'm better," murmured Abby, wincing as the cuff tightened.

"Look at me," ordered Gem. Abby found her face but something seemed off, something wrong with her vision. "You're not better," Gem analyzed. "You've got nystagmus."

Nystagmus, Abby thought dimly. A neurological derangement of eye muscles. Made the eyes twitch rapidly back and forth.

"No, I don't," she scoffed. Her head suddenly seemed too heavy and lolled back against the wall.

"What? The half-life can be twelve hours? Maybe longer?" Gem cried into the phone. Aghast, holding Abby to steady her. "No, we're not close to an emergency room! It's a really long way…Yes, I've called the cops. In fact, they're here now."

They heard the heavy commotion of boots up the steps and into the clinic, the room suddenly crowded with rangers.

"Hey, Gem. What's the problem?"

"What a mess! What's all this on the floor?"

"Hey, Doc. You feel okay? You look really pale."

"Did you say you might want a helicopter?"

Gem turned and snapped. "You haven't called the goddamn chopper yet? Look at her—she's been poisoned!"

A small sob broke in her throat. Then she bit her lip and collected herself and started over, quickly explaining everything, even as she kept talking with Poison Control.

Abby watched dully. Someone ordered the helicopter, someone started organizing a search for Turbo. Brisk commands, many calls. A radio kept blurting loud and fuzzy, garbled. Someone rushed out and someone rushed in, Abby couldn't keep track. She felt them look at her, say "He did what?" Gem reported Abby's vitals and oxygen into the phone and now a physician came on the line.

Abby felt her chin go wet, something dripping. She reached up to check but her hand lost its way and collided with her nose instead.

"You're drooling," Gem said, taking her hand and holding it, wiping her chin. She shook her shoulder lightly. "Try to swallow, Abby. Come on, you can do it. You don't want to aspirate."

Chagrined, Abby focused and made herself swallow, her throat muscles thick and awkward. She tried to stand up to reach her phone, to call Pepper, but instead, she tilted away from Gem and would have collapsed to the floor, but one of the rangers saw her start to slide and seized her. He and Gem pulled her onto an exam table.

"Take it easy," the ranger said, his worried face close, supporting Abby's arm as Gem looped a tourniquet around it, starting an IV. Abby knew him, he was funny and kind and he always teased her about the Grand Canyon, how she lived there on the edge of a big drainage ditch. Only she couldn't recall his name…she tried to read his nametag but the letters wiggled away. She must have looked distressed because he patted her arm and said "Hang in there," then he looked hard at Gem, his mouth stiff and angry. Abby saw muscles work in his jaw. "I can't believe it. Turbo? That little twit?"

"That little twit's gone fucking psycho," Gem ground out between clenched teeth as she threaded the needle into a vein. "Someone better find him fast, before he kills somebody."

"Is there an antidote?" he asked hopefully.

Gem flashed him a desperate look. "No—we have to keep her going."

Abby heard bits of talk, people coming and going. Roadblocks. Search parties. Psychotic oxygen. She just needed a nap, she thought, then she would be okay. But Gem was in her ear, telling her to stay awake, to keep talking, so Gem would know she was all right.

"I'm not awake," Abby explained carefully.

"Yes, you are," Gem insisted. "Open your eyes. Take a deep breath."

"You're so bossy," Abby muttered, trying. Breathing took all the energy she could muster.

"Chopper's landing," someone announced, and then Abby was moving, jostling, floating, now outside where the chalked half-moon hung crookedly above in a blurry charcoal sky, Gem alongside holding the IV bag, watching her closely. Something flickered and glowed erratically through the trees, orange and yellow flames dancing, lights and shadows. Abby stared, mesmerized.

"What the hell," someone said, "is Snow Lodge on fire?"

"Two fires, it looks like," came another voice, "Snow Lodge and the dormitory, too."

A thin scarlet noise keened through the night, then another joined it, the long shrill sounds twining around each other. Sirens.

"Turbo," Abby whispered, a twinge of fear. But no one heard her.

Then she was bumped and raised and inside the helicopter, Gem climbing in with her. A bald man in a flight suit settled next to Abby, smiled briefly at her as his eyes shrewdly ran over her, assessing her. He quickly hung the IV bag, attached a blood pressure cuff, and clamped a pulse ox on her finger.

"Hey there," he said cheerfully, bending to her. "I'm Jack, your friendly paramedic of the skies. We met a few weeks ago, remember—I transported that guy from Germany with the heart attack? How're you feeling right now?"

Abby narrowed her eyes.

"You're not Jake," she said slowly, trying to recall something.

"Nope, I'm Jack. Let's get you outta here, okay?" He looked meaningfully at Gem, pointed to the digital oxygen reading, and said, "Only eighty-eight." He turned a dial and pulled oxygen tubing over Abby's head, and slipped the prongs into her nose.

"Two infinities," Abby mumbled.

Gem shook her arm vigorously. "Abby. Take a deep breath. Right now, I mean it."

Abby tried, had a hard time locating her lungs, figuring out how to breathe. She felt a giddy surge as the helicopter rose, tilted, and started moving. The pilot called out, "Look at those flames. What the hell's going on here?"

Gem's and Abby's eyes connected for a second. They knew.

"Two infinities?" Jack asked Abby, sifting through his supplies, extracting an Ambu bag and setting it close by. "Does that make sense?"

"Eighty-eight," Gem explained. "Two figure eights, you know. Like two infinity signs. Two infinities."

"And beyond," Abby managed to say. Her tongue lethargic.

Jack let out a short laugh, even as he tugged a tourniquet around her other arm. "Really? Buzz Lightyear?"

Gem rolled her eyes. "She's kind of a nerd."

"I'm starting another IV," he said briskly, efficiently inserting the line and releasing the tourniquet, opening up the fluids. "Her blood pressure dropped a little."

Abby wanted to sleep. The rackety rotors lulled her. Suddenly Gem's voice came loudly in her ear, inches away, and she painfully pinched her arm.

"Abby! Wake up! Take a breath!" Abby's eyes opened, saw Gem's face right in front of her. "Don't you dare quit breathing."

Abby really tried. She discovered a way to open her mouth but still she wondered about her lungs, where they might be, how to connect with them. She liked her lungs, they were good lungs, they were in good shape from running and they had always worked so well for her. She heard Gem call out to the pilot, pleading with him to go faster, heard him saying it can't go any faster or I'll break it. She heard Jack talk to someone on a phone or radio or something, heard the words *impending respiratory arrest.* That's not good, she thought, who are they talking about?

"Abby, look at me," Gem called out from far away, maybe a mile or two.

Abby moved her fingers, tried to reach for her, felt desperation twist inside her because she still couldn't find her lungs—shrunken, withered, lost. It seemed terribly sad.

"Zem," Abby said, her lips listless, barely moving.

"What? Good job, keep talking." Gem's voice brightened.

"Zem." Abby wanted to open her eyes but now she couldn't find them either. She felt terrible, overwhelmed with sorrow, swamped with doom. "Zem. Wha'sappening? My dying?"

"No, goddammit!" Gem shouted and shook Abby's whole body so hard that Abby startled and managed a little gasp, her eyes coming open. Abby saw Jack reach across and grip Gem's shoulder, Gem's look of anguish. His bald head shone like the moon. So cold, she thought, I'm freezing. Her limbs shivered violently and someone pulled a blanket up over her legs.

"Getting close," the pilot called.

She was too weary. Gem kept saying her name but her voice was tiny, warped and metallic, far away down a long tunnel.

"Oxygen still dropping," Jack said. "Hand me that Ambu bag."

She just wanted to sleep. Her eyelids fluttered and she saw a dark shape, felt a rubbery circle around her nose and mouth. There came a great puff and rush of air, filling her throat and opening her lungs. There they are, she thought, my lungs—what a relief. Then again, another puff of sweet wonderful air. Now she could sleep.

Come on, stay here, Jack demanded, and she felt his knuckles sharp and rough against her sternum.

Ouch—that really hurts, stop that, she wanted to say.

But there were no more words inside her. She let go, and they all faded away.

24

Chirp, chirp, chirp.

It sounded like crickets. Or maybe birds. Was she camping? The persistent tweeting came relentlessly, intruding on her sleep. Something soft and warm encased her hand, then slightly squeezed. Abby blinked and gazed into the troubled, hopeful blue eyes of John Pepper.

"Hey," she said. A smile tugged her lips. Her voice felt creaky, dormant.

"Hey, yourself," he said, squeezing her hand tighter. "Sleepyhead."

Abby looked around. She lay propped in a firm white bed. White walls, white lights, white ceiling, white sheets. A web of lines around her, IV and chest lead and pulse ox. The chirping emitted from a cardiac monitor. She took a breath and her lungs filled immediately like they should. Her lungs in fact felt crowded with air, her blood running rich with oxygen.

"ICU?" she asked.

"Idaho Falls." Pepper nodded. He searched her face and put his hand along her jaw, his thumb traced her mouth and his fingers brushed her ear. Abby grinned, and he closed his eyes in relief.

"How long?" she asked. She studied every line and crease of his face, his long straight nose and high forehead, his fine lips, his brown beard now a little longer than usual, his rumpled hair. His grave blue eyes, darkly sunken. He looked haggard.

"Two nights. It's morning now."

Abby's eyes widened. "I've been here two nights?"

"You really, really did not want to wake up yesterday," he said. "Then all night long you were in and out of it. Last night. You were pretty confused."

She remembered nothing of that. "When did you get here? How?"

"I drove three hundred miles an hour," he said, twisting the corner of his mouth.

"No. Really." She raised her hand and tested her fingers, opening and closing. Wonderfully adept and normal.

"Let's just say I owe a certain pilot a very big favor." A dire look came and went across his face.

"I'm sorry," she breathed, taking his hands. She could hardly imagine what he must have gone through. She wondered who had called him, what they said. How he reacted.

"Good lord, Abby. It's not like it was your fault."

It felt somehow like her fault. Slowly things came back to her, scraps of clues, shreds of knowledge. She needed to sort it out, put it into piles and stitch it into place, but she couldn't right now.

"Where's Gem?" she asked. She had a whirling memory of the helicopter, the clashing rotors, Gem and Jack bent over her, the rush of oxygen. Two infinities.

"I just sent her out for breakfast, with William. She's been here most of the time. Until I got here, she wouldn't leave you at all."

Abby smiled. Then something jarred inside and she went cold, looked down to gather herself. Her eyes climbed back to him and his face darkened, knowing what she would say.

"Where's Turbo?" Barely audible.

Pepper's expression tightened and he shook his head no. "Not now. We'll talk about that later. Scoot over."

He nudged her over and climbed into bed with her, pushing off his shoes with his toes. He rearranged the lines and draped his arm around her, pulling her against the hollow of his shoulder. She felt him kiss the top of her head.

"Seems like I remember doing this once before," he remarked. His fingers lightly stroked the scar on her forehead. "Is this how it's going to be, if we stay together? You getting tangled up in some fiasco and me climbing into your bed afterward?"

Abby snuggled to him. "What do you mean, if?"

He hugged her tightly. "I think I'm going to have to put you in a goddamn bubble."

He leaned his head back, sighed deeply, and fell asleep.

An older nurse came in, short gray hair and a calm wise face, wearing dark blue scrubs dotted with tiny moons and stars. She beamed at Abby, checking the monitors. Abby said hi and wiggled her fingers in greeting from within Pepper's slumbering embrace.

"Good morning. It's so good to see you awake. And alert." The nurse spoke quietly, not wanting to wake Pepper. "Thank goodness he's asleep. He's hardly slept since he's been here, he's been so worried about you."

"He hasn't slept for two nights?" Abby felt incredibly upset.

"Barely. We were plotting to put sedatives in his coffee. And he wasn't eating much, either. We kept ordering him trays, and he ate maybe a few bites." She went through the neuro checks as much as she could without moving Abby from his clasp. "How do you feel?"

Abby grew more aware every moment. Events came seeping back, into ever-sharpening focus. And where was Turbo now? Why hadn't John told her? Which meant he was probably still out there, not yet apprehended. She feared he hurt someone else, caused more damage. So many times, he said they'll be sorry. Her heart flopped as she suddenly remembered the flames. She wondered what had burned and what else he had done, what else he might do. After two nights, the infection in his leg would be severe. She imagined the wound, inflamed and swollen, thick with pus. His filthy face swam before her, hurry hurry hurry. She shuddered.

"Do you need another blanket?" The nurse watched her closely.

Abby nodded. She wanted a dozen blankets and she wanted to burrow under them all. She closed her eyes and made herself quit thinking about it, pushed it away. The new blanket came toasty warm from the heater and soon she was sweating and had to throw it off.

A security guard passed her door, tipped his head to peek in and saw her looking back. He touched the brim of his hat, some sort of salute, then moved on. Abby realized Turbo could be nearby, sick or injured or both, lying in a bed just around the corner. Her emotions cartwheeled and she reached for the nurse call button. She had to know.

Before she pressed the button, though, voices came from the hall and Gem and William appeared. Abby forgot Turbo and put out her arms, embracing Gem for a long moment, both reluctant to let go. Gem straightened at last and looked at Pepper.

"Thank heaven. I'm so glad he's finally sleeping—he was starting to worry me."

"So I've heard," Abby said.

William bumped Gem over and hugged Abby himself. "Welcome back," he managed, his voice choked.

The nurse reappeared with permission from the hospitalist, saying that Abby could get up in a chair and eat a little.

"Just thick liquids to start with," she apologized. "To make sure you won't aspirate."

That was fine with Abby, suddenly hungry. She felt weak but stable, her feet and legs obediently moving where she asked them to go, holding her up. She slid cautiously from under Pepper's arm and into the bedside chair, presented with a fine meal of applesauce and chocolate pudding. The nurse winked and unfastened the cardiac monitor, noting that nothing was wrong with her heart. Then she unclipped the pulse ox, too. "Your oxygen levels have been normal for almost twenty-four hours. On room air."

Abby felt lighter, unencumbered. Gem and William pulled up chairs and warily watched her eat as if she might need intervention any minute. She put down her spoon and regarded Pepper tenderly, his lips parted as he breathed, one leg sideways off the bed. Then she switched back to the others.

"You have to tell me. Everything," Abby pleaded. "And you have to tell me where Turbo is. What he's done."

Gem and William exchanged a heavy look.

"You have to," Abby insisted, frustrated. "Stop trying to protect me—I'm not delicate or fragile. I'm just a little weak. But I'm getting better and better every minute and you're all making me crazy."

"All right, me first," Gem said slowly. "Then William can tell you about Turbo. But if you get too tired, or if you feel upset, or if you need us to stop, you have to say so."

Abby nodded, and Gem related the rest of the helicopter flight. How they bagged her airway until reaching the emergency room. How the emergency physician waited, ready to perform intubation, and started the procedure when suddenly Abby began breathing again on her own. So she never got intubated, but they monitored her diligently through the night, the equipment ready.

"I might have missed one or two of your breaths overnight, but I don't think so. I'm pretty sure I watched every dang one of them," Gem admitted. She looked gravely at Pepper and her small features crumpled. "I should have been the one to call him. But I couldn't. I just sort of lost it, I think…the ER doc had to tell Pepper." She sighed. "Then all the next day—yesterday—you just wouldn't wake up. You were sort of awake off and on last night, but you were out of it."

Abby took Gem's hand. "Thanks for everything. If you hadn't come back that night…"

They all sat silent. No one said it, that Abby would have died.

Abby shifted to William.

He looked sideways at Gem, and Abby felt her cold fear return. Why were they being so strange? If Turbo was in custody, they would just tell her, wouldn't they? William looked like a different man in jeans and a plaid shirt, wearing wire-rimmed glasses. His cinnamon hair now pleasantly shaggy around his ears. A two-day dark-red stubble roughened his face. He looked professorial in a weary, untidy sort of way.

"I've never seen you in glasses," Abby commented, trying to lighten the mood.

"I haven't had much sleep," he admitted. "I can't wear my contact lenses all the time." He looked at Abby, his brown eyes somber and tired, and leaned forward with his elbows on his knees. "But first I need to say how sorry I am. That this happened to you. That we didn't pay attention, when you started thinking it might be Turbo. I feel awful."

"Don't be silly. There was no proof. And who would have thought he would do this?" Abby pointed at herself. Then her heart tripped and she flew a look toward the door, biting her lip. "I just have to know one thing. I—I have to know. Is he here? Turbo? In this hospital?"

"No, no," they exclaimed together, appalled.

"He's not here," Gem assured her. "You're safe, okay?"

Abby nodded, tried to relax. She knew her expression must have been disturbing because Gem's eyes brightened with tears, but she blinked them away.

"It's just sort of a long story. And you should probably hear it from the start," William said, almost reluctantly. "It will make more sense that way." He looked at Pepper, slouched over in the bed. "Should we wake him up?"

"Does he know?" Abby asked, and William nodded. "Then let him sleep."

"Okay. So. Back to that night." He swallowed hard. "By the time I got there, you and Gem were already on the helicopter. I was pretty upset—to put it mildly. I couldn't understand what happened, until I found some guys who had been there, and they told me everything. They said how bad you looked, all weak and limp. I guess it took them a few minutes to calm me down." He paused, then went on.

"At first I helped with the fires, but we actually put them out fairly easy. They weren't planned well. He threw some loose papers and kindling in the stairwells and splashed some gasoline on the outside of the buildings. The stairwell fires went out by themselves, and the exterior didn't burn much—he must have only used a little gasoline. The flames looked bad at first, but it was a short flare. The rain earlier that day helped, because everything was damp. We found a small water bottle with traces of gasoline."

"So no one was hurt?" Abby sighed with relief.

"No, no one else." William stopped and sat there, looking at his hands. Abby saw him feel it again, worried sick about her and Gem, off in the sky. "So we had to find Turbo, but we hardly knew where to start. You know how huge the complex is, hundreds of rooms and cabins and places to hide. Or maybe he'd left, run off into the countryside. Roadblocks were set up, but we knew he didn't have a car. Of course, he could have stolen one, or tried to hitchhike. Not that anyone would pick him up, the way he looked. We talked about tracking dogs.

"I helped raid his room. I don't normally do enforcement, I'm just a seasonal interpretive ranger, but everyone was scattered. Turbo had a roommate until last week, but I guess that guy got fed up with him, just quit his job and left. Anyway, the room was full of newspapers and messy notebooks. And veterinary drugs, bottles and bottles of stuff. Syringes and pills. Bags of apples, mostly going rotten. The place smelled like apple cider."

"Was there more pentobarbital?" Abby asked.

"At least four vials. Bright pink, right? I guess they dye it pink like that so the vets never make a mistake and use it by accident. I mean, in a cow or horse. Because it's so deadly. Did you know that's the same drug they used to execute convicts on death row?"

Gem whirled on him. "Don't tell her that. What are you thinking?"

William blinked, but Abby actually laughed. "It's okay, Gem. I already knew that…it's in the news all the time. Besides, William and I always talk about deadly things. You know, volcanoes and meteors and stuff."

"Anyway." William glanced at Gem, then went on. "His notebooks were crazy. All about closing the park, no more humans, leaving the animals alone. About animal rebellions. Wild animals taking over. Pages and pages, ranting about his evil supervisors and his coworkers and the ranchers and pretty much everyone on up to the president. He thought the government was plotting to kill all the wild animals so there would be more room to raise livestock. That he had been chosen to fix it."

Abby was not surprised, just unhappy. If only she'd convinced him to talk about it, maybe she could have done more. Somehow intervened, tried other tactics. She focused and saw them watching her.

"I just wish I'd gotten through to him," Abby said. "That I tried harder. Took more time."

"I knew you would do this," said Gem, aggravated. "So just stop it, okay? You did try hard and you took lots of time with him. More than anyone else ever would have done. I don't think anyone could reach him—he was too paranoid."

Skeptical, Abby motioned for William to continue.

"Nothing really got accomplished that night. Someone arranged for dogs to come—we had plenty of scent. Nobody really slept because we were searching as much as we could, going through the basin with flashlights, checking all the crazy nooks and crannies of the Old Faithful Inn, places like that. I even climbed over that locked gate and went up to the old orchestra platform at the top of the Inn. Scariest thing I've ever done, but someone needed to look and I wasn't going to let Perkins go." William smiled. "I could almost feel those stairs swaying, but it was probably my imagination. I mean, no one's gone up there in decades, not since the earthquake. It was pretty scary, looking all the way down.

"Anyway, Turbo could have been right under our noses and we wouldn't have known. Then early in the morning, we started getting calls about a crazy guy out on the road, shouting and stopping traffic.

"I was talking with Perkins, so I went with him. Perkins felt really upset because he listened to your phone message that morning, the one you'd left the day before about Turbo. I think he blamed himself, because if he'd come by he might have…" William shook his head, let that go. "When we got there, traffic was backing up. We approached slowly on foot because we didn't want to spook him, and we didn't know if he was armed.

"He was marching back and forth across the road, in and out between cars. It was that stretch where the big herd hangs out, where there's always bison jams. Bison grazed all around, but they're used to the road. Turbo stood shouting and flapping his arms, yelling at people to leave and never come back. You could see tourists put up their windows and lock their doors. He looked a terrible mess, all dirt and blood and sweat. Someone along the road said 'Watch out! There's a zombie,' and I'm not sure if they were kidding. The bandages on his thigh had soaked through, all bloody, dripping down his leg. Pretty creepy.

"Hi, John." William nodded at Pepper, now awake and listening.

"Keep going," Pepper said, glancing over at Abby. She tilted her head his way but her eyes stayed on William.

"Then he saw us—there were four of us, more on the way. First he tried to get into a car, ran up and down pulling on door handles, but luckily everyone had locked up. Then he started shouting and swearing at us and he climbed up on the hood of a car, smearing blood all over. Even the bison stared at him then, getting nervous. Perkins told us to hold back and he approached him alone, trying to calm him down. He said let's go sit and talk about this, let's make some plans.

"Turbo listened real suspicious-like, quiet for a minute. Then he started yelling again, calling Perkins a liar and worse, pointing at everyone, saying we would all be sorry.

"He jumped off the car and ran into the field. Well, he limped and fell and he got back up, sort of staggering. Perkins ran after him, and we all started moving. But then Turbo entered the herd, shouting at the bison to rise up and follow him, to come with him to safety. I mean, he jumped back and forth between them, waving his arms, reaching out and touching them, lunging at them. And of course they all panicked and jerked away and took off, charging every which way. I mean, bam! Like a big explosion, a giant stampede—it's a good thing people were in their cars. Perkins rushed back to the road, and we all moved between the vehicles just to be safe.

"A huge cloud of dust rose up and caught the sunlight, this big white haze and we couldn't see a thing, just heard snorting and bellowing and hooves pounding. You could see the shapes of running bison, like ghosts, through the cloud."

He looked closely at Abby.

"He was trampled. Turbo's dead."

25

Abby felt like she had been kicked in the gut.

She needed a moment. Abby closed her eyes, remembering the first time she saw Turbo with his wounded hand. Maybe not a broken dish after all, maybe an accident with his own knife. His dysmorphic anxiety, the way he worried about his ribs. His tired spells, probably from ingesting pentobarbital in the bison's organs after he killed them. The borderline test for barbiturates. The brucellosis.

He had not meant to hurt her—she understood that. And even though she would wish for the rest of her life that she had reached him, she also knew Gem was right. She had tried.

Exhaustion suddenly overtook her.

"Everyone quit staring at me. I'm okay…I had to know. It would have been worse if we'd waited." She moved back to the bed, let Gem help steady her even though she didn't need it. She curled up with Pepper and they slept most of the afternoon.

After that, Abby recovered rapidly from the drug. Although tired, she wolfed down a normal supper and requested discharge that evening. But everyone insisted she stay one more night, much to her frustration. Transportation became complicated. William had to return to work and Gem went with him, while Pepper flew back to the canyon the next morning.

That left Marcus to come get her, driving over one hundred miles each way. The hospital physician would not condone Abby getting behind the wheel for one more day, worried that her reflexes might still be impaired.

"I can't believe we only have two weeks," Marcus moaned as they moved down the road. He beamed frequently at Abby, thrilled to be her taxi, relieved and chatty. He wore a purple shirt and yellow plaid shorts. "I still haven't found another job. I had two leads, but they're not appealing. One is a pediatric practice, and the other is with a urologist. Don't get me wrong—I love kids, but I enjoy adults too much. And urology is so…limited. Not enough ups and downs. Ha ha, pun intended. I'm used to variety now. I'll always want to work with a family physician. You've ruined me."

Abby smiled, leaning back. Despite her protests, she was glad not to drive. Cirrus feathered the light blue sky, smeared with hazy contrails, and small boisterous cumulus bubbled at the horizon, stained pink by distance. She couldn't get enough of it. "I wish you could come work with us at the canyon. If only Priscilla would give up on Pepper and leave."

"You have to promise to call me immediately if that happens. I would love to work with you two."

"There aren't any golf courses close by," she warned.

Marcus shrugged. "It's not that far to Flagstaff."

"Do you really think you'll play again?"

"Maybe. Probably. I actually had a good time at Big Sky, not counting you-know-who."

"So now he's Voldemort?" Abby wondered why there seemed to always be a Voldemort in her life.

Marcus nodded and made a frightened face.

Their conversation moved to Gem and William, wondering if they would stay near each other. Marcus felt certain they would; Abby was more cautious. She thought Gem might bolt.

Marcus looked sideways at her.

"What?" said Abby.

"I'm not sure if I'm supposed to tell you. But everyone else knows, so you should, too."

"Now what?" Abby wanted no more surprises.

"Gem might not want me to—"

"Too late. You already said something. And since when were you afraid of Gem? If you don't tell, then you'll have to be afraid of me."

Abby almost laughed, because no one was afraid of her. She remembered her old wish, longing to be tougher, more critical. Less vulnerable and gullible. It remained to be seen whether this latest disaster would aggravate her messy brain. The nightmares seemed temporarily wiped away. Which reminded her that she had two voice messages from her psychologist. Abby missed the appointment with Karen two nights ago while she lay in the hospital. Although John already let Karen know what happened, Abby really should call her tonight. She should call Lucy, too. And Pepper, of course. Abby sighed.

"You good?"

Abby nodded. "Sure. I just—I don't know how this will play out. I was just starting to do better."

"Don't overthink it. That was always my problem. Wait and see if it comes to you. Maybe it won't."

"Maybe." She wasn't convinced.

"Hey." Marcus touched her hand, looked at her a little longer than he should, considering he was driving. "Please know that you can always call me. I can be your—what you call it—support system."

Abby smiled. "Thanks. That really means a lot to me. And likewise."

"So hey. Do you want to know what I was going to tell you?"

"Absolutely." Move along, she commanded herself.

"It's mostly good, and partly not, okay?"

They reached West Yellowstone and Marcus worked through the tourist traffic. Then they turned east and left the town behind, the landscape becoming rugged, cliffs and small canyons, the road bending through. Sunlight baked the car and Abby felt warm and secure; Marcus drove steadily, tireless and talkative, and Abby started to think maybe she could put this behind her. The entire escapade seemed almost as if it happened to someone else.

Marcus went on. "Here's the thing. The company is throwing you a farewell party. Apparently you've been a huge success, which we all knew. They made buckets of money." Marcus batted his eyelashes. "For which I take a little credit…I do know my way around those billing codes, and I get them out fast. But of course, you do the work. Anyway. It's a big party at the Inn with food and drinks and probably some silly little speeches. It's right before you leave."

"I don't want that," Abby protested.

"I figured." Marcus hesitated. "I think FirstMed is doing this for goodwill, because they're afraid you'll hold them liable for what happened to you. That they didn't provide enough security."

Abby shook her head. "It never occurred to me."

"Well, it occurred to lots of us. We've been upset and angry, to tell you the truth. Turbo broke into the clinic easy as pie that night—there's not even an alarm on the building. And Pepper did make a big deal about it when he visited."

"He did?" Abby knew only that he talked with Perkins.

"Yeah, I think he had a big argument with FirstMed about it."

"Why do you know this and I don't?"

Marcus smiled. "I get around. But you know what? Everyone agrees with him. And we kind of want this party. This sounds sappy, but we really will miss you. Not just me and Gem. Everyone around here."

Abby sighed. "Fine. I guess I'll survive. But thanks for telling me. If there's anything I don't need right now, it's more surprises."

"Gem was going to tell you soon." Marcus frowned. "And there is a downside."

"What?"

He made a face. "Wrigley will be there. I suspect he's behind some of it."

She cringed a little inside, thinking of the chocolates. Then she reminded herself to be tougher. "Well. I can deal with that. I haven't even seen him in over a month. How bad can he be, right? You guys will be there."

"Right." Marcus nodded. "And maybe Pepper can come?"

Abby shook her head. "Not likely. He missed too much work because of a sudden trip to Idaho Falls. Something about his girlfriend. She's really high maintenance." She paused while Marcus laughed.

"He was originally going to come on my last day, help me pack up and drive back with me."

"We'll just have to call him, then. Almost as good."

"Not exactly," Abby replied, now grinning.

"Hey. Keep it clean."

That evening, visitors filled Abby's cabin and she had to kick them out when it got late. She drew a new cartoon, showing stick-figure Pepper asleep in the hospital bed, next to wide-awake, energetic Abby. She walked it over to the mailbox before going to bed.

Marcus refused to schedule patients the next day, to give Abby more recovery time, though she was busy with messages and charting. The next day, the clinic teemed with the usual routine checks and unexpected problems. Some patients were tired and slept too much, while others couldn't sleep no matter how tired they felt. There were children with runny noses and runny eyes and runny bowels. There were lusty new relationships that needed testing, and old relationships on the rocks, causing stress.

The only trace left from Turbo was a faint amber discoloration on the floor where the Betadine spilled, the linoleum permanently stained. Abby stared at it now and then and tried to avoid making analogies about tarnished brains.

They all met for supper in the cafeteria. Gem offered Abby to stay with her a few nights, but Abby declined and changed the subject.

"What's going on with our supervolcano, anyway?" Abby asked William. She had not checked the YVO site in days.

William looked glum. "It's really quiet. The lowest seismic activity in months. All the new vents are dwindling and the seismographs are just plain boring. Even the dome under the lake is subsiding a bit. It's all rather disappointing."

"Come on, now," Abby said. "You didn't really want to see the country buried in ash, did you? The world in volcanic winter?"

William smiled, rueful. "I suppose not."

"Look at him," Gem said cheerfully, pecking his cheek and sliding her hand around his waist, her fingers dipping into his hip pocket. "You gotta love this guy. He was so looking forward to the end of the world. Right, Willie?"

Abby's eyebrows rose. Willie? He colored slightly, picked up Gem's other hand, and stroked the tattooed snake with his thumb, something like affection. Abby decided that maybe Marcus was right.

Later they walked Abby to her cabin, as if it was something they always did.

26

Abby assumed her last stretch would be uneventful. She had already faced far too much drama for one short season.

The rumblings beneath Yellowstone remained tranquil. The vast deep lake of magma kept the geysers steamed up, kept the mud boiling and the vents hissing, but for now, nothing spectacular or world altering seemed imminent.

One week to go.

Dave Turner, the bearlike, curly-bearded mechanic who Abby treated for shingles the first month she arrived became suddenly lethargic and quit eating. He had just tuned up Abby's car for her drive back to Arizona. Now he could barely drag himself through the day. When the whites of his eyes turned yellow, his wife pulled him into the clinic.

"Not good," said Abby. "You've lost seven pounds."

"I'm not even hungry," he groaned. "I feel like I could puke all day long. And all I want to do is sleep. I'm exhausted just walking to the shop."

Normally an energetic, enthusiastic man, Dave helped everyone out regardless of how busy he might be. Abby's exam confirmed jaundice, a mustard tint in his eyes. His right upper abdomen felt tender, the edge of his liver too prominent, swollen and sore.

"A lot can go wrong with your liver," Abby said.

In a hazy corner of her mind, she imagined Turbo up to his elbows inside a bison, carving off a wet slice of raw liver, raising it to his teeth. Although these associations were fading, she wondered if they would ever completely disappear. After her hospitalization, the first time she performed her relaxation exercise and mentally colored her stress points her entire body lit up bright green. But she was able to dial it down, reduce it to that soft mossy shade, a rewarding accomplishment. Needless to say, she and Dr. Goh had much to discuss.

When Abby's thoughts suddenly strayed like this, she invented a switch in her mind. Now she flipped that switch off and shut it down, a trick she grew better at every time.

She focused on Dave. "The most common problem would be a liver infection, like hepatitis, usually caused by a virus. Or it could be a toxin or chemical that's causing damage. Or a blockage, like a stone."

Dave blinked in dismay. "How do you do figure it out?"

"It's challenging," Abby admitted, "but not much different from what you do, when you diagnose what's wrong with an engine. We start with the most obvious, then work our way down the list. And I ask a whole bunch of questions to narrow it down."

Dave's history was unremarkable: no new sexual contacts, no IV drug use, no tattoos or needle exposures, no transfused blood products. No drugs, legal or not. Not much alcohol, only a few beers a week after a difficult day in the shop. Perhaps chemical exposures at work, but nothing obvious. No travel, just occasionally to West Yellowstone for supper at his favorite Mexican restaurant.

Abby ordered the blood tests; depending on those, he might need an ultrasound to see if his bile duct was blocked. Which meant seeing a doctor in West Yellowstone.

"Nope. I just want you as my doctor," Dave insisted. His rumbly voice rose from deep in his chest. "I like how you explain things, and how thorough you are. It makes me feel better."

"This is my last week," Abby reminded him. "You'll need monitoring for a while, no matter what. And you probably won't stay here much longer either, right? What do you do in the winter, after things close down?"

Dave laughed, a growling chuckle. "People say I'm part bear, so I tell them that I hibernate. And right now I feel like I could curl up and sleep all winter, no kidding. But actually I go stay with my brother in Yuma, where my wife and I have winter jobs at his trailer park. We take care of the snowbirds and their RVs, which always break down. Lots of work."

Abby warned him that he might be contagious, giving him precautions about hand washing and sharing, blood contact, and unprotected sex.

After he left, Gem confessed her own concerns.

"I don't worry about hep B, because I was vaccinated for that. But there's my tattoo, and hep C…" Gem scrolled through the computer. Her hand brushed the hair behind her neck where the little tattoo hid. "I should have been more careful, but I was kind of rebellious those days."

"Reputable tattoo businesses use clean new needles," Abby assured her. "You should be okay unless you had it done in some seedy kind of place."

Gem fretted. "It wasn't exactly the Neiman Marcus of tattoo parlors."

"You should get tested if you're worried. Actually, all adults should be checked for it."

"And there's still no vaccine for C?"

Abby shook her head. "Not yet. You'd think there would be by now, what with all the hep C cases and the liver transplants they need. And the high cost of treatment meds. But the hep C virus is tricky, and the vaccine just isn't ready."

"And it's not spread sexually, right?"

Abby smiled. "No, not C. Hep B is most contagious sexually, but you're vaccinated."

"It's really a pain in the neck to have a boyfriend you care about." Gem frowned.

"That seems a pretty good problem to have."

Dave Turner tested positive for hepatitis A. He felt relieved because Abby told him it would resolve within a month or two, and frustrated because he had no idea where he contracted it. Abby filed her report with the state health department and discovered there were other cases from West Yellowstone, linked to the restaurant Dave liked.

"It's probably the kitchen help problem," Abby told him. "Someone who works there, most likely preparing food, has hepatitis A. Then they use the bathroom but they don't wash their hands. And the virus moves on to its next victim. The health department is working on it."

"Gross. I may never eat out again." He reluctantly promised to follow up with another physician. Relieved, Abby invited him to her farewell party.

The last day came.

It seemed unreal to imagine no longer working with Gem and Marcus, no more lunches under the pines scrutinized by the bright eyes of greedy ravens. No longer watching Old Faithful spew, no more misty walks across the upper basin, the raw sulfur. But Abby also sorely missed the canyon, its jagged stair steps down through the ages, the wide reaches and the great ruddy river below, perpetually delving into the stone. And of course Pepper, who she missed every single minute, missed like one of her own hands, like her own breath. And Dolores and Ginger, all eagerly awaiting her return. Priscilla, not so much. But having the party that Friday night helped everyone exit the clinic quickly to get ready, staving off goodbyes. Already nearly packed, Abby had most of her belongings stuffed in her car.

Gem and Marcus would remain one more week to help shut down the place, to sort out and pack up supplies, but Abby would be gone. William would be gone, too, back to the university.

Everyone looked forward to the party. Abby wore her best jeans and bought a new top from the gift shop, a flowing dark red tunic with gauzy sleeves. Tiny scattered spangles made her think of galaxies.

An impressive turnout—many came to see Abby off. Others simply came because there was a party. Definitely a handful of people Abby had never seen before, but she didn't care and it wasn't her money. Wrigley watched for her, his hair gleaming and boots polished, a gracious smile, and he presented her a large bouquet of flowers in a glass vase. A big embrace, too long, too close, smashing himself against her. Abby pulled back and thanked him, smiled briefly, then turned to others. What a useless gift, she thought, since she was leaving tomorrow. Well, maybe Gem could enjoy the flowers. No, Gem would rip them to shreds. Maybe she could give them to Hannah.

Abby talked with Gem and William and Marcus, then visited with Dave Turner and his wife, pleased to see Dave eat a little bit. There was Hannah and her partner, and then Perkins and countless others she knew fairly well and barely knew at all. Nearly all the rangers came who helped put her on the helicopter, and they hugged her and recalled how worried they were that night. Finally, Abby managed to fill a plate and sit down, joined instantly by Wrigley, pulling his chair close. He smelled heavily of beer and barbeque, and he twisted open another dripping bottle that he plucked from an icy tub.

"Can I get you a drink?" he asked, leaning a little against her.

Abby smiled tightly. "I don't drink. You probably forgot."

"No, I remember. Just checking." His eyes traveled across her and he licked his lips. "That red is a great color on you. You look gorgeous."

"Thanks," she said briefly, taking a few bites, not looking at him. She glanced across the room, planning her escape, and saw Gem watching them with a narrow look on her face.

He took a long swig of beer then leaned to her ear and said quietly, "Do you have any plans for after this party?"

"Excuse me?" Abby was astounded.

"You know." He sat back and drained the beer, reached for another although he didn't open it. His voice lowered confidentially. "After everyone leaves, I would love to take a walk with you. It's a beautiful evening, and we could talk about your experience here. Whether you're coming back next year, what you might want. What you need." He moved his lips close again, his beer-breath wafting across her face. "I bet there are things that you need, aren't there? Things that you like?" He dropped his hand on her shoulder and his fingers stirred her hair.

Abby shifted sharply away from him, scooted her chair back.

"Mr. Wrigley. Rex." Abby flushed with resentment. "I have nothing to talk to you about. I'm not walking with you, and I'm not returning. End of story."

He raised his hands in innocent protest and smiled broadly. "No offense, no offense. You can't blame a man for trying, right? Here." He rooted in a pocket, pulled out a small white box tied with a slender pink ribbon. "A little token. For all that you've done this summer, for all my employees here who've used your services. It's made my job much easier." He placed it on the table by her plate.

"That's really not necessary," Abby said, standing up and nodding toward Gem. "I have to go talk to someone right now."

"Good move," Gem said when Abby joined her. "I was about to come over."

Abby shook her head, annoyed. "Now I need to get a new plate of food since I can't go back there."

They watched him where he sat by himself, staring around the room, a squinty, critical look. Then an older woman with teased gray hair, overdressed and her face creamy with foundation and ruby lipstick, leaned over him and said something, sat down. She worked in the reservations department and had come to the clinic a few times, but Abby couldn't remember her name. A sour smile came and fled across Wrigley's face, and now he looked as if he wanted to escape.

Marcus tapped his glass with a fork, calling for silence. He dressed formally for the occasion, a yellow-and-green checkered shirt with a jarring blue bowtie. He'd lost some weight, Abby noticed. Marcus beamed at her.

"I just want to thank Dr. Wilmore—Abby—for making this the best summer ever." He raised a glass of wine in her direction, and more glasses went up. "She showed me that dedication and excellence are not drudgery, but a great adventure. I never thought about the clock, never thought about taking time off, never wished I was anywhere else. All I've wished is that the season was longer."

Marcus sat down and Abby looked embarrassed and everyone applauded. A few others said kind things, with some references to how the place nearly killed her off, that maybe she should just stick with grizzly bears when she felt like risking her life. Gem tried to talk, then gave Abby a hug instead. Abby worried that Wrigley would say something, but he remained planted in his chair, glum and drunk. He seemed pathetic and Abby almost felt sorry for him. Almost. The older woman still sat there but had turned away, chatting with someone else. A small village of beer bottles surrounded his plate, glinting in the light. Then his eyes jumped up straight at Abby and she quickly looked away.

Her turn. Abby tried to put a few thoughts together, and had Gem and Marcus stand with her.

"We are a team. I never dreamed I would have the privilege of working with such wonderful friends. I will never ever forget this." She thanked everyone for developing medical problems that brought them in to meet her, and thanked Gem and the rangers for saving her life.

People laughed and got a bit rowdy, all good fun. The next time Abby glanced over to check on Wrigley, he was gone. Good, she thought. Go sleep it off.

The staff set up dessert, coffee and tea and tempting bite-sized cakes and pies. Abby circulated and found herself back at the table where Wrigley once sat. She picked up the small white box.

"What's that?" Gem asked.

"Something from Wrigley. A token, he said." Abby made a face.

"What the hell. Go ahead, open it." Gem's eyes gleamed.

The others were watching, so Abby reluctantly pulled the ribbon and slid off the lid. Nestled in white cotton lay a delicate silver necklace, a chain so fine it was barely a glistening thread, with an elegant small "w" pendant adorned by two tiny diamonds, twinkling in the light. Abby compressed her lips, imagining the expense, incensed that he would give her something with his own initial before she realized it was also her initial. Which would have been comical in other circumstances.

Gem saw her face and reached for the box, eyed the necklace critically.

"Yuck," she said.

William's look said that that jewelry was out of his league, but Marcus took it and held it to the light.

"I'd say a few hundred dollars. Probably more."

"Obviously, I'm not keeping it." Abby snatched the box, crammed on the lid. She looked off to the side of the room, where a door led down a hall. "Isn't his office down there? Is that door locked?"

William shook his head. "I don't think the hall door is locked. Though his office might be locked. It's the one with a little sign that says MANAGER. Down near the end, on the right."

"If it's closed up, maybe I can slide it under the door. If not, then I'll leave it at the front desk. He's got to have a mailbox or some-thing," Abby said with resolve. She could barely stand holding it in her hand.

"Want me to go with you?" Gem asked. William had his arm around her. They only had one more day together.

"No, of course not. I'll be right back." Abby started for the door.

"Wait a minute," said Gem. She pulled Abby's phone from her bag, tapped it, then handed it back to her. "Just in case."

Abby rolled her eyes and slipped the phone into her pocket. The connecting door was unlocked, the dim hallway deserted, with fire-wood stacked along the wall behind the door. Abby hurried to the end, found the MANAGER sign, and pushed the door open. Perfect. The desk light had been left on, a low yellow glow. Abby put the box on the desk blotter and turned to go, but then saw notepaper and pens and debated whether to leave a brusque note.

"I thought you'd come."

Abby startled and yelped, whirling toward the voice behind her. Wrigley sat sprawled in an old leather armchair and he did not look good. His eyes drooped, his face pallid in the weak light, his collar and underarms damp. He held his hand splayed over his left chest, which rose and fell with his breathing.

"Are you all right?" Abby moved toward him, her own agenda for-gotten. "Are you having chest pain?"

He slowly shook his head and raised one shoulder. "Sort of. I don't feel so great."

"Tell me," Abby insisted, shifting quickly into medical mode. "What are you feeling—does your chest seem heavy? Are you nauseated or short of breath?" She bent and picked up his wrist, found his pulse steady if a little fast. She wished she had her stethoscope. His face was clammy and she undid his upper shirt button, opened the collar.

"Listen," she said earnestly. "Are you okay here for a minute? I'm going to go get some help. I want to send you to the ER, so they can check out your heart."

"Wait. Feel this, right here." He looked down at his chest and he rubbed the left edge of his sternum, wincing.

"Does that hurt when I push there?" Abby pressed against the spot. Maybe it wasn't angina after all, maybe it was rib pain. She made quick plans: it wouldn't take long to run to her cabin and get her stethoscope, and she could have Gem sit with him meanwhile.

He covered her hand with his, curled his fingers around it. His large palm hot, moist. "I always wanted to be your patient."

Abby scowled and tried to take her hand back, but his grip tightened.

"Maybe you should listen to my heart," he said. His mouth bent crookedly. "Maybe you should examine me all over."

"Are you serious?" Abby cried, glaring. She mentally stumbled to switch her frame of mind, still uncertain if he was ill. "This isn't funny."

"Like I said, I knew you'd come. I saw that look you gave me." His lips parted and he stared brashly at her, up and down. Then he hauled on her hand and she swerved on one foot, lost her balance, and half fell onto him.

"No! There was no look," Abby exclaimed, struggling to right herself. "Leave me alone. Stop it!"

"Hold still," he crooned. His fingers trailed down her face. "So pretty. So lonely."

Abby recoiled and shoved her arm stiffly against his chest. She pushed away, got her feet under her and began to stand, turning away. "Quit touching me—let go of me!"

"I should have known," he snarled, his face suddenly cruel. He sat up straighter, still holding her wrist, her sleeve. He pulled powerfully and she heard fabric tear, and she unbalanced and fell dizzily backward on him again. His fingers thrust into her hair behind her neck and he jerked, wrenching back her head and watching her gasp.

"I should have known, you little tease." He yanked again on her hair. "You quiet ones always like it rough, don't you?"

Abby made a strangled sound of protest, tried to call out, but he jammed his mouth painfully against her lips, ramming his tongue deep into her, tasting rankly of beer and grease. She tried to turn her legs, her hips, bend herself away, but he sank his elbow into her lower abdomen, pinning her. He was a large, strong man and she was overwhelmed. She couldn't talk, could hardly breathe, his tongue a wet squirming slug filling her mouth. Then his arm snaked up under her shirt and he grabbed her breast as he crushed his mouth against hers and groaned, his fingers hooking deep into her flesh. She felt him lump up beneath her, the stiff bulk of his erection.

Something inside Abby snapped, something beyond rage. Everything went red and black and she convulsed, exploding with a strength she'd never had, kicking striking bucking until she felt something give, and she twisted and ripped painfully away and tumbled onto the floor. She scrambled madly on her hands and feet toward the door when he grabbed her ankle and jerked, flattening her against the rug.

"Come back here," he jeered. "You should show me some gratitude, you little bitch."

Abby swiveled and kicked up at him. Her foot connected and suddenly he wasn't there and she thrashed up and out the door and scrambled down the dim hallway. She glanced over her shoulder to make sure he wasn't following, when she heard the door open to the dining room and she turned back in time to run smack into John Pepper and his outstretched arms. She flung herself around him and held on like she was drowning.

"Surprise! Guess who's here," he crowed happily. "I just managed to—"

He stopped, realizing that her clutch was not normal, felt her sob of relief. He peeled her away and his frosty eyes ran quickly over her, her frantic expression, her swollen upper lip, the small tear in her sleeve. Her messy hair. His face went dark and he gripped her like steel while Abby stared blankly at him, barely able to process his presence, speechless with anger and fear.

She saw a heavy wrought-iron poker propped against the firewood and she lunged for it, seized it.

"I'm going to kill him," she swore, utterly outside herself. She felt as if she'd been doused with kerosene and lit on fire, whirling to go back down the hall, wielding the poker. Pepper grabbed her arm and she swung around violently, nearly striking him in the head with the poker as he wrestled it from her hand.

"Damn it, Abby, let go," he exclaimed, ducking. He kicked the door open and called for Gem. Both their hands were smeared with soot, and now Abby had a smudge across her cheek where she had swiped herself in the struggle. Gem heard the alarm in Pepper's voice and pulled William with her.

"Where the hell is he?" Pepper demanded hotly, holding the rescued poker over his head even as Abby kept reaching for it. "Stop it, Abby, for god's sake. What's his name?"

"Wrigley," spat Gem. "William, show him where Wrigley is. We're okay, just go with him." Gem took Abby's other arm with both her hands, tugged on her. "Come with me, Abby. I mean it. Let them handle it."

Abby managed to focus on Gem's face, looked back and forth, managed to catch her breath and quit fighting for the poker. She felt Gem's hand plunge into her pocket.

"Wait." Gem locked her arm around Abby and tossed the phone to the men. "Listen to this. It's all recorded."

They bent over the phone, their contorted faces lit by the screen as Gem pulled Abby out through the door and into the restroom nearby.

"Marcus," Gem called. "Bring us some ice."

A few heads turned but nobody really noticed. Conversations continued loudly and the dessert buffet was popular, everyone busy with coffee and sweets, the crowd diminishing as people left.

Abby paced to the mirror and stared at her face, touched her puffy upper lip, relieved to see it was only mildly swollen. She turned to leave but Gem held her arm.

"What happened?" Gem insisted, wetting a paper towel and rubbing at the soot on her cheek.

"I can't—" Abby fumed. She couldn't settle. She dodged and headed for the door, but Gem caught her hand and pulled her back.

"Leave it. Let them handle it. Right now it will only be worse if you're there. What did he do?" Gem repeated, persistent but gentler.

Abby clenched her teeth, the words grating. "He grabbed me by the hair and he held me down and he kissed me and he grabbed me. He was too strong and I couldn't get away. I couldn't breathe and I couldn't get him off me. He was horrible and sweaty and mean and drunk and—"

Marcus pushed through the restroom door with a cup of ice and a cloth napkin filled with ice cubes. His sudden appearance halted Abby's stream of words and she clamped her lips. Gem reached for the cold pack, but Marcus shook his head and gently held the icy napkin up to Abby's lip.

"It's not too bad," he said softly to her. His fingers were tender and his face was murderous.

"Then I got away," Abby mumbled against the ice. "Nothing else happened. So it was nothing." Abby felt suddenly ashamed. Compared to what Gem had endured, this was truly nothing. Get over it, she thought severely to herself. You're fine.

"Good for you," Gem said vigorously. "You took care of it. And it's not nothing."

The door swung open and a young woman entered, poking in her purse. She halted and peered up at the three of them and the ice pack and she slowly backed out. "I'll go somewhere else," she said, and fled.

Abby took Gem's offered comb and dragged it roughly through her tangled hair, but she kept pacing and couldn't be still.

"I can't just wait here," she insisted. "I have to see Pepper. Please don't stop me. I won't do anything stupid."

"Okay, but we're going with you," Gem said, close behind.

Pepper and William emerged from the hallway, their faces stony and flushed. Pepper threw his arm around Abby, but William stayed by him with an alert and wary face. Marcus took the ice away.

Abby remained too agitated. She still felt on fire, felt like she had insects buzzing inside her, her arms and legs electrified. Seeing Pepper's rigid, silent face somehow made her worse, and she didn't know what to say or what to do. She shuddered and pulled back from him and then turned around and clutched him and then let go again. Wondering what he must think, how she had let this happen. How she could have been so clueless, so—

Her distress broke through and he saw her torment, her restless misery.

"Come on, come with me," he said, taking her hand. He asked the others not to leave, heading for the door with long, determined strides, drawing Abby with him.

A moonless night, coal black. He walked so rapidly she had to jog now and then to keep up. They passed Old Faithful, exhaling softly, and forged on until they reached the bridge and wheeled around back past the Inn, all the long way down the slope past Castle Geyser, its mound glowing ghostly wet in the starlight. They finally turned and headed back to the bridge yet again. They didn't speak. They just gripped hands and paced and paced under thousands of stars littering the sky and flaming over them like feverish bonfires, burning recklessly through trillions of miles, until Abby finally tired out and the insects settled down and her limbs unwound. She pulled on him to slow, to stop.

"Okay," she said breathlessly. "I'm okay."

He bent down and held her face, fiercely kissed her forehead. Then he touched her lip delicately with his fingertips. "Does it hurt?"

"Hardly. Barely. It's nothing."

"It's not nothing," he said harshly, his face hardening.

Abby took his hands. She felt the warm swelling on his right knuckles, raised his hand and saw the scuffed broken skin, smudges of blood.

"Oh, John," she moaned. "What happened?"

"I fucking hit him," he said violently. His lip raised in a snarl, barely restrained.

Abby felt terrible. That she had caused this sensitive, caring man to become so inflamed. To injure himself, to cause harm, to act so crudely against his nature.

"I'm so, so sorry," she said quietly. She stroked his face. "I can't believe I didn't see this coming. That I let this happen."

"What the hell, Abby," he said, flaring again. "It's not your fault. Don't you ever say that again."

He moved them to a bench, sat her down, looked intently into her eyes. "He attacked you. You didn't let it happen, whatever the hell that means. You were just being yourself, trying to help. I listened to it and I—" He stiffened, looked up at the sky. "I don't think you know how you are, Abby. You don't understand how good you are. How you are always so generous with people. You don't judge. You—"

"Yes, I do," she retorted. "I can't even—"

"No," he cut her off. "You don't. You always give people a second chance, and then a third chance, too. You always forgive."

Abby looked away. "You mean I'm soft. Gullible."

She felt him suppress his frustration.

"You're not," he said. "You're plenty tough enough when you need to be. But mostly you're compassionate. You give everyone the benefit of doubt. And that backfires on you sometimes. But thank god that hasn't changed you. I don't know why, but it hasn't. You're still kind. You put me to shame."

The thin trail of steam from Old Faithful suddenly thickened and rose. Abby sighed and leaned into him, laced her fingers in his. Her fire had burnt out and now she felt like ash, reduced to powder, silvery and insubstantial. The geyser sputtered then climbed, soaring and crashing and ascending into the night, charging up over itself, roaring and hissing and splashing back down until it wore itself out and subsided, gurgling and trickling away. The breeze was high and she and Pepper were glazed with a fine mist, and briefly they sparkled.

Abby felt emptied as well. She knew that right now she needed to talk about something else. Anything. Something better than what just happened. It felt stupid and needless and unworthy. They hadn't even discussed how he was suddenly there, what plans had changed. She still needed to know what exactly happened with Wrigley, where he was now, what had been said.

Soon, but not this minute.

"Did you know," Abby said slowly, searching her brain, nodding at the shiny base of Old Faithful glistening in the weak light, the hot water still burbling away down the ruined mineral slopes. "Did you know that Saturn has a little icy moon, called Enceladus? And Enceladus has geysers. Only it's so cold up there that when the geysers erupt, they throw out ice crystals instead of steam and hot water. And then, because Enceladus is small and has so little gravity, those ice crystals spew up and out over endless miles, and they become part of Saturn's rings."

His arm went snug around her. "If you say one more word about ice geysers in space, you will never get rid of me."

Abby faintly smiled and said "Enceladus."

Pepper threw his arms out. "That does it. It's hopeless. Now there's nothing I can do to get away from you." He stood and pulled her up. "Come on. Those guys are probably still waiting for us. And there's a whole lot we need to talk about."

27

Gem sat by William, talking with Marcus, while Perkins and Santana stood near, conversing quietly, too. Everyone else was gone, the dessert buffet strewn with stained napkins and crusted plates, looking like the aftermath of a culinary battle. Someone had rescued a handful of confections and lined them up on the table where they sat. William gave Pepper a cautious look and began to stand, but Pepper shook his head and motioned him to stay seated as he and Abby pulled up chairs.

"What happened with Wrigley?" Abby asked William. With her adrenaline down now she felt steady, matter of fact, ready for anything. But she wanted to hear it from William.

William blew out a breath, glanced at Pepper. "It wasn't pretty. Wrigley was very intoxicated and sloppy, and he tried to deny everything. I'm not sure he even knew who we were, but he acted like we were all buddies—really disgusting. Until we showed him your phone, the recording. Then he got flustered, and then he blamed it on you. You know, that you tried to seduce him. That's when John hit him. I should have been quicker, should have seen that coming. Not that I blame him." William gave Pepper an inscrutable look; Pepper's face stayed impassive but his grasp on Abby's hand was almost painful.

William went on. "Wrigley rebounded faster than you'd think, considering how drunk he was. He jumped up and swung at Pepper." William shook his head. "I had to use a restraining hold on him, I'm afraid."

"Wrigley was that combative?" Abby asked.

William looked at her as if she was dense. "No, I used a restraining hold on Pepper. Wrigley missed him, of course—he couldn't have hit the broad side of a barn—but then Wrigley called you a name, something I can't repeat. So Pepper slugged him again. It's a good thing I was there, or I'm not sure he would have stopped."

Abby looked at Pepper; his glacial eyes locked onto hers and defied her to react. She turned his hand and examined his knuckles again, which looked worse in brighter light. Puffy, scraped, still oozing blood.

Marcus leaned over to see, then started making another cold pack, muttering. "Guess I should have kept the first one."

"It's fine," Pepper said, covering his knuckles with his other hand. "Don't worry about it." Marcus handed him the ice-filled napkin and he put it in place.

Perkins stepped over to Abby, his face grave. "That's when William called us for help, and we were already right here. We escorted Wrigley to his room, put someone outside to keep him there. I don't think he's going anywhere very fast. He wasn't walking so well—he was sort of guarding his crotch."

Abby shrugged when they looked at her. "I kicked out at him and something connected, but I didn't know where. I just took off."

Gem started to smile, then wiped it away.

"Well." Perkins rubbed his chin, fingered his salty moustache. "I need to ask if you want to press charges."

Hannah came up and held her arm. "Are you okay? Are you injured?"

Abby shook her head. "I'm not really hurt. He didn't hit me. He just held me down and grabbed me—" She would not describe the details but knew she should say something. "He was just rough and nasty. He tried to kiss me." She touched her lip.

Perkins sighed. "I hate to say it, but that might not even make a case for misdemeanor assault. In some states it would. Anyway, we're going to keep him overnight no matter what."

"I'm so done with this," Abby said forcefully, determined that Wrigley would not spoil another minute of the evening. "I appreciate everyone's concern, but I don't want to talk about it or think about it—at least not tonight. I've got better things to do. I want to say my goodbyes. Wrigley can go to hell."

Abby handed out the desserts. Marcus looked at her and told a funny joke, and Abby reminded herself to thank him later for that because they all laughed and relaxed a little. Pepper explained that Dan Drake agreed to moonlight at the last minute, freeing him to rush to Yellowstone, even though he arrived far later than he expected. He tried to call Abby on the way but couldn't get a signal, and then his phone ran out of charge. Which clarified his sudden appearance after dinner, when he went down the hall to find her. To Abby it seemed like she had been gone forever, but it was actually not very long.

"I've got some other news," Pepper went on. "Our wonderful receptionist Ginger just announced her wedding plans, and her fiancé Diego has a new job in southern Arizona, close to his family. So in a few months we'll need someone at the front desk." Pepper looked at Marcus. "Someone who knows what they're doing."

Marcus stared back with disbelief. "Are you really serious? This isn't a joke?"

Pepper nodded. "I'm totally serious. Mind you, the other receptionist—Priscilla—can be challenging to work with. It's not the best offer in the world. You might want to meet her first, check the place out."

Marcus grinned and straightened his bowtie. "How soon can I sign?"

"Don't you want to know the salary, the benefits?"

"Nope, it doesn't matter. Besides, it's the same medical company. Nothing that different."

"Good," said Pepper. "And you can help me keep an eye on Abby. Because I'm not letting her out of my sight for at least a year."

Abby groaned, then hugged her friend. "I'm so excited, Marcus."

Pepper shook Marcus's hand to seal the deal, which made Pepper wince with pain. Marcus picked up the cold pack and handed it back to him.

"Congrats, Marcus," Gem said, grinning. "And I'll tell you what I've decided, too. But first, because William's too shy, I want to share what Edna Dillon did. It turns out that she left William enough money to pay off his college loans and to cover the rest of his education. Until he gets his doctorate. She wrote that if she had a son, she hoped he would have been like William."

William shook his head. "They don't care about that."

"Yes, they do," Gem assured him. "And for me—I'm taking a job at the university health center in Missoula, where William is. Don't worry," she smiled a little wickedly, "we're not moving in together. Not yet. I mean, we barely know each other." William's face colored, and he mumbled something under his breath about them knowing each other pretty dang well. "And I'm thinking of going back to school, maybe to be a nurse practitioner," she added. "This summer has changed me, made me think differently about medicine. About myself."

Abby's eyes widened and Gem went on rather formally. "Maybe someday, Dr. Wilmore, you'll quit underestimating yourself. But knowing you, probably not."

"I hope that's all the announcements," Abby said. "I don't think I can take anymore."

They talked a long time, slowly winding down. Pepper sat quiet, solemn, and never moved from Abby's side, but she eventually made him smile about his clever negotiations for a new receptionist. No one wanted to call it a night, or end the summer, and the conversation gradually circled back to volcanoes and earthquakes, as it always did. Gem asked William something about Mount St. Helens and he shifted into lecture mode. Serious, he picked up a champagne bottle and fiddled with it.

"Pretend this is Mount St. Helens," William said, tilting the bottle. He had nudged the cork until it was nearly out, wedged precariously. "You can see how the cork is holding in the lava—I mean, champagne—but it wouldn't take much to dislodge the cork, which is like the big bulge that formed on the side of St. Helens. There was all this pressure just underneath, just waiting."

He made the bottle tremble. "Little earthquakes kept rumbling under St. Helens, all the time. Finally those tremors shook the mountain enough to shift that bulging slope, make a few cracks, and"—he barely grazed the cork—"Boom!" The cork sprang free and champagne burst from the bottle, gushing up then flowing down his hand. He sobered. "No one knew when it would happen. And sadly, dozens of people died. Including scientists who were way too close, and even some campers a long way off. But luckily it was on the weekend, when the lumber crews weren't there, or it could have been hundreds."

Everyone sat silent. Thinking about St. Helens, thinking about Yellowstone. Any minute, Abby thought, or maybe not for thousands of years. No one knew what went on down there, hundreds of miles beneath them. Humans skated like tiny particles on a thin skim of continent, heedlessly exploring Yellowstone, a very unwise place. She stared at the bottle, now half-empty as Gem and William caught the champagne in a glass and started sharing it.

"What was the last big seismic event here?" Pepper asked.

"Hebgen Lake in 1959," William replied without hesitation. "A seven-point-three earthquake triggered a landslide that killed twenty-eight people at a campground." William shook his head. "There have been plenty of other quakes, too, but that was the worst. I mean, there are always earthquakes here, over a thousand every year, but they're mostly too mild to be felt."

Pepper stood, his arm around Abby. His mouth still looked tight but he managed a small smile.

"We need to get out of here, first thing tomorrow. If Yellowstone erupts anytime soon, or if there's any big earthquakes, I don't want anyone blaming Abby. The way trouble finds her, I need to get her away from here."

28

They got away early despite little sleep.

Gem and Marcus were mentally tuned to their friends' departure and showed up to wave them farewell. Then along came William, drowsy and rubbing his eyes. Abby declined to say goodbye, saying instead she would see them soon. She had dealt with enough finalities lately. Instead, she saluted Old Faithful, exuding its warm misty breath, and she promised to return, while Pepper scowled playfully and wondered aloud if he should worry about her.

"Because I have a personal relationship with a geyser?" she asked.

They took turns driving and napping, delighting in each other's company as if embarking on an adventure instead of simply returning to work. He brought a book, and they swapped reading out loud while the other drove. Pepper mimed odd voices when it was his turn to read, making her laugh; when Abby tried to perform the voices, Pepper said she sounded like chipmunks and that made him laugh. Determined to get as far as possible that day without jeopardizing safety, he set his sights on Kanab.

They made good time and called ahead for a room in a rustic motel. That would leave them just a few hundred miles the next day, that long eastward out-of-the way loop around the Colorado River to reach the South Rim.

Abby let loose, brimming with relief, and talked about everything, especially how she fulfilled her summer goal and became more independent, more confident. She felt good about that. And how she knew enough about living on a supervolcano to last a long while.

Pepper's research team completed the sodium study in hikers, and it looked certain to be published the next year. Somehow, during that unlikely discussion, they made a commitment to one another, that they would never live apart again.

They left nothing out, not Turbo, not Wrigley. Once when he was driving, Pepper took her hand and held it for a long time as she spoke, as she explored and poked at her feelings. What to do about Wrigley, how and when Abby would file her complaint. Perkins had promised to help.

Throughout the day they sailed across lower Idaho and into Utah, past secluded watchful mountain ranges and clattering creeks and south into the realm of stony slabs and broken red rock. The wind tore at the car, filled the sky with an unruly profusion of thin gauzy cirrus and thick clotted cumulus, high and low vapors, streaming over them.

They reached Kanab near suppertime.

"Are you up for a little hike?" Pepper asked. "If I don't move my legs a bit, they may never straighten out again. There's a nice trail just outside of town."

Although the weather was hot for hiking, they wore T-shirts and shorts and they were, after all, from Arizona. Heat felt like a familiar companion and, of course, they had water, knowing that on a bad day that made the difference between life and death. The parking lot at the dusty trailhead stood empty, as if waiting just for them. Abby stuffed the water into her small backpack and soon they tramped along, enjoying the warm late sun and wind, the complicated clouds shuttling sunlight and shadow back and forth.

Pepper stopped at a scenic spot, let himself down on a large flat stone under a scrubby tree. He sat with his knees up and drew Abby between his legs, her back against his chest. She heard him sigh and relax as he pulled out her ponytail and played with her hair. Settled comfortably, she put her hands on his knees, her forearms along his thighs.

"Nice armchair," she observed contentedly, running her palms over his legs as if evaluating the fabric on furniture. "A little bit hairy."

"Mm," he mumbled, nuzzling her ear. "Only the very best models come in the hairy version."

Abby laughed, reaching back over her shoulders and threading her fingers in his hair. He slowly ran his hands down her inner arms and along her sides, sliding across the outer curves of her breasts. He brushed against the unseen bruises, and Abby's breath clipped and she flinched away. Her arm dropped in sudden reflex, her elbow clamping against his hand.

Pepper froze. She sensed him figuring it out, felt his anger rise.

"What did he do?" he asked quietly. Too quietly.

"It's just a bruise," she said slowly, aware that she should have told him, should have shown him. But she hadn't noticed until later, getting ready for bed, hadn't realized that Wrigley's grip left marks, and last night she simply could not face starting it up again. She just wanted to be left alone, and she worried how Pepper would react. It should have been obvious that she couldn't pretend it wasn't there. She wondered what she'd been thinking, though she knew she wasn't thinking at all. Just feeling. Craving some sort of privacy.

Little birds flickered through the tree, sunlight sifting through them.

He tried to move his hand but her arm stayed, pinning him. As if she could put it off.

"Abby." His voice tight. "Please. Let me see."

She nodded and moved her arm. He slowly raised her T-shirt, then gently eased her bra over her breast. She heard his quick hiss of breath and they both looked at it, mottled purple and dark red, the tender moons of contusion.

"Is this what you meant when you said he grabbed you?" His voice low and furious.

"Yes." She drew the word out. "I just—I didn't see it until later."

"Is there anything else? Anything at all?"

She shook her head. Except for Pepper's fingers, softly slipping her clothes in place, she felt him turn to rock, every muscle rigid. She understood it. An indignant part of her embraced his fury, and she knew she was not done with this. But she also knew it was not what she wanted, not right now.

"John." Abby turned herself to face him.

His eyes like arrows into hers, subzero.

"John," she repeated. She put her hands on both sides of his face, searched him. "I don't need angry Pepper right now. I really need gentle Pepper. Please."

He closed his eyes, clenched them tightly, and his hands gripped her arms. "I can't help it. I want to hurt him."

She felt such distress, seeing him fight himself. Her eyes burned and she tried to make it stop, tried to resist it, but she was too upset and a tear slipped down her cheek.

His eyes opened and his face changed. He touched the tear, wiped it away. "Oh, Abby. Please don't cry."

"I'm not crying." She shook her head and sniffed.

"I see tears. That's called crying," he said kindly.

"Just one. I think there's something in my eye, that's all." A little defiant.

He sighed.

"What do you want me to do?" He pulled her to him, wrapping his arms around her.

"I don't know." She nestled, then shifted her head and gave him a firm glance. "Should I take you for a walk? To calm you down?"

His face twitched and he almost smiled. They sat a long time, watching the small drab birds flit from branch to branch. Watched the sinking sun as it turned the sky into pale vanilla, the clouds like smooth sherbet scoops, orange and lemon.

"Do you want to hike any farther?" he asked quietly.

She took her time responding. "No, I'm too tired."

"Do you want to go take a nap?"

She considered. "No, I'm not tired enough."

She felt him sigh again, couldn't tell if he was amused.

"Do you want to get something to eat?" he asked.

"No, I'm not hungry." It was becoming a game. Long pauses between suggestions and answers.

"We could go for a drive."

"No, I'm tired of the car."

"Should we just sit here and watch the sunset?"

"No, it's too slow."

"Do you want to chastise me some more?"

She imagined the quirk at the edge of his mouth. "No, I already did that."

He kissed the top of her head. "Do you have any idea what we should do?"

She tilted her face back to him, then lightly kissed his lips. "I want to make love."

"Now?"

"Yes."

"Here?"

"Yes."

"It's kind of a public place."

"There's big rocks we can hide behind. And there's no one. The parking lot was empty."

"It's kind of gritty around here." His eyebrows rose, now clearly amused.

"I don't care. I'm pretty sure our motel has a shower."

He was already up, leading her off the trail. They found a tiny hollow behind the rocks, a sandy floor, permeated by the faint dusty fragrance of sagebrush and pinyon and a muted pink glow from red stone. Small slivers of wind trickled through, tickling their skin.

They went slowly, as if discovering each other for the first time, and she touched him everywhere and he stroked every inch of her and her bruises, too, murmuring that contusions also need love. Which went straight to her heart because it was exactly what she needed and she knew again, profoundly, why she was with this man. Then he accelerated and she forgot about that and the grit and dirt and everything but his touch. When they finally recovered and rose, he carefully brushed the sand off her.

The drive the next day seemed effortless, scurrying over the parched rusty lands, through the bronze boulders and brittle burnt arroyos, circling east to where the Colorado River moved shallowly across the broken landscape and could still be bridged. Where the Grand Canyon was still only a small river's dream. By midday they were in the trees and then they were home. Abby stood in the yard and stretched, inhaling the dry clean scent of pine and stone. She took a moment to imagine the ages assembled below her on this high thrust of the earth, the disintegrated mountains and dried up oceans, the great crumbled forests, all shoved up by unimaginable forces millions of years ago. Still moving, still shifting.

Abby unpacked in the bedroom, thinking how great it would be when Marcus joined them. Trying to guess what the interactions might be like between him and Priscilla, wondering how Marcus would manage with her. Abby pulled clothes from her duffel, sorting, when the house thumped.

The house thumped, as if a giant hand picked it up a few millimeters and let go. The wood clunked and the windows shivered. She stopped, immobile, then hurried to the kitchen where Pepper stood making a sandwich.

"What was that?" he asked. "Some sort of sonic boom—?"

She grabbed his arm and dragged him outside. The forest strangely silent. As if every tree and every creature, every bird and mammal and insect, held its breath.

"Earthquake," she said. Then it came again, barely a bump, much more subtle.

Then nothing.

They waited a long time, looking at each other, staring around them, mute. Waiting for the planet's intricate shelves to move, to slide or drop. Maybe just below them, maybe miles away, a trundling rocky chain reaction of unstable stone. Maybe far away, near the Pacific Coast, the long-awaited clunk of massive tectonic plates colliding, juddering and diving, jolting the entire continent. Not likely, but…

Nothing. Slowly the birdsong returned, a squirrel chittered and ran down a tree. An erratic horsefly buzzed, zigzagging past.

"That might have been a big one," Abby said. "Somewhere."

Pepper still looked cautious. "How closely linked are quakes between here and Yellowstone?"

Abby shook her head. "I don't know. Not very. But do you remember that Hebgen Lake earthquake that William told us about? The one in 1959 that buried those campers?"

He nodded.

"That came only a month apart from a major quake here—the one that caused the big rockslide at Mather Point." Abby raised her eyebrows. "Geologically speaking, that's less than a blink apart."

"Let me find my phone," Pepper said. "I'm calling William."

But Abby had already dialed. It was William's last day with Gem for a few weeks, until she joined him at the university. Abby hated to bother them, but she just needed to talk to him. She considered him her personal geologist, after all.

William knew nothing about the earthquake, but got quickly excited. He checked the YVO seismographs while Abby waited, but nothing had happened there. He promised to get back to her later after more study, but it looked like a local event. Not the big one.

Later that day, as they raked and cleaned up their yard, Pepper admitted he realized what triggered the earthquake.

"It must have been us, yesterday, on that trail near Kanab." He wore a poker face.

Abby shook her head and touched his beard. "Are you telling me that you think you made the earth move?"

Pepper shrugged and looked lofty. "You tell me."

Abby thought about the terrain under her feet, the limestone over two hundred million years old that once heaved as an ocean, suspended with sea fossils, now immobile. A place where ancient corals and sponges thrived, those flinty ghosts in this unlikely display of fractured rock. And deeper, the flattened desert dunes and crushed primitive trees, far down to the bottomless granite and schist, those solid remnants of hot flowing rock.

Here. There. Gone.

She looked down and scuffed the ground with her foot, made a rind of gray dust, then looked up at him and smiled.

"You might be right," Abby said.

Acknowledgments

So many thanks…

To my generous and resilient first-draft readers: Ted Cavallo, Cheryl Pagel MD, Kelly Luba DO, and Cindy Alt.

To Cheryl Pagel MD, for her bison know-how from living on the National Bison Range in Montana, especially about how bison like apples. And for her wholehearted support on that trip to Yellowstone and the Museum of the Rockies in Bozeman.

To the best-ever psychologist, Kristine Goto PHD, for her amazing knowledge and guidance about anxiety disorders and treatments.

To the excellent and enthusiastically helpful veterinarians, Dan Klinksi DVM and Melissa Miller DVM, and veterinary technician Kim Russell CVT (veterinary anesthetist, large animal/equine), for their valuable information about livestock sedatives and drugs.

To all the helpful publishing experts at the University of Nevada Press: especially marketing manager Sara Hendricksen, because without her enthusiasm and support from the beginning, I never would have had this opportunity; but thanks also to project editor Sara Vélez Mallea; acting director Joanne M. Banducci, marketing assistant Iris Saltus, and copyeditor Luke Torn.

To Neil DeGrasse Tyson PHD and his talk on *The Late Show with Stephen Colbert*, informing us about ice geysers on Enceladus.

For the generous and helpful rangers, staff, and paramedics in the Old Faithful area, the Upper Geyser Basin, and Norris Geyser Basin who answered all my pestering questions in June 2017. To my readers, please support our national parks—they are magnificent and they are struggling.

And my apologies to everyone for what I got wrong, or when I altered situations to fit the plot and action. The description of the mud pot area is not precisely accurate, and there are some liberties with the Old Faithful Inn.

And more…

Thanks to the many literary resources about Yellowstone, volcanoes, and everything else:

- Achenbach, Joel. "When Yellowstone Explodes," *National Geographic* vol. 216, no. 2 (Aug. 2009).
- Olson, Steve. *Eruption: The Untold Story of Mount St. Helens.* New York: W.W. Norton and Company, 2016.
- Peterson, David. Editor. *Postcards from Ed: Dispatches and Salvos from an American Iconoclast.* Minneapolis: Milkwood Editions, 2006.
- Thompson, Dick. *Volcano Cowboys.* New York: Thomas Dunne Books, St. Martin's Press, 2000.
- Whittlesey, Lee H. *Death in Yellowstone.* Lanham, Maryland: Roberts Rinehart Publishers, 2014.

Also, many other online references helped impart details regarding medicine, geology, and astronomy:

- National Park Service, multiple Yellowstone websites, https://www.nps.gov/yell/index.htm.
- Museum of the Rockies, Bozeman, Montana, http://www.museumoftherockies.org/.
- Centers for Disease Control and Prevention on brucellosis and measles, http://www.cdc.gov.
- Neurology MedLink on subacute sclerosing panencephalitis, http://www.ninds.nih.gov/disorders/subacute_panencephalitis/subacute_panencephalitis.htm.
- Dinosaur details, https://en.wikipedia.org/wiki/Triceratops.
- About the chemical element iridium, http://en.wikipedia.org/wiki/Iridium.
- The latest news, images, and videos from America's space agency, pioneering the future in space exploration, scientific discovery and so much more, https://www.nasa.gov.

- Visit the prominent *constellation*, Orion, located on the *celestial equator* and visible throughout the world, https://en.wikipedia.org/wiki/Orion_(constellation).
- Observe the extrusive *igneous rock* with a very high silica content, rhyolite, http://geology.com/rocks/rhyolite.shtml.
- And state fossils galore, https://en.wikipedia.org/wiki/List_of_U.S._state_fossils
- http://www.amsmeteors.org/meteor-showers/meteor-shower-calendar/; http://hvo.wr.usgs.gov/volcanowatch/archive/2000/00_01_27.html.

The Author

Sandra Cavallo Miller is a retired family physician in Phoenix who spent most of her career in academic medicine, but she was always a writer in her secret heart. Little fiction has been written about women physicians and modern primary care, and she enjoys showing the personal and medical challenges in an entertaining way. You are likely to find her hiking or on a horse, or off somewhere under a tree, reading about volcanology and astronomy.

Check out her website at www.skepticalword.com, and you can contact her at skepticalword@gmail.com.

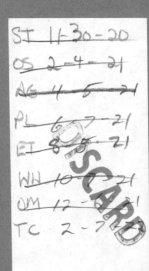